More Praise for Alistair MacLeod's

NO GREAT MISCHIEF

"An extraordinary novel." — Adam Mars-Jones, *The Observer*

"You will have scenes from this majestic novel burned into your mind forever. It's hard to think of anyone else who can cast a spell the way Alistair MacLeod can." —Alice Munro

"The book deserves to be a popular success." —A. J. Anderson

"*No Great Mischief* is a lesson in the art of storytelling. Not only does it show by example (which it does magnificently), but its subject is the way stories work, the sources of their power and the means by which they are kept alive." —Hal Jensen, *Times Literary Supplement*

"The author has created a painfully beautiful myth in which the long-ago is in many ways more present than modern existence. I doubt that this inspired and elegiac novel will ever leave those who are lucky enough to read it." —Kerry Fried

"The retold family stories are without exception gripping and quite moving, and are graced by stunning little gasps and leaps of felicitous phrasing. It confirms his reputation as one of Canada's most sensitive and stylish writers of fiction." —*Kirkus Reviews*

"This sturdily textured debut novel never hesitates or meanders." —*Library Journal*

No Great Mischief

ALISTAIR MacLEOD

NO GREAT MISCHIEF

W. W. Norton & Company

New York • London

For information about permission to reproduce selections from this book,
write to Permissions, W. W. Norton & Company, Inc., 500 Fifth Avenue,
New York, NY 10110

For information about special discounts for bulk purchases,
please contact W. W. Norton Special Sales at
specialsales@wwnorton.com or 800-233-4830

Manufacturing by RR Donnelly, Bloomsburg

Library of Congress Cataloging-in-Publication Data

MacLeod, Alistair.
No great mischief / Alistair MacLeod.—1st American ed.
p.   cm.
ISBN 0-393-04970-1
1. Young men—Nova Scotia—Cape Breton Island—Fiction.
2. Brothers—Nova Scotia—Cape Breton Island—Fiction. 3. Family—Nova
Scotia—Cape Breton Island—Fiction. 4. Scots—Nova Scotia—Cape Breton
Island—Fiction. 5. Cape Breton Island (N.S.)—Fiction. I. Title.
PR9199.3.M3342 N6 2000
813'.54—dc21   00-021801

ISBN 978-0-393-34119-5 pbk.

W. W. Norton & Company, Inc.,
500 Fifth Avenue, New York, N.Y. 10110
www.wwnorton.com

W. W. Norton & Company Ltd.,
Castle House, 75/76 Wells Street, London W1T 3QT

1   2   3   4   5   6   7   8   9   0

This book is for Anita, "mo bhean 's mo ghraidh."
Appreciation also to our children: Alexander, Lewis,
Kenneth, Marion, Daniel, and Andrew.
Not to forget our lost son Donald.

No Great Mischief

I As I begin to tell this, it is the golden month of September in southwestern Ontario. In the splendid autumn sunshine the bounty of the land is almost overwhelming, as if it is the manifestation of a poem by Keats. Along Highway 3 the roadside stands are burdened down by baskets of produce and arrangements of plants and flowers. Signs invite you to "pick your own" and whole families can be seen doing exactly that: stooping and straightening or staggering with overflowing bushel baskets, or standing on ladders that reach into the trees of apple and of pear.

On some of the larger farms much of the picking is done by imported workers; they too, often, in family groups. They do not "pick your own" but pick instead for wages to take with them when they leave. This land is not their own. Many of them are from the Caribbean and some are Mennonites from Mexico and some are French Canadians from New Brunswick and Quebec.

On the land that has already been picked over, the farmers' tractors move across the darkening fields, ploughing down the old crops while preparing for the new. Flocks of hopeful and appreciative gulls follow raucously behind them.

Once, outside of Leamington, my grandmother, who was visiting at the time, burst into tears at the sight of the rejected and overripe tomatoes which were being ploughed under. She wept for what she called "an awful waste" and had almost to be restrained from running into the fields to "save" the tomatoes from their fate in the approaching furrows. She was fifteen hundred miles from her preserving kettle, and had spent decades of summers and autumns nurturing her few precious plants in rocky soil and in shortened growing seasons. In the fall she would take her few surviving green tomatoes and place and turn them on the windowsills, hoping they might ripen in the weakened sun which slanted through her windowpanes. To her they were precious and rare and hard to come by. The lost and wasted tomatoes which she saw outside of Leamington depressed my grandmother for days. She could not help it, I suppose. Sometimes it is hard to choose or not to choose those things which bother us at the most inappropriate of times.

I think of this now as my car moves along this rich and golden highway on its way to my eventual destination of Toronto. It is a journey which I make on Saturdays, and it is a drive which I begin early in the morning although there really is no reason why it should begin at such an early time. In the fall and in the spring I take the longer but more scenic routes: Highway 2 and Highway 3 and even sometimes Highways 98 or 21. They are meandering and leisurely and there is something almost comforting in passing houses where the dogs still run down to the roadside to bark at the wheels of the passing cars – as if, for them, it were a real event. In the more extreme seasons of summer and winter, there is always the 401. The 401, as most people hearing this will know, is Ontario's major highway and it runs straight and true from the country that is the United States to the border of Quebec, which some might also consider another country. It is a highway built for the maximum movement of people and of goods and it is flat and boring and as efficient as can be. It is a sort of symbol, I suppose, if not of the straight and narrow at least of the very straight or "the one true way." You can only join it at certain places and if your destination is directly upon it, it will move you as neatly as the conveyor belt moves the tomatoes. It will be true to you if you are true to it and you will never, never, ever become lost.

Regardless of the route of entrance, the realization of the city of Toronto is always something of a surprise. It is almost as if a new set of reflexes must be mastered to accommodate the stop and go of the increased traffic, and more careful thought must be given to the final destination.

In the downtown area along Yonge Street and to the west, the anti-nuclear protestors are walking and carrying their signs. "One, two, three, four," they chant, "we don't want a nuclear war." "Two, four, six, eight, we don't want to radiate." Marching parallel to them and on the opposite side of the street an equally determined group glowers across the strained division. "Pacifists, Communists Love You," "If You Don't Like What This Country Stands For, Go Somewhere Else," "Canada, Love It or Leave It," proclaim their signs.

In the area around Queen Street West which runs between

Yonge Street and Spadina Avenue, I begin to look more carefully and to drive more slowly, thinking that I might meet him in the street, almost as if he might be coming to meet me, regardless of the direction of my approach. But today he is not seen, so I manoeuvre my car for a short way through the back alleys with their chained-down garbage cans and occasionally chained-down dogs, and over broken glass which is so crushed and flattened it is now no threat or danger to any tire. The makeshift fire escapes and back stairways lean haphazardly and awkwardly against their buildings, and from the open doorways and windows a mixture of sounds comes falling down: music and songs from various countries and voices loud on the verge of quarrel and the sounds of yet more breaking glass.

In the autumn sunshine, I lock my car in the afternoon alley and step between walls into the street crowded with bargain shoppers and barking proprietors and seekers of refuse. In the grimy windows hand-lettered cardboard signs offer almost everything, it seems, at less than its true worth.

Between these storefront doors, there are often other doors that the casual person might not notice because they seem so commonplace. They are often painted brown and may or may not have numbers above them, often with one digit missing or hanging crookedly from their nails. When you open these doors, there may or may not be a row of mailboxes, some bearing names stuck on with grey adhesive tape. Almost all of these buildings, though, have a wooden stairway that leads steeply up to a hall lit by a yellow forty-watt bulb, and along this hallway and sometimes along other hallways above it are the people who live above the street-level stores. Contrary to the myth, few of the people who live here are the owners of the stores beneath them. They are, instead, people who do not own much of anything. Generally even their furniture, such as it is, is not their own and when they move, as they often do, they do not look in the Yellow Pages for any selection of moving companies.

Although there are some couples, most of the people are single and most of them are men and most of them are beyond middle age. Sometimes there are whole corridors occupied by men only. They are generally in those buildings where the apartments are very small or consist of a single room. In such corridors there is a small bathroom at one end and it serves all the residents of the floor. It is the kind of bathroom where the lock never works and people who sit on the toilet hold one foot against the door to keep it closed. Sometimes potential users shout at the closed door, "Is there anybody in there?" much as they might if they were members of a large family in the early rush of pre-breakfast hours. Inside the bathroom the toilet paper is chained down by an elaborate system of interwoven links, and the dim light bulb is surrounded by a wire cage so it will not be stolen and taken back to one of the rooms. In the old salvaged sink, one of the taps will never shut off properly and there is generally a yellowed stain left by the constant trickle of the running water. Hot water is often scarce, and sometimes on the upper floors it does not exist at all.

Behind the closed doors one can hear vague sounds. The most dominant one is, perhaps, that of men coughing and spitting. Almost all of the men smoke quite heavily, some of them rolling their own cigarettes, sitting in their underwear on the edges of their beds. There is also the sound of radios and of the very tiny portable television sets which sit on tables or on top of the nearly empty refrigerators. Few of the people eat very much. Many of the rooms do not contain stoves, or ones with workable ovens. Tomato soup is heated on top of hot plates and filled with crackers. The smell of burnt toast is often present, and sometimes jars of instant coffee or boxes of tea bags sit on windowsills or on archaic radiators beside packages of purchased cookies so laced with preservatives that they may sit there for months without any signs of change.

It is into such a doorway that I turn now, leaving the sun behind me on the street. And it is such a stairway that I climb, towards the hallway above. This is the third time that he has lived at this address in recent years, circling back and making agreements with the landlord for whom he, at one time, did some work as a handyman. The landlord nearly always takes him back because he is reasonably dependable, and they have at least a few years of some sort of shared past. The landlord, who sells wine in brown paper bags to his tenants, has his own share of problems, which he is quite willing to share with anyone who will listen. It is not easy, he says, having tenants who move in the night without paying their rent; or who steal and sell some of the furniture he and his wife have provided; or who make duplicate keys to lend to their friends. It is not easy, he says, having the police call him at home in the evenings, when he is watching television, to report disturbances; and it is not easy for him when people stab one another with kitchen knives in quarrels over their wine; or when they are found dead in their urine-soaked beds, strangled and choked on strands of their own vomit, and he does not know any next of kin to contact. Generally, he says, the bodies are "given to science." "But," he adds, "that's the good thing about you. I always know who to contact – just in case." He is a short, portly man who has prospered greatly since coming from Europe as a child. He is proud of his children, who have all gone to university and who smile with perfect teeth from their pictures in his wallet.

As I move down the hallway, I am troubled, as always, by the fear of what I might find. If my knock is unanswered and if the door is locked, I will listen with my ear close to the keyhole for the sound of his uneven breathing. If I do not hear that, I will go back to the street and the neighbourhood and visit the taverns where the draught beer glasses sit in sloppy unwiped puddles which drip onto the floor and where the men have trouble zipping up their trousers as they weave erratically out of the washrooms.

But today when I knock, his voice says almost immediately, "Come in."

"The door's locked," I say, after trying it.

"Oh, just a minute," he says. "Just a minute." There is the sound of three unsteady steps and then a tremendous crash, followed by a silence.

"Are you all right?" I ask.

"Oh yes," comes the answer, "just a minute. I'll be right there."

The lock is turned and the door is opened, and as I enter, he is standing there, holding on to the doorknob for support with both of his huge hands, swaying sideways as the door moves inward and towards him. He is in his sock feet, and his brown work pants are held up by a broad brown leather belt. He wears no outer shirt other than the white, now yellowed, woollen underwear which he wears during all seasons.

"Ah," he says, speaking in a mixture of English and Gaelic. "Ah, *'ille bhig ruaidh*, you've come at last." He steps backwards, pulling the door towards him and still clutching its knob for support. There is a gash above his left eyebrow, caused, it seems, from the crashing fall against the steel frame which protrudes beyond the mattress at the foot of his bed. The blood flows down his face beneath his ear, and then under his chin and down his neck until it vanishes into the hair on his chest beneath his underwear. It does not drip on the floor, although one almost expects to see it, eventually, perhaps emerging beneath the cuffs of his trouser legs. But for now it seems to follow the contours of his face, as the mountain river follows the land before falling into the sea.

"Did you hurt yourself?" I say, looking around for something such as Kleenex to staunch the flow.

"No," he says. "What do you mean?" and then following the direction of my gaze he takes his left hand from the doorknob and touches his cheek. He looks at the blood on his fingertips with surprise. "No," he says. "It is nothing, just a scratch."

He relinquishes the doorknob completely and staggers backwards until he falls in a jangling sitting position upon the protesting springs of the unmade bed. When his hands are removed from the doorknob they shake violently; but now, sitting on the edge of the bed, he places them on either side of him and holds the bedframe's steel. He hangs on to it fiercely, until his huge and broken knuckles whiten, and then finally his trembling hands are stilled.

"As long as I have something to hang on to," he says, swaying back and forth, "I am okay."

I look around the small familiar room and its spartan neatness. There is no evidence that he has eaten today and there does not seem to be any food visible. In a wastebasket beside the sink, there is one of those amber bottles in which oversweet and low-priced wine is sold. It is empty.

"Do you want anything to eat?" I ask.

"No," he says, then after a pause, "nothing to eat." He emphasizes the last word and smiles. His eyes are as dark as my own, and his hair, which was black, is now a rich, luxurious white. It is the only thing about him that has continued to flourish, rising above his forehead in succeeding waves and, because it is untrimmed, now extending over his ears and too far down his neck. It is almost a sign, as is the case with so many men who eat too little and drink too much. Almost as if the alcohol were a mysterious kind of plant food, causing the topmost leaves to flourish while the plant itself grows numb.

He looks at me expectantly, smiling in the old affectionate way. "My cheque does not come until Monday," he says.

"Okay," I say. "I'm going out to the car. I'll be right back."

"All right," he says. "Leave the door open."

I go out into the hall and past the quiet closed doors and down the stairway into the street. The sun is shining brightly, which is almost a surprise, after the dimly lit interior. I pass through the space between the buildings to my car. Opening the trunk, I take out the bottle of brandy which I have purchased the night before in case of these exact circumstances. Brandy always works the fastest. I put it inside my sports coat and press it tightly against my ribs with my left arm and then retrace my route. The door is ajar and he is still sitting on the bed's edge, hanging on to control his shaking hands.

"There is a shot glass in the cupboard," he says as I take out the brandy bottle. I go to the cupboard to look for the shot glass. It is easy to find as there is not much else. It is a souvenir of Cape Breton with an outline of the island on it and some of the place names. It is a gift to him from my children, purchased as part of a bar set two summers ago. "Uncle Calum will like this," they said, being too young to intend anything as sophisticated as irony.

I pour the brandy into the shot glass and walk across to the bed to offer it to him. He removes his right hand from the bed and grasps the glass, but it flies out of his hand immediately, bouncing against my thigh and falling to the floor. It does not break, and now I can see and feel the stain of the brandy as it spreads its dark outline on the left leg of my trousers. He replaces his hand quickly on the bed, as if it has been burned.

The mug without the handle does not work any better, although he is able to grasp it with both hands for a moment before the contents spill on his own crotch and between his legs to seep into his bed. I go a third time to the cupboard and get a plastic bowl, the unbreakable kind that mothers buy for babies in high chairs. I splash some of the brandy into the bottom of the bowl and take it to him. He places both of his huge hands beneath it and raises it to his lips while I continue to steady the rim that is closest to me. He makes slurping sounds as he tilts his head back and the brandy gurgles down his throat. Because he has tipped the bowl too far some of the brandy spills along the outside of his face and runs down his chin to mingle with the blood still flowing from the gash. I splash some more brandy into the bowl and give it to him. Almost immediately it begins to take effect. The shaking of his hands becomes less agitated as his dark eyes become more clear. Like the patient who receives the anaesthetic, his fear and trembling are reduced.

"Ah, *'ille bhig ruaidh*," he says. "We have come a long way, you and I, and there are no hard feelings. Do you remember Christy?"

"Yes," I say. "Of course I remember Christy."

"Ah, poor Christy. How she always kept her part of the bargain." He pauses and then changes the subject. "I have been thinking the last few days of *Calum Ruadh*," he says with an almost apologetic shrug.

"Oh yes," I say.

"He was our great-great-great-grandfather, right?"

"Yes, he was."

"Ah yes," he says. "I wonder what he looked like."

"I don't know," I say, "other than that he was supposed to be big and of course *ruadh*, red. He probably looked like the rest of us."

"Like you, maybe," he says.

"Well, you're big," I smile, "and you have Calum, his name."

"Yes, I have his name, but you have his colour." He pauses. "I wonder if his grave is still there?"

"Yes, but it is very near to the cliff's edge now. The point of land is wearing away. Some years faster than others, depending on the storms."

"Yes, I imagine so," he says. "It was always so stormy there. It is almost as if his grave is moving out to sea, isn't it?"

"Yes, I guess that's one way of looking at it. Or the sea coming in to meet him. But the big boulder with his inscription on it is still there. We had the letters rechiselled and then painted them in with a new marine waterproof paint. They will last for a while."

"Yes, for a while. Although they'll eventually wear away too, and someone will have to recut them again – like before." He pauses. "It is as if with the passing of time he moves deeper into the rock."

"Yes," I say.

"Deeper into the rock before he falls into the sea, perhaps? Do you remember how when the gales would blow, the spray from the sea would drench the boulder until it glistened?"

"Yes."

"And when the boulder was wet you could see the letters more clearly?"

"Yes." I say. "That's right. You could."

"Yes, more clearly in the storm than in fair weather. I have been thinking of that now, although I can't remember if I ever thought about it then."

He gets up from the bed and retrieves the mug without the handle from the floor. He is steadier now, and his hands no longer tremble. He takes the brandy bottle and sloshes some of the contents into the mug which a few moments ago he was unable to control. He is rising out of one state into another. Next he will achieve a kind of plateau where he will level off for perhaps an hour and then, depending on how much more alcohol he consumes, he will begin to go down what seems like the other side of the mountain. The late afternoon and early evening may or may not see him spitting blood or swaying in the shadows as he attempts to urinate in the sink, fumbling at the front of his trousers with his right hand while supporting himself with his left against the wall. And I will have to leave him then, to follow my headlights through the city and then back down the highway. Each of us repeating his own small history.

"Didn't I mention this to you the last time you were here?" he asks, breaking my thoughts and returning to the subject of *Calum Ruadh* and his gravestone.

"No," I say at first, hoping to save him embarrassment, and then, "Yes, yes you did."

"Ah yes," he says, "'*ille bhig ruaidh*. Will you have a drink? Have a drink with me?" He offers me my own brandy.

"No," I say. "No, I don't think so. I'd rather not. I have a long drive ahead of me. I have to go back."

"Ah yes, you have to go back." He gets up, still holding the brandy bottle, and walks to the window which looks out on the back alley, on the erratic fire escapes and the resting garbage and the ground-down glass.

"It is a nice day out there," he says, as if looking at another country. "A nice September day. The blackfish are jumping off the *Calum Ruadh*'s Point. I can see them: the way they shine, so black and glistening. But they had better not come in too close. Do you remember the one who came to shore?"

"Yes, I remember him."

"And how we hoped that the storm would take him back out, but it didn't."

"Yes, he couldn't get back out."

"No," he says, turning from the window, "he couldn't. Do you remember our parents?"

"I'm not sure," I say. "Some things. I'm not sure how many of the memories are real and how many I've sort of made up from other people's stories."

"Ah yes," he says. "And your sister, Catriona, the same."

"Yes," I say. "The same."

He drinks again. This time directly from the bottle, which is now emptying rapidly.

"Poor Grandma and Grandpa," he says. "They were good to you. As good as they knew how."

"Yes," I say. "They were."

"'Always look after your own blood,' Grandma said." His mood changes in an instant and he seems suddenly angry and suspicious. "I suppose that's why you're here?"

I am caught off guard by the sudden shift, trapped in the net of my own guilt and history.

"No," I say. "Why no. Not really. No, it's not that way at all."

I look towards him, trying to gauge his mood as he sways slightly on the balls of his sock feet before me. The golden September sunshine slants indirectly through the window behind his back and seems to silhouette him as the dust motes flicker in its beams. He appears like the actor in the spotlight of the afternoon performance. He is poised and potentially dangerous, and in spite of all the years of abuse, his body still responds to the old tense signals. He rocks forward now on his toes and then backwards on his heels while holding the brandy bottle lightly in his left hand, as if he might throw it. The fingers of his right hand open and close slowly and rhythmically; now into a fist and now into an extended hand. Then he laughs and the moment is past.

"Ah yes," he says. "Yes, *'ille bhig ruaidh*. I was only thinking. Go and get some more liquor. Brandy if you want, or wine or beer, and we will drink away the day together. And the night."

"All right," I say, stepping towards the door, perhaps too quickly, and feeling ashamed for seeming so eager to abandon the room I have driven so many miles to enter.

"What would you like? Beer? Wine?"

"Oh," he says. "It doesn't make much difference. It doesn't make much difference."

"Okay, I won't be too long."

"No big rush," he says. "Take your time. I am not going anywhere and I have this." He swings the amber brandy bottle and its contents back and forth in his left hand. "I will sit here and wait."

I go out into the hallway and close the door behind me and then slump with temporary relief. It is the slump of students when they close the door of the examination room behind them, or of those who leave the dentist's office after being told, "The fillings will be two weeks from today – but *not* today." Or of the witness released from his cross-examination in the box.

As I stand in the hallway I hear him as he begins to sing on the other side of the door. He sings softly but resolutely – singing to himself in the manner that the drunken or the near-drunken often use to communicate with themselves:

"Chi mi bhuam, fada bhuam,
Chi mi bhuam, ri muir lain;
Chi mi Ceap Breatuinn mo luaidh
Fada bhuam thar an t-sail."

He is singing *"Cumha Ceap Breatuinn," "Lament for Cape Breton,"* which is one of those communal songs often sung by large groups of people or in situations where one person sings the verse and the group sings the chorus. It means something like:

I see far, far away.
I see far o'er the tide;
I see Cape Breton, my love,
Far away o'er the sea.

As I walk down the hallway I move out of earshot of the singer who recedes with each of my steps, but as I begin to descend the steep, sad stairs, beneath the forty-watt bulb, the song continues and I am almost surprised to realize it is no longer coming from him but from somewhere deep within me. It rises up to the extent that my own lips move in an almost reflex action:

"Gu bheil togradh ann am intinn
Bhi leibh mar a bha

Ged tha fios agam us cinnt
Ribh nach till mi gu brath."

There's a longing in my heart now
To be where I was
Though I know that it's quite sure
I never shall return.

It is as if there is no break between his ending and my beginning; although the subject matter is much different, the verses
and chorus come easily to my mind in the way, I suppose, that
middle-aged former boy scouts remember the verses of "She'll
Be Coming Round the Mountain" and "Oh, My Darling
Clementine." Sounds planted and dormant and flowering at the
most unexpected times.

I am a twentieth-century man, I think, as I step out onto the
street. And then another phrase of my grandmother's comes to
mind, "*whether I like it or not.*" I am a middle-aged man this
September and indeed there is not much of the twentieth
century left. If I continue to journey towards its end I will be
fifty-five when the century closes, which is either young or old,
perhaps, depending on your own point of view and attitude
towards age and time. "We will live a long, long time," said my
grandfather of the *clann Chalum Ruaidh*, "if we are given the
chance – and if we want to." I try to square my shoulders in the
September sun – as if I were auditioning for the part of "twentieth-century man" in a soon-to-be-released spectacular. "Ah,"
haunts the voice of my oldest brother, "ah, *'ille bhig ruaidh.*

You've come at last. We have come a long way, you and I, and there are no hard feelings." The voice pauses. "I have been thinking the last few days of *Calum Ruadh*. I wonder what he looked like?"

"I don't know," I say. "I don't know. Only what I have been told."

"Ah," says the voice. "Stay with me. Stay with me. You are still the *gille beag ruadh*."

2   *Still* the *gille beag ruadh*. The phrase means "the little red boy" or "the little red-haired boy" and it was applied to me as far back as my memory goes. I remember thinking of it as my name and responding to it rather than to "Alexander," which is what is on my birth certificate. And even on the first day of primary school, sitting behind my twin sister in my new clothes and clutching my newly purchased crayons in my too clean but sweating hands, I failed to respond when my true name was called from the roll.

"That's you," said a cousin, poking me from across the aisle.

"Who?" I said.

"That's you," he said. "That's your name."

Then, taking matters into his own control, he raised his hand and, pointing towards me, said directly to the teacher, "That's him, *gille beag ruadh*, Alexander."

Everyone laughed because I had missed my own name and the teacher, who was not from the area, became very flushed, probably because of the Gaelic phrase she did not understand. Thankfully, however, we were of the generation who were no longer beaten because we uttered Gaelic, "beaten for your own good," as the phrase seemed to go, "so you will learn English and become good Canadian citizens." Instead she merely asked, "Is your name Alexander?"

"Yes," I said, having regained some shreds of composure.

"In the future, please answer when your name is called from the roll," she said.

"I will," I said to myself, making a sharp mental note to be on the lookout for the foreign sound in the future.

And also at that first recess, several bigger boys approached me, and one said, "Are you *gille beag ruadh*?"

"Yes," I said, at first responding from habit and then, remembering my most recent lesson, "no, I'm not. Alexander. I'm Alexander."

However, it seemed to make no difference: "The *Calum Ruadh*'s hair is red. It sets fire to their bed," he chanted.

Again, under attack, I felt my lower lip trembling and I was afraid that I might cry.

"Leave him alone," said another bigger boy in the group. "You're part *Calum Ruadh* yourself," and he ruffled my hair as he led the group away. I ran to join my sister, who was waiting for me a few yards away, and we went to play on the slides, which we had been told was a good thing to do at recess.

The *Calum Ruadh* who seems so present in thought and conversation in today's Toronto was, as I mentioned earlier, my great-great-great-grandfather. And he came from Scotland's Moidart to the New World in 1779. Sometimes it seems we know a lot about him, and at other times very little. "It is all relative," as they say. No pun intended. There are some facts and perhaps some fantasies that change with our own perceptions and interests.

These seem the facts: He was married in Moidart to Anne MacPherson, and they had six children, three boys and three girls. While these children were still quite small, Anne MacPherson became ill and died "of the fever," leaving him with what my grandparents referred to as "his care," meaning his motherless children. Later, his wife's younger sister, Catherine MacPherson, came to keep house for him and to look after her nieces and nephews and eventually to marry the man who was their father. They had six more children, again three boys and three girls. Anyone who knows the history of Scotland, particularly that of the Highlands and the Western Isles in the period around 1779, is not hard-pressed to understand the reasons for their leaving.

They already had friends and relatives in North America. Many of them were in the Cape Fear River area of North Carolina — nearly all of them men, fighting at the time in the American War of Independence. Some of the older ones were on the side of the revolutionaries because they had decided to fight for a new life in the New World, and others fought on the British side because they remained stubbornly loyal to the British cause. At night they sang Gaelic songs to one another across the mountain meadows where they would fight on the following day. Singing Gaelic to their Highland friends and relatives across the glens of North Carolina: "Come on over and join us." "You're on the wrong side." "Don't be fools." "The future is with us."

Calum Ruadh was fifty-five in 1779 and had been twenty-one "at the time of the Forty-Five" when the call had gone out to "rise and follow Charlie." Again there were friends and relatives singing and saying to one another: "Don't be fools." "You're on the wrong side." "Your loyalty is misplaced." "Think about it." Pressures from above as well as from all sides.

He and his wife and family had apparently talked about leaving for some time, and had made their plans quietly and contacted the emigration agent and agreed to meet him and his ship in one of the sheltered coves along the coastline, where he was picking up families such as theirs. Bound for Nova Scotia, "the land of trees," although *Calum Ruadh*'s destination was Cape Breton, where, he had been told in a Gaelic letter, there would be land for him if he would come.

They were to leave on August 1, and the crossing would be perhaps six weeks with favourable winds. But in the weeks prior to the departure, the former Catherine MacPherson became ill and they did not know what to do. In the end they decided to go, having sold their cattle and given up the precious end timbers to their house, which in that land and in that time were hard to come by. Ironically, leaving a land with too few trees for one that was to have, perhaps, too many. They came down to the shore and waited, *Calum Ruadh* and his ill but hopeful wife and his twelve children. His eldest daughter was already married to a man named Angus Kennedy from the Isle of Canna and they waited also. One sees them in imagination's mist, shuffling their feet and watching the horizon while the shapes of friends and relatives move in and out of the shadows. "Perhaps you're making a mistake." "You could be fools." "The future is uncertain."

They waited there, *Calum Ruadh* holding his violin and perhaps resting his foot on the wooden sea chest with its neatly divided compartments. All of them with some small provisions and with their money secreted inside their shoes. He was unaware that the French Revolution was coming and that a boy named Napoleon was but ten, and had not yet set out to conquer the world. Although he was not surprised, later, at the number of his own relatives who died before and during Waterloo, still shouting Gaelic war cries while fighting for the British against the resistant French. General James Wolfe, whom he perhaps did not remember from the Forty-Five, was already dead twenty years, dying with the Highlanders on the Plains of Abraham — the same Highlanders he had tried to exterminate some fourteen years before.

It is unlikely that *Calum Ruadh* had many thoughts of Wolfe in that August of 1779. His mind was likely filled with more immediate concerns as he prepared to leave Moidart — another MacDonald leaving Moidart yet again — although this time not to "rise and follow Charlie," although that image and that music may have haunted the recesses of his mind.

As they waited on the shore, the dog who had worked with them for years and had been left to the care of neighbours ran about in a frenzy, sensing that something was wrong, and rolling in the sand and whining in her agitation. And when they began to wade out to the smaller boat which would take them to the waiting ship, she swam after them, her head cutting a V through the water and her anxious eyes upon the departing family she considered as her own. And as they were rowed towards the anchored ship, she continued to swim, in spite of shouted Gaelic threats and exhortations telling her to go back; swimming farther and farther from the land, until *Calum Ruadh*, unable to stand it any longer, changed his shouts from threats to calls of encouragement and, reaching over the side, lifted her soaked and chilled and trembling body into the boat. As she wriggled wetly against his chest and licked his face excitedly, he said to her in Gaelic, "Little dog, you have been with us all these years and we will not forsake you now. You will come with us."

"That always got to me, somehow," I remember my grandfather saying, "that part about the dog."

The voyage was a bad one. The quarters below were cramped and overcrowded and were apparently modelled partially on those of the transport ships used to carry Highland soldiers to fight in the New World and partially on the quarters of the slave ships plying from Africa to ports of that same New World. Overcrowding being a matter of simple economic greed.

In fair weather the people could come above decks and move and clean themselves, but in this year of the stormy August crossing, they were unable to do so, and were forced to remain below in their own stench and confinement. Three weeks out, the former Catherine MacPherson died. Her death brought on, again, "by the fever" and no doubt hastened by the overcrowding and the wormy oatmeal and the tiny measures of brackish water. She was sewn in a canvas bag and thrown overboard, never to see the New World on which she had based such hopes. One week after her death the wife of Angus Kennedy gave birth. The child was called Catherine and was known ever afterwards as "*Catriona na mara*," "Catherine of the Sea," because of the circumstances of her birth.

As I said, these seem the facts, or some of them anyway, although the fantasies are my own. And as is the case with the Gaelic songs, I do not choose nor will myself to remember them. They are just there, from what, even in my relatively short life, seems like a long time ago. I remember my grandfather telling me the story one afternoon in early spring as we were out at the woodpile making kindlings – he chopping them and I carrying them in to dry. I was, perhaps, eleven and the geese were winging northward, flying over the still iced-in rivers and lakes – seeming fools for being so early yet being geometrically true to their intended course and purpose.

"After they landed on the shores of Pictou," he said, "*Calum Ruadh* broke down and wept and he cried for two whole days and I guess they were all around him, including the dog, and no one knew what to do."

"Cried?" I said incredulously. Because even by then I was conditioned by movies where the people all broke into applause when they saw the Statue of Liberty which their ship was approaching. Always they seemed to hug and dance and be *happy* at landing in the New World. And also the idea of a fifty-five-year-old man crying was a bit more than I was ready for. "Cried?" I said. "What in the world would he cry for?"

I remember the way my grandfather drove the axe into the chopping block – with such violent force that it became so deeply embedded he had difficulty in getting it out later – and he looked at me with such temporary anger in his eyes that I thought he would snatch me by my jacket front and shake me. His eyes said that he could not believe I was so stupid, but they said so only for a moment. He was, I suppose, somewhat like the teacher at the blackboard who explains and draws diagrams and gives examples, and then upon asking the question of under-standing finds that no one has received his message – and fears in anger that everyone's time has been utterly wasted. Or, perhaps, it is merely the mistake that adults sometimes make in talking to children, thinking that they are talking to other adults who share their knowledge and their views. Explaining the facts of life to those who have as yet no interest in such a subject, and who would probably be more interested in eating cookies.

"He was," he said, composing himself and after a thoughtful moment, "crying for his history. He had left his country and lost his wife and spoke a foreign language. He had left as a husband and arrived as a widower and a grandfather, and he was respon-sible for all those people clustered around him. He was," he said, looking up to the sky, "like the goose who points the V, and he temporarily wavered and lost his courage.

"Anyway," he went on, "they waited there for two weeks, trying to get a shallop to take them across the water and here to Cape Breton. And then, I guess, he got better and 'set his teeth,' as they say, and resolved to carry on. It's a good thing for us that he did."

"What's a shallop?" I asked, my curiosity getting the better of my fear of ignorance.

He was not angry at the question but only laughed as he set about trying to free the embedded axe from the chopping block.

"I don't really know," he said. "It's just the word they always used, 'shallop.' It's sort of a small open boat. You can row it or use sails. Sort of like a dory. I think it's originally a French word."

As I gathered the kindlings that fell from his axe, another V of geese flew north. These seemed somehow lower, and it was almost as if one could hear the strong and regulated "whoosh" of their grasping, powerful, outstretched wings.

One sees the little group of people even now, as if we could, in imagination's mist, rowing or sailing in their shallop or shallops across the choppy fall sea. Looking along the Cape Breton coastline, which would become the future subject of "*Chi Mi Bhuam*," although they had no way of knowing that then. Nor did they know, probably, that once they landed they would be there "forever" – none of them in that boat ever returning to the mainland during their natural lives. One sees them with the "saved" dog, perhaps, in the shallop's prow, the wind spray flattening the hair along her skull while she scanned the wooded coastline with her dark intelligent eyes. When the boat landed on the gravelled strand, the cousins who had written the Gaelic letter and the Micmacs who were at home "in the land of trees" helped them ashore and continued to help them through that first long winter.

Official settlement was not appreciated in Cape Breton at that time because of the many political and colonial uncertainties, but in 1784 Cape Breton was constituted a British province and those who were already "inhabitants" petitioned for the land they had been working. *Calum Ruadh*, after walking the hundred or so miles to Sydney, received "the paper" outlining in some formal sense his land in "the colony of Cape Breton." He was sixty years old at the time. Thirty-six years later, after Cape Breton was re-annexed to Nova Scotia in 1820, he obtained new papers for the new province, but by this time there were local magistrates and he did not have to walk. It was probably just as well, as he was ninety-six at the time of the re-annexation and he had been in the New World for forty-one years. He continued to live for another fourteen years, giving his life a strange sort of balanced structure; living to be one hundred and ten years old; fifty-five in Scotland and a second fifty-five "in the land across the sea." Of the second fifty-five, he spent five as a sort of energetic squatter and thirty-six as a "citizen of Cape Breton" and fourteen as a citizen of Nova Scotia. When he died, in 1834, it was thirty-three years before Confederation.

He was never a married man in the new country and that is, perhaps, why his grave seems doubly lonely, set as it is on the farthest jutting headland that points out to the sea, where it is caught by all of the many varying winds. Most of his children are buried in the early "official" graveyards beside their wives and husbands and sometimes, in the larger plots, surrounded by their own children and children's children as well. Families in death, as they were in life. But *Calum Ruadh* is buried all alone, apparently where he wanted to be, marked only by a large boulder with the hand-chiselled letters which give his name and dates and the simple Gaelic line: *Fois do t'anam.* Peace to his Soul.

3 *In* the years that followed, some of *Calum Ruadh*'s many descendants expanded his original land holdings, while others moved farther along the coast and others deeper inland. Nearly all of them had large families, which led in turn to complex interrelationships and complicated genealogies, over all of which his name continued to preside. I remember as a high-school athlete, travelling to hockey games in communities which seemed a great distance away, sometimes playing in arenas but more often on windswept ponds beside the sea. And after our games we would be invited into the homes of our hosts, where we would inevitably be quizzed by their parents or grandparents. "What's your name?" "What's your father's name?" "What's your mother's father's name?" And almost without fail, in the case of myself and my cousins, there would come a knowing look across the face of our questioners and they would say, in response to our answer, "Ah, you are the *clann Chalum Ruaidh*," as if that somehow explained everything. They would pronounce *clann* in the Gaelic way so that it sounded like "kwown." "Ah, you are the *clann Chalum Ruaidh*," meaning "Ah, you are the children (or the family) of the red Calum." We would nod and accept this judgment, as the ice and snow dripped off our shin pads to form puddles on the linoleum floors. And later, when we were out of the house and thinking ourselves more sophisticated than we were, we would laugh and sometimes imitate the people and their identification. "What is your father's father's father's father's name?" we would ask one another, carving our initials in the snow with our hockey sticks, and then answering our own questions, "Ah, now I know, you are the *clann Chalum Ruaidh*," and we would laugh and flick snow at one another with the blades of our sticks.

There are a few physical characteristics of the *clann Chalum Ruaidh* which seem to have been passed on and, in some cases, almost to have been intensified. One seems a predisposition to have twins, most of whom are fraternal rather than identical. And another has to do with what is sometimes called "colouring." Most of the people are fair-skinned, but within families some of the individuals have bright red hair while that of their brothers and sisters is a deep, intense and shining black. When my twin sister was seventeen, she decided for reasons of girlish vanity to dye her hair with a silver-blondish streak which rose from her forehead and swept in undulating waves through the heavy blackness of her own natural hair. Later, tiring of the effect, she attempted to dye the streak back to black, but could find no dye that would make it as black as it was before. I see her now, sometimes, in memory, sitting in her slip before her mirror and biting her lip in frustration close to tears, looking like those heroines of the Scottish ballads with "milk white skin and hair as black as the raven's wing" and wishing to be someone else. My grandmother had little sympathy for her plight, saying with straightforward firmness, "It is good enough for you, for tampering with the hair God gave you."

It was months before her hair grew to its own blackness again, and then almost simultaneously and ironically the first few strands of premature whiteness began to appear as they so often do, coming to the dark-haired at a very early age.

Many of the red-haired people also had eyes that were so dark as to be beyond brown and almost in the region of a glowing black. Such individuals would manifest themselves as strikingly unfamiliar to some, and as eerily familiar to others. When one of my sons was born in southwestern Ontario, the hospital staff said, "Either his hair will turn dark or his eyes will turn blue. Most red-haired people have blue eyes. No one looks *like that*." There seemed little reason for me to say anything, given the circumstances of my own physical presence.

And once, years after my sister had married the petroleum engineer she met at the University of Alberta, her eleven-year-old son was pushing his bicycle up the incline of Calgary's Sarcee Trail on a sunny summer afternoon. He was met, he said, by a car filled with men and bearing a banner which said "B.C. or Bust" strung across its grille. It passed him and then stopped in a slew of roadside gravel, and then, grinding into reverse, roared backwards towards him where he stood half frightened and clutching his handlebars. "What's your name?" said one of the men, rolling down his window. "Pankovich," he answered. And then one of the men in the back seat ("the one with the beer in his lap," he said) leaned forward and asked, "What was your mother's last name?" "MacDonald," he answered. "See," said the man to the car in general, "I told you." And then another of the men reached into his pocket and passed him a fifty-dollar bill. "What's this for?" asked my nephew named Pankovich. "It is," said the man, "for the way you look. Tell your mother it is from *clann Chalum Ruaidh*."

And then the car bearing "B.C. or Bust" moved into the flow of the summer highway, heading for the rolling foothills and the distant shimmering mountains.

"Mom," said my nephew on arriving home, "What's kwown calum rooah?"

"Why?" she asked, startled. "Where did you hear that?" And he told her his story and she, some of hers.

"I remember it so clearly," my sister said to me later. "I was fixing my hair because we were going out to dinner that evening. It just struck me so suddenly that I started to cry, and I asked him what licence plates were on the car, but he said he hadn't noticed. I would have liked to have found out who they were, and to have thanked them somehow – not for the money, of course, nor for him, but somehow for myself." She extended her hands in front of her and then moved them sideways as if she were smoothing an imaginary tablecloth hung in air.

4 Both my twin sister and I were raised by our paternal grandparents and both of them were "of the *Calum Ruadh*," which meant that they were cousins. So was our maternal grandfather, although we did not know him quite as well nor for as long; and in the manner of the more unknown, he seems now more intriguing. He was what was called "a come by chance," which meant that he was illegitimate

and had been fathered by one of the *Calum Ruadh* men who went to work in the woods near Bangor, Maine, but never returned. Apparently my grandfather's parents planned to marry in the spring when the husband-to-be would return with the money to begin their married lives; and his bride-to-be had given herself to him in that fall – in the manner that young girls give themselves to equally young soldiers before they depart for war – hoping they will come back, but uncertain and fearful as well. He must have been fathered in late October or early November because his birthday was August 3, and one has even now a haunting sympathy for them all. For the girl who discovers in the depth of winter she is pregnant by a man she cannot reach. And for the man who died, crushed beneath the load of logs on the skidway, perhaps without realizing he had set a life in motion, which would in turn result in even such a life as mine.

Apparently he was killed in January, although word did not filter out for some time, as it was a great distance and the season was winter and there were no telephones and postal service was uncertain and most of the people involved were still unilingually Gaelic-speaking. He was buried there, in winter, in the woods of Maine, and in the spring a cousin brought back his boots and his few possessions in a bundle. He had not been working long enough to earn anything substantial, and what he had put aside for his wedding was needed for his burial. As I said, one has a haunting sympathy for them all, for him and for the girl waiting in the depth of winter for a dead man who might free her of her shame. And for her also later in the hot summer months before the birth, poor and desperate and ashamed, with unknown expectations for her coming fatherless child.

Perhaps because of the circumstances of his conception, my maternal grandfather was an exceedingly careful man. He became an exceptional carpenter, finding great satisfaction in the exactitude of a craft where everything would turn out perfectly if you took the time to calculate it so. He did not marry until he was middle aged and had already designed and built his compact, perfect house within the town; and within his marriage he fathered but one perfect child, who was my mother. After the death of his wife in childbirth, he lived for a long time by himself, rising at exactly six a.m. and shaving and trimming his neat reddish moustache. His house was spotless, and within it he knew where everything was all of the time. And in the little building behind his house where he kept his shining tools it was the same. He was the kind of man you could go to with a request such as, "Do you have a screw nail that is exactly 1 1/8 inch long?" And immediately he would go to the perfect little jar and there it would be.

Before going to bed he would set out his breakfast dishes for the next morning; again with great precision, his plate face down and his cup inverted upon its saucer with its handle always at the same angle, and with his knife and fork and spoon each in its proper place, as if he were in a grand hotel.

His shoes were always polished and in a shining row with their toes pointing outward beneath his neatly made bed, and his teapot was always placed on exactly the same spot upon his gleaming stove. "He is so clean, he makes you nervous," said my other grandfather, who, while he had a great affection for him, was a very different kind of man.

Although he had a shot of whisky when he got up and one before he went to bed, he drank very little compared to many of the men his age, and although he could sometimes be inveigled into going to the taverns he never remained long and did not like them. "He's always getting up to get a cloth to mop the table," my other grandfather would complain, "and he sits far back from the table like this" (giving an imitation of a man at a table – close but distant) "because he's afraid someone will spill beer on his pants. And he can't stand the washrooms with all that piss on the floor."

Neither did he like ribald songs nor off-colour stories in either English or Gaelic, and his face would redden at almost any sexual reference. Again, I suppose because of what he considered to be a certain ill-prepared sloppiness in his painful past. And stories about the man who rides the girl and then goes away were not, for him, particularly funny.

When my sister and I were small children we would visit him more out of duty than affection because he was the kind of man who did not appreciate muddy boots on his always scrubbed floor, nor did he appreciate having his hammer mislaid, nor his saw left out to rust in the rain. And if he were not home and we left scrawled childish notes on his door, he would encircle all the misspelled words with his carpenter's pencil and later on our next visit ask us to spell them correctly because he so wanted everything to be "right."

He was a strong taskmaster at homework, but not without his own humour. I remember one night, while staying with him, attempting to memorize history dates. "Confederation, 1867," I chanted aloud. "Think of me," he said with a twinkle in his eye. "I was born here in 1877. I am only ten years younger than Canada, and I am not very old." It seemed an amazing thing at the time for he *did* seem old and so did Canada and I was not that strong at making distinctions, and did not realize what was young and what was old.

Although he was older and "different" than my other grand-parents, they had a great affection and respect for him – not only because his only daughter had married their son and they shared that resulting pain, but I suppose also because he was their cousin and part of "*clann Chalum Ruaidh*," although none of them remembered the young man who had fathered him in another century and who died on the winter skidway in the snow near Bangor, Maine.

"He has always stood by us," said Grandma. "He has always been loyal to his blood. He has given us this chance." "This chance" involved the story of how my grandparents became dwellers of the town rather than of the country. They had spent their early married years on the *Calum Ruadh* land, living with their in-laws for a while and then constructing their own unfinished house. They were always short of money and uncer-tain of their future and, apparently, even considered going to San Francisco, where Grandma's sister, who had married Grandpa's brother, had already gone and where they seemed to be prosper-ing. But in the end they did not go. "The old people did not want us to go" was one explanation, but it seemed they really did not want to go themselves, although the idea persisted as fantasy, especially with Grandpa when he was in his cups. "*I*," he would say, rising unsteadily but grandly from his chair and holding his glass in his hand, "could have gone to San Francisco."

For a number of years, as their children came, they lived the uncertain "normal" lives of their time; Grandma washing her clothes in the brook and slapping them on the rocks and tending her precious garden in its stony soil. Grandpa fishing in the waters off the *Calum Ruadh*'s Point for a while in summer, and caring for his animals and working haphazardly in the woods in winter.

When they began to construct the new hospital in the town ten miles away, my other grandfather began to work there as a carpenter and eventually to take small contracts on certain portions of it, and when it began to rise above the ground as a sort of monument to the future sick, few people knew as much about it as did he. He realized that when it was completed it would have to be maintained, and decided to groom Grandpa for the job. "He would come at night," Grandma would say, "with his blueprints all so neat and exact, and I would wipe away everything from the table and he would spread them out and we would study them by the kerosene lamp, and he would point out all the pipes and cables and which connected to which and he would show us how all the newfangled switches and latches worked, and then he would ask us questions, just like the teacher, and invent problems and ask how they might be solved. And sometimes he would explain things in Gaelic. Then he would have one drink of whisky and play a tune on the violin – which always seemed so strange in him, you would never think of him as playing the violin – and then he would go. He never spent the night with us. I used to think it was because we did not have an indoor bathroom and he was always so clean – 'fastidious' I heard him called once. Anyway it got so that *I* knew everything about the inner workings of the hospital myself."

When it dawned on the authorities that the new hospital

would need a maintenance man, Grandpa was, as he said, "really ready." There were apparently some periods of tension when it seemed he might be on the wrong side of politics, but he was so dazzling in his interview that he simply overwhelmed any such opposition and was hired for the job. "I'm all set for life now," he apparently said, patting his new pipe wrench in his new coveralls. "To hell with San Francisco."

This was "the chance," as I said, that led to my grandparents becoming dwellers of the town instead of dwellers of the country. It was, of course, but a short distance physically, and hardly any mental one at all. They lived on the outskirts of the town and they had a "yard" which consisted of almost two acres and they brought with them their chickens and their pig and their ever-present *Calum Ruadh* dogs, and for a while they even kept a cow. Their relatives visited them constantly, and because the town was also on the sea and because of the indented shoreline, they could look down along the coast and see the point of land from whence they came, and on clear nights they could see the lights glowing like earthbound stars where the distant dark horizon curved down towards the sea.

They were tremendously happy people, grateful for "the chance," and never seeming to think much beyond it. "He is a really smart man," said my other, more reflective grandfather of Grandpa, "if only he were more thoughtful."

Still, it was he who had engineered the maintenance job for Grandpa and steered him towards it, almost, it seems, like the vocational guidance teacher, looking at the job and looking at the student and deciding (and hoping) that each might prove suitable for the other.

For his part, Grandpa would say, "I know *one thing* really well and that's how to run this hospital. That's enough for me."

During their early married years, it seems, it was decided that Grandpa would earn whatever he could, and that he would then give everything there was to Grandma, except for a small allowance for tobacco and beer. She would then do almost everything else, which was no small accomplishment, considering that during their first twelve married years they produced nine living children. Before "the chance," the earnings were erratic and unpredictable and Grandma was frequently hard-pressed, but after it, she too, like her husband, felt "all set for life," and after her early years of "making do" with little, she felt privileged and almost "rich" beyond any of her earliest expectations. She was frugal and capable because, as she said, "I always had to be," putting patches on the patches and hardly ever throwing anything away. And she believed with great dedication in a series of maxims. "Waste not, want not" was one, and "Always look after your blood" was another.

"He is the nicest man you could ever be around," she frequently said of Grandpa. "And I should know. I have been sleeping with him for more than forty-five years. Some men," she would add in ominous seriousness, "are nice as pie in public but within their own homes they are mean and miserly to those who have to live with them all the time. No one, perhaps, knows this except those who are captives within their houses. But he is never like that at all," she would add, brightening at the very thought. "He is always cheerful and happy, and there is more to him than some people think."

5 *I* think of my grandparents a great deal, and, as in the manner of the remembered Gaelic songs, I do not do so consciously. I do not awake in the morning and say, as soon as my feet hit the floor, "Today I *must* remember Grandma and Grandpa. I will devote *ten whole minutes* to their memory" – as if I were anticipating isometric exercises or a self-imposed number of push-ups to be done on the floor beside my bed. It does not work that way at all. But they drift into my mind in the midst of the quiet affluence of my office, where there is never supposed to be any pain but only the creation of a hopeful beauty. And they drift into the quiet affluence of my home, with its sunken living room and its luxuriously understated furniture. And they are there too on Grand Cayman or in Montego Bay or Sarasota or Tenerife or any of those other places to which we go, trying to pretend that, for us, there really is no winter. They drift in like the fine snow in the old *Calum Ruadh* house in which my brothers used to live; sifting in and around the window casings or under the doors, driven by the insistent and unseen wind, so that in spite of primitive weather stripping or the stuffing with old rags, it continued to persist, forming lines of quiet whiteness to be greeted with surprise.

I see my grandparents even now, in terms of their gestures and certain scenes. The way she would touch his inner thigh from

39

behind, as he stood on the ladder, helping her with the spring housecleaning, which he hated but always did; and the way his knees would buckle at the surprise of the touch until he had composed himself and was able to turn, laughing, towards her, looking down from his ladder while holding the curtain rod or the cleaning cloth in his hand.

As they became older and he became somewhat deaf, they reverted almost totally to Gaelic – especially when they were alone. It was the language that one heard emanating from their bedroom late at night – his voice a bit too loud, the way it often is with the somewhat deaf who cannot hear the volume of their own utterances. It was the language of their courting days and they had always been more at ease with it, although, especially after "the chance," they had become quite adept at English. If one passed the sometimes slightly opened door of their bedroom in the early morning, they were to be seen always sleeping in the same position. He, lying on his back, on the outside of the bed with his lips slightly parted and with his right arm extended and curved around her shoulders. And she, with her head upon his chest while the outline of her right arm extended down beneath the blankets, towards the familiarity between his legs. They were tremendously supportive of one another, never denying each other anything which came within their framework of knowledge. And confidently certain of how their lives should be.

Sometimes when he stayed too long at the taverns, as he sometimes did in his later years, he would exhaust his money and send a "runner" to Grandma, asking for more so that he might extend his socializing. She always gave it to him, saying, "He does not do this often. And it is little enough when you consider all he has given to us." And once when a rather cryptic neighbour said, "If he were my husband, he would not get another cent," Grandma, in her own indignation, said, "Yes, but he is not *your* husband. You look after your husband and I'll look after mine."

On one Christmas Eve, we waited and waited for him throughout the late afternoon and the early evening. He had gone to get his last-minute presents, but "must have stopped along the way," as Grandma put it. "Maybe he took too much money for the presents," she added. "Anyway, he will come by 6:30, because he knows that there are things to do, and that we must go to church later tonight, and anyway the taverns close at six on Christmas Eve."

Sure enough at 6:30 he arrived; in a taxi, no less, accompanied by a number of erratic friends who helped him open the door and carry in his precious packages and then vanished back into the taxi, amidst off-key choruses of "Merry Christmas."

"Hullo," said Grandpa, weaving unsteadily across the kitchen floor. "*Ciamar a tha sibh?* Merry Christmas to all. Is everybody happy?"

He wobbled to his chair at the end of the kitchen table, where he sat swaying almost regularly, as if sitting on the deck of a departing, pitching boat. "How is everyone?" he said, waving to us blearily, his hand moving back and forth before his face, as if he were cleaning an imaginary windshield. "Great day to be alive," he added, and then he sort of crumpled and fell off his chair in a rapid yet amazing sequence. It was like looking at those films which show the destruction of the building which has been cleverly laden with dynamite and then, in a matter of seconds, folds up and seems to vanish soundlessly before your eyes. A few tremors and shocks and then it crumbles.

"Holy Jesus, get that boat up before the tide rises" was one thing he said from the floor and the other was "Be sure that all the valves are shut off before you do it." Two rather curious statements: one from his life before "the chance" and the other, perhaps, from after it, referring to the hospital. And then he was sound asleep. Even Grandma was a bit taken aback, looking down on him as he slept so peacefully, his mouth partly opened and his arms outstretched.

"Whatever will we do?" she mused, and then brightening she said, "I know." And going to the box of leftover Christmas tree decorations she began to extract various ornaments and strands of foil rope and even a rather tarnished star. She placed the star at Grandpa's head and deftly strung the rope about his limbs, and placed little balls and stars at strategic places on his outstretched limbs. She strung some Christmas icicles across his chest, where they looked vaguely like outworn war medals, and then sprinkled him with some artificial snow. The latter caused him to crinkle his nose, and it seemed for a moment that he might sneeze, but he slept on. And when she was finished her decorating, she took his picture. When Grandpa stirred later in the evening, he was at first almost afraid, seeming somewhat like Gulliver among the Lilliputians, awakening to find himself covered with small strands of silver foil, and for a while not really realizing just where he was nor what had happened to him. He did not move for a bit, allowing only his eyes to move about the room, until they finally came to rest on Grandma, who was sitting quietly in a chair not far from his feet. Then he lifted his right hand very slowly, looking at the snow and icicles that fell from it and at the green ball fastened to his middle finger.

"We thought that we would finish decorating you for Christmas," she said, looking at both my sister and me. And then she began to laugh. Slowly, like someone trying to extricate himself from a wired and potentially explosive bomb, Grandpa sat up, moving carefully and trying not to disturb his strands and streamers. When he stood up and looked down at the place he had vacated, it was almost possible to see his outline on the floor, like a sort of reverse snow angel, with bits of artificial snow and some of the ornaments outlining the former boundaries of his limbs. Later that night, at church, when he turned his head in certain directions, the golden muted lights reflected on the wisps of artificial snow still found within his hair.

After the picture was developed, he kept it in his wallet for years until it began to crease and fall apart the way such pictures do and then he had Grandma dig out the old negative so that another copy might be made.

I think of it now as one of those "joke" pictures taken for high-school yearbooks and which, years later, seem to reveal more than was ever realized at the time.

6 *M*y twin sister and I were the youngest children in our family, and we were three on March 28 when it was decided that we would spend the night with our grandparents.

After he returned from naval service in the war, my father had applied for the position of lightkeeper on the island which seemed almost to float in the channel about a mile and half from the town which faced the sea. He had long been familiar with boats and the sea and, after passing the examination, was informed in a very formal letter that the job was his. He and my mother were overjoyed because it meant they would not have to go away, and the job reeked of security, which was what they wanted after the disruption of the years of war. The older generation was highly enthusiastic as well. "That island will stay there for a damn long time," said Grandpa appreciatively, although he later apparently sniffed, "Any fool can look after a lighthouse. It is not like being responsible for a *whole* hospital."

On the morning of March 28, which was the beginning of a weekend, my parents and their six children and their dog walked ashore across the ice. Their older sons, who were sixteen, fifteen, and fourteen, apparently took turns carrying my sister and me upon their shoulders, stopping every so often to take off their mitts and rub our faces so that our cheeks would not become so cold as to be frozen without our realizing it. Our father, accompanied by our brother Colin, who was eleven, walked ahead of us, testing the ice from time to time with a long pole, although there did not seem much need to do so for he had "bushed" the ice some two months earlier, meaning he had placed spruce trees upright in the snow and ice to serve as a sort of road guide for winter travellers.

During the coldest days of winter, the so-called "dog days," the ice became amazingly solid. It was a combination of drift ice from the region of the eastern Arctic and "made" ice which resulted from the freezing of the local channel. In extremely cold winters if the ice was smooth, it was possible to move freely from the island to the mainland and back again. One could walk, or skate, or fashion an iceboat which would skim and veer with cutting dangerous speed across the stinging surface. People would venture out on the ice with cars and trucks, and on one or two weekends there would be horse races to the delight of all. The sharpshod horses would pull light sleighs or even summer sulkies as they sped around yet another track staked out by temporary spruce. At the conclusion of their races, their owners would hurry to cover them with blankets as the perspiration on their coats began to turn to frost. They seemed almost, for a few brief moments, to be horses who had prematurely aged before the eyes of those who watched them, their coats of black and brown turning to a fragile white. White horses frozen on a field of ice and snow.

My parents welcomed the winter ice because it allowed them to do many practical things that were more difficult to accomplish in the summer. They could truck their supplies over the ice without the difficulty of first hauling everything to the wharf and then trying to load it on the boat which swayed below and then, after transporting it across to the island, having to hoist it up out of the boat to the wharf's cap and then again having to transport it up the cliff to the promontory where the lighthouse stood. They took coal and wood across in the winter, and walked and traded animals, leading them by their halters across the treacherous and temporary bridge.

Also in the winter their social life improved, as unexpected visitors crossed to see them, bringing rum and beer and fiddles and accordions. All of them staying up all night, singing songs and dancing and playing cards and telling stories, while out on the ice the seals moaned and cried and the ice itself thundered and snapped and sometimes groaned, forced by the pressures of the tides and currents, running unabated and unseen beneath the cold white surface. Sometimes the men would go outside to urinate and when they would return the others would ask, "*De chuala?*" "What did you hear?" "Nothing," they would say. "*Cha chuala sion.*" "Nothing, only the sound of the ice."

On March 28 there was a lot for my family to do. My older brothers were going to visit their cousins in the country – those who still lived in the old *Calum Ruadh* houses neighbouring the spot which my grandparents had left when they became people of the town. If they could get a ride they were going to spend the weekend there. Even if they could not get a ride, they were planning to walk, saying that ten miles on the inland sheltered roads would not be as cold as a mile and a half straight across the ice. My parents were planning to cash my father's cheque, which they hoped my grandparents had picked up at the post office, and my brother Colin was looking forward to his new parka, which my mother had shrewdly ordered from the Eaton's sale catalogue when such heavy winter garments were reduced by the coming promise of spring. He had been hoping for it since before Christmas. My sister and I were looking forward to the visit with our grandparents, who always made a great to-do about us and always told us how smart we were to make such a great journey from such a far and distant place. And the dog knew where she was going too, picking her way across the ice carefully and sometimes stopping to gnaw off the balls of snow and ice which formed between the delicate pads of her hardened paws.

Everything went well and the sun shone brightly as we journeyed forth together, walking first upon the ice so we could later walk upon the land.

In the late afternoon, the sun still shone, and there was no wind but it began to get very cold, the kind of deceptive cold that can fool those who confuse the shining of the winter sun with warmth. Relatives visiting my grandparents' house said that my brothers had arrived at their destination and would not be coming back until, perhaps, the next day.

My parents distributed their purchases into haversacks, which were always at my grandparent's house, and which they used for carrying supplies upon their backs. Because my parents' backs would be burdened and because my brothers were not there, it was decided that my sister and I would "spend the night" and that our brothers would take us back to the island when they returned. It was suggested that Colin also might stay, but he was insistent that he go, so that he might test the long-anticipated warmth of the new parka. When they left, the sun was still shining, although it had begun to decline, and they took two storm lanterns which might serve as lights or signs and signals for the last part of the trip. My mother carried one and Colin the other, while my father grasped the ice pole in his hand. When they set out, they first had to walk about a mile along the shore until they reached the appropriate place to "get on" the ice and then they started across, following the route of the spruce trees which my father had set out.

Everyone could see their three dark forms and the smaller one of the dog outlined upon the whiteness over which they travelled. By the time they were halfway across, it was dusk and out there on the ice they lit their lanterns, and that too was seen from the shore. And then they continued on their way. Then the lanterns seemed to waver and almost to dance wildly, and one described an arc in what was now the darkness and then was still. Grandpa watched for almost a minute to be sure of what he was seeing and then he shouted to my grandmother, "There is something wrong out on the ice. There is only one light and it is not moving."

My grandmother came quickly to the window. "Perhaps they stopped," she said. "Perhaps they're resting. Perhaps they had to adjust their packs. Perhaps they had to relieve themselves."

"But there is only one light," said Grandpa, "and it is not moving at all."

"Perhaps that's it," said Grandma hopefully. "The other light blew out and they're trying to get it started."

My sister and I were playing on the kitchen floor with Grandma's cutlery. We were playing "store," taking turns buying the spoons and knives and forks from each other with a supply of pennies from a jar Grandma kept in her lower cupboard for emergencies.

"The light is still not moving," said Grandpa and he began hurriedly to pull on his winter clothes and boots, even as the phone began ringing. "The light is not moving. The light is not moving," the voices said. "They're in trouble out on the ice."

And then the voices spoke in the hurriedness of exchange: "Take a rope." "Take some ice poles." "Take a blanket that we can use as a stretcher." "Take brandy." "We will meet you at the corner. Don't start across without us."

"I have just bought all his spoons and knives," said my sister proudly from the kitchen floor, "and I still have all these pennies left."

"Good for you," said Grandma. "A penny saved is a penny earned."

When they were partway to the shore, their lights picked up the dog's eyes, and she ran to Grandpa when he called to her in Gaelic, and she leaped up to his chest and his outstretched arms and licked his face even as he threw his mitts from his hands so he could bury them deep within the fur upon her back.

"She was coming to get us," he said. "They've gone under."

"Not under," someone said. "Perhaps down but not under."

"I think under," said Grandpa. "She was under, anyway. She's soaked to the spine. She's smart and she's a good swimmer and she's got a heavy, layered coat. If she just went down, she'd be down and up in a second but she's too wet for that. She must have gone down, and then the current carried her under the ice and she had to swim back to the hole to get herself back out."

They went out on the ice in single file, the string of their moving lights seeming almost like a kind of Christmas decoration; each light moving to the rhythm of the man who walked and carried it in his hand. They followed the tracks and walked towards the light which remained permanent in the ice. As they neared it, they realized it was sitting on the ice, sitting upright by itself and not held by any hand. The tracks continued until they came to the open water, and then there were no more.

Years later, my sister and I were in Grade XI and the teacher was talking to the class about Wordsworth and, as an example, was reading to us from the poem entitled "Lucy Gray." When she came to the latter lines, both my sister and I started simultaneously and looked towards each other, as if in the old, but new to us, we had stumbled upon the familiar experience:

"They followed from the snowy bank
Those footmarks, one by one,
Into the middle of the plank;
And further there were none!"

"And further there were none!" But on March 28 we were tiring of our game of store and putting the cutlery away as our grandmother prepared to ready us for bed while glancing anxiously through the window.

Out on the ice the dog began to whine when they came near the open water, and the first men in the line lay on their stomachs, each holding the feet of the man before him, so that they might form a type of human chain with their weight distributed more evenly than if they remained standing. But it was of no use, for other than the light there was nothing, and the ice seemed solid right up to the edge of the dark and sloshing void.

There was nothing for the men to do but wonder. Beyond the crater, the rows of spruce trees marched on in ordered single file in much the same way that they led up to the spot of their interruption. It was thought that perhaps only one tree had gone down and under. The section of the ice that had gone was not large, but as my grandfather said, "It was more than big enough for us."

The tide was going out when they vanished, leaving nothing but a lantern – perhaps tossed on to the ice by a sinking hand and miraculously landing upright and continuing to glow, or perhaps, set down after its arc, wildly but carefully by a hand which sought to reach another. The men performed a sort of vigil out on the ice, keeping the hole broken open with their ice poles and waiting for the tide to run its course. And in the early hours of the morning when the tide was in its change, my brother Colin surfaced in one of those half-expected uncertainties known only to those who watch the sea. The white fur hood of his parka broke the surface and the half-frozen men who were crouched like patient Inuit around the hole shouted to one another, and reached for him with their poles. They thought that he had not been a great distance under, or that his clothes had snagged beneath the ice; and they thought that, perhaps, since he was not bearing a backpack, he had not been so heavily burdened and, perhaps, the new material in his parka possessed flotation qualities that had buoyed him to the top. His eyes were open and the drawstrings of his hood were still neatly tied and tucked beside his throat in the familiar manner that my mother always used.

My parents were not found that day, or the next, or in the days or months that followed.

7   *In* the morning my sister and I were having our porridge, mapping little rivers on its surface for the milk to follow and sprinkling it too liberally with brown sugar, and still for the most part unaware of what had happened. My grandmother hugged my sister fiercely to her and my grandfather ruffled my hair, "Poor *'ille bhig ruaidh*," he said. "Things will never, ever again be the same for you."

The wake for my brother Colin was held at the home of my grandparents, two days and two nights with the funeral on the third day. *Clann Chalum Ruaidh* came from great distances as well as from nearby, and it seemed the house would burst. The women sent in vast quantities of food; roasts fully cooked and surrounded by vegetables, and accompanied by containers of gravy; mounds of biscuits and homemade bread; and plates heaped high with pastries. And there were more than enough men to dig the grave in the frozen snow-covered cemetery, passing the pick from one to the other and watching the sparks fly up from the frozen earth.

When the mourners entered the house they went immediately to the casket to say their prayers, and then they would turn to offer their condolences. Many of them looked instinctively for my parents, because it was to the parents that one turned when a child was lost. And then they would remember, and compose themselves and look for the other closest next of kin. They would go towards my grandparents or my uncles and aunts or my stricken older brothers, embracing the women and shaking hands with the men and saying, "Sorry for your troubles. Sorry for your troubles." Throughout much of the wake many of them, in spite of themselves, kept looking towards the door as if expecting to see my parents coming in; coming home; called home by "a death in the family." But they never did come at all.

Throughout the days and nights of the wake, *clann Chalum Ruaidh* slept on chairs, and in the hallways, and sometimes on the floor in bedrooms where the beds were already full. And most of them took shifts, sitting up all night beside the small corpse of my brother Colin so he would not be alone. He lay in perfect stillness throughout it all, but with that type of perfection that still seems somehow to be in waiting. As if waiting for my mother to check his necktie or to make sure his fingernails were clean. As if she were to say, "You will be the centre of attention. Everyone will be looking at you."

Throughout the days and nights there was much conversation as to how and why it had all happened. Everyone agreed that my father was "a good man on the ice" and it was true that they had crossed over the same route earlier in the day. It was true, also, that the currents and tides were running freely and had perhaps eaten away more of the underside of the ice than anyone had realized. And it was, after all, the end of March and the sun had been shining, although it did not seem to have been that strong. It all remained, somehow, most inconclusive.

It was generally decided that it was an "act of God," as the insurance companies might term it, although *clann Chalum Ruaidh* referred to it as "God's will" and trusted in His Mercy. Some others who had read or misread the Book of Job saw it as an example of God's justice and His punishment, and cast about for reasons. Perhaps since my parents had taken the job on the island they had not gone to church as often as they should have? Perhaps they had engaged in pre-marital sex in the time before their marriage? Who was to know? Who was to find reasons?

Others told stories of forerunners; of how they had seen "lights" out on the ice "at the exact spot" years before, and of how such harbingers could now be seen as prophecies fulfilled.

Throughout the wake, my other grandfather made only irregular appearances because he was not a man for communal mourning. And later he volunteered to cross the ice and "look after the island" until a permanent replacement could be found. He took his violin with him and once or twice in the still evenings and when the wind blew towards the land it was possible to hear the laments he apparently thought he was playing only to himself. He played better than most people realized he could, and the music was even more haunting to those who understood its source. He played "The Cobh's Lament" and "Glencoe" and "Patrick MacCrimmon's Lament for the Children."

"We have suffered a great loss, but we have other children and we have each other," said Grandma. "Nobody knows the depths of that man's sorrow."

In the time after the wake, the older *Calum Ruadh* men who often sat around my grandparents' kitchen would sometimes offer my sister and me handfuls of coins because they could not think of anything else to do. Sometimes they would refer to us as the "lucky" children and sometimes as the "unlucky" children. "*M'eudail* on the little girl," they would say or, "Poor *'ille bhig ruaidh*, you have a long road ahead of you."

They say that beneath the ice there is always a layer of air between it and the actual water. And that if you are swept under, the thing to do is to try to turn on your back until you can almost press your mouth and nostrils against the underside of the ice which will, at least, allow you to breathe. And then you must keep your eyes open so that you can see the hole that you came through, and try to work yourself back towards it. If you close your eyes in the freezing salt, you may become disoriented, and therefore doomed, because you do not have much time. And if the currents are running strongly, they may take you under such a distance, and so quickly, that your most rapid reaction may prove, in the end, to be too slow.

I have often thought of my parents as upside down beneath the ice. Almost the way you see potato bugs on the underside of the leaf. Their hands and knees pushing upwards in something resembling a macabre fetal position, trying to press their mouths against the underside of the top which kept them down. Trying to breathe in order that they might somehow stay alive.

In the weeks that followed their loss, the sun shone brightly and the currents were strong, and the ice turned black beneath its own whiteness, as if eaten by a hidden cancer which only now began to make itself visible. And within a few days what had been a white and seeming certain expanse became but a view of bobbing cakes and swirling chunks, turning and reflecting in the light and grey-blue water.

Twice, before the breakup, the dog left my grandparents' house and crossed to the island looking for her people, and twice my uncles crossed to bring her back. The second time Grandpa tied her with a chain to the doorstep, but she whined, or "whinged," as they said, so visibly and so mournfully that the next morning Grandpa let her go. "Because she was breaking my heart," he said.

Immediately, she raced down to the shore and started across, running low across the level ice and hurling herself without hesitation into the open water, swimming to the nearest pan and then leaping from one pan to the other while Grandpa watched her progress through his binoculars. "She made it," he said, finally turning from the window. "Poor *cú*."

She was still there, waiting for her vanished people to rise out of the sea, when the new lightkeeper, "a man from the way of Pictou," nudged the prow of his boat against the wharf on the island's rocky shore. She came scrambling down the rocks to meet him, with her hackles raised and her teeth bared, protecting what she thought was hers and snarling in her certainty. And he reached into the prow of his boat for his twenty-two rifle and pumped four bullets into her loyal waiting heart. And later he caught her by the hind legs and threw her body into the sea.

"She was descended from the original *Calum Ruadh* dog," said Grandpa when he heard the news, pouring himself a water glass full of whisky which he drank without a flinch. "The one who swam after the boat when they were leaving Scotland. It was *in* those dogs to care too much and to try too hard."

On May 15, my other grandfather came across his daughter's purse while on one of his early-morning walks along the shore. It was still clasped tightly and inside it there was not much of value or interest to the larger world. There was a ten-dollar bill wrapped tightly within a handkerchief and the saleslip and guarantee for Colin's parka – in case it should not prove to be quite adequate.

Some pointed out that it was ironic that my grandfather should find the purse, that it should somehow "come" to him. But Grandma said he found it because he walked along the shore each morning after rising; that he found it because he looked, and there was nothing mysterious about it at all. Nothing else, as I said, ever "came" nor was ever "found." My grandfather kept the purse for many years until he gave it to my sister the week before her wedding.

This is the story of how my sister and I, as three-year-old children, planned "to spend the night" with our grandparents and remained instead for sixteen years until we left to go to university. This is a story of lives which turned out differently than was intended. And obviously much of this information is not really mine at all – not in the sense that I experienced it. For, as I said, while our parents were drowning, my sister and I were playing store. And in the generations a long time before, we did not see *Calum Ruadh*'s faithful dog swimming after her family to a life beyond the sea. And we did not see our great-great-great-grandmother, the former Catherine MacPherson, sewn into a canvas bag and thrown also into that same sea. But still, whatever its inaccuracies, this information has come to be known in the manner that family members come to know one another because they share such close proximity. Or as Grandma would say, "How could you *not* know that?"

"There are a lot of things I don't know," said Grandma, "but there are some things I really believe in. I believe you should always look after your blood. If I did not believe that," she would say, "Where would you two be?"

8 Now in Toronto in the late September sun, I stand and hesitate in the country of Queen Street West. Here beyond the expensive restaurants and the region of towers, the battle between restoring and destroying goes on. "For Sale," say some signs. "For Rent," announce others. The cranes with their wrecking balls are silent but poised, surrounded by the mounds of rubble which they have recently erected.

The people pass and jostle in the street, speaking in various dialects of Chinese, speaking Greek, Portuguese, Italian, English. Items in the windows claim to be "Imported." Brazen but wary pigeons flap their blue-grey wings and sometimes land to walk or waddle like pompous businessmen along the busy sidewalks. In the distance the protestors and counter-protestors move and mill. "Pacifists, Communists Love You." "If You Don't Think This Country Is Worth Defending, Go Somewhere Else."

Once at an orthodontists' conference in Dallas, a man noted my name tag and said to me, unexpectedly and improbably, "Who are these Ukrainians one is always hearing about in Canada?"

"They're people from the Ukraine," I said. "That's where they're from."

"No," he said. "There's no such place. They're Russians. I looked it up on the map."

"No, they're not Russians. The map changes."

"When I look at a map," he said, "I believe those lines. I believe it like I believe in an X-ray."

"But an X-ray shows you more than the obvious lines," I said rather pointlessly. "It tries to show you what's beneath."

"Look," he said, "lines are lines, right? Either they're there or they're not. There aren't any Ukrainians. They're Russians."

"It's not that simple," I said pointlessly again.

"I hear the Communists are taking over the medical system in Canada," he said. "That's why I asked the question."

"No," I said. "That's not that simple either."

"You keep saying everything's not that simple," he said. "To me there's a right way and a wrong way and medicine is free enterprise. I bet I make triple what you do."

"Probably so," I said. "But I make enough."

"You should come to Texas," he said. "In our business, you've got to go where the money is and now the money is here in Texas. This is where the rich are, and they're willing to pay to be beautiful."

He looked again at my name tag. "With an Irish name like that," he said, "you'd be in like Flynn. I changed my name. I mean my grandfather or someone did. To be more American. To fit in or whatever."

"What was it before?" I said, looking at his tag, which read, "Hi! My Name Is Bill Miller."

"I don't know," he laughed. "Who cares? It's all in the past. Look, do you guys consider yourselves Canadians first or North Americans first?"

"Well . . ." I began.

"Never mind," he said, laughing again and punching me lightly on the shoulder. "You're going to say it's not that simple. Have a good day." He moved easily into the crowd.

I hesitate now, to consider my purchase. At times like this I never know what to buy. Perhaps I should buy vodka because it is supposed to contain fewer impurities. Perhaps I should buy the brown molasses-like ales from the British Isles because they contain "food value" and will keep the consumer alive for a while and after a fashion. "The *clann Chalum Ruaidh* will live for a long time," said my grandfather. "If they are given the chance and if they want to."

A young woman wearing a black T-shirt walks towards me. The slogan on the front reads, "Living in the past is not living up to our potential."

9 *A*fter the death of my parents, my three brothers moved back to the old *Calum Ruadh* house my grandparents had lived in before the time of "their chance" which had allowed them to become "people of the town." It had not been lived in permanently for many years, although various people lived in it during the summer months when life was not so hard or desperate. My brothers were considered too young to do the necessary maintenance required of the lightkeeper and, as I said, the job went almost immediately to "the man from Pictou," who, like my father, was a veteran and had apparently been on a waiting list for such a civil service position.

None of my brothers returned to school after our parents' death and it seems no one suggested that they should, or made any attempt to force such an action on them. Since moving to the island, they had been largely taught by my parents, although sometimes they attended the town schools. But now that, like so much else, seemed "over" and of the past. They turned instead towards the house and the land beside the sea, taking with them the remnant objects of our parents' lives, objects to which various additions were gradually made.

When Grandpa and Grandma had become "people of the town," they had given various possessions they no longer needed to their friends and relatives: fishing nets, saws, chains, sets of harness, a colt, a calf. All of these, or items like them, came back to my brothers after a generation of absence and often much improved. The young mare, Christy, came that way and three young cattle and a dory which, while old, was newer than the one left behind by Grandpa. By the time the rotted ice had vanished, my brothers had their own few lobster traps ready, or were preparing to fish with various relatives, and attempting to plant a few potatoes and an acre or two of oats. Again, I say this now as if I knew about their lives, or heard the midnight stifled sobs of the youngest of my older brothers. But that was the spring my sister and I were more interested in the groundhog. We had just learned of the concept and it seemed of the most magnificent importance. "Do you think he will see his statue this year"? we had constantly asked our mother. "Not statue, shadow," she had replied, often adding, "I hope not. I don't think we could live through another six weeks of winter."

It is hard when looking at the pasts of other people to understand the fine points of their lives. It is difficult to know the exact shadings of dates which were never written down and to know the intricacies of events which we have not lived through ourselves but only viewed from the distances of time and space. I think of this at times amidst the soft brown decor of my office where we never, ever raise our voices and where the gentle music attempts to soothe and dispel fear. And where the well-to-do sit with folded hands in attitudes of patient trust. Hoping that I might make them more beautiful than they were before. "Trying to improve on God," as Grandma once sniffed.

"This will not hurt at all," I say softly, showing them the diagrams and the X-rays, the "before" and the hopeful "afters", tracing the fine lines of their jaws in pictures, discussing overbites and protrusions, looking at the present and to the future in terms of "what might be."

I think of how little I know or knew of my three brothers the spring that I and my sister were three and when they were fourteen, fifteen, and sixteen and our brother Colin was no more. Sealed forever in the perfection of the Eaton's parka tied by our mother's hands or behind the still, small necktie, which on his final appearance she did not touch at all.

I think of my brothers' lives only as I viewed them later. Going as the *gille beag ruadh* to visit them in the summer or sometimes in the winter. Travelling at first in sleighs or wagons behind their horses and later in the old cars they were always buying or trading or working upon. Marvelling at the lives they seemed to be living, which were so different from mine or from my sister's. And I do not know whether the specific memories come from the time when I was eight or ten or twelve or the years before or after, or how they stand out from the general ones which seem to pervade a longer length of time.

For a long time in the house where my brothers lived, there was neither plumbing nor electricity, and heat came from two stoves filled with wood they hauled with their horses from the shore. Some of the wood was driftwood and so filled with the "dried" salt water that it hissed and sputtered and gave off small explosions within the stove. Some of it was the near-useless black spruce they cut themselves with their bucksaws and crosscut saws from the stands where it grew so near the sea. Some of the trees had been exposed to the wind from the ocean for so long that particles of sand had become embedded within their trunks, into the very centre of their being, it seemed. And when the saw passed through them in the early darkness of the fall and winter evenings, streaks of blue and orange flame shot from them like the temporary streamers of a light show, flaring forth from the deep wood's heart. Steel on sand, unseen in wood. "It is there in the daytime too," said my brothers of the fire from the trees, "only you can't see it then. It makes it hard to keep an edge on the saws."

In the winter evenings my brothers would sit around their kitchen table bathed in the orange glow of their kerosene lamp, their gestures becoming exaggerated shadows thrown upon the walls, almost like friezes or the cave paintings of primitive men. Sometimes they would listen to their large box-like radio or play cards – "45's" or "Auction," either among themselves or with various friends and relatives, many of them of the *clann Chalum Ruaidh*, who came to pass the time of the long winter evenings. When they spoke it was often in Gaelic, which remained the language of the kitchen and the country for almost a generation after it became somewhat unfashionable in the living rooms of the town. In the time following their return to the old *Calum Ruadh* house and land, my brothers spoke Gaelic more and more, as if somehow by returning to the old land they had returned to the old language of that land as well. It being still the language of the place in which they worked.

Sometimes they would take the lids off the kitchen stove to provide more light and then the actual flames would flicker and flare in constantly changing patterns of orange and red and black, constantly changing patterns of colour and shadow within the stove and emanating from it to the surrounding walls and the dusky overhead ceiling. Sometimes those gathered would merely watch the fire and its shadows, but at other times it seemed to move them to tell stories of real or imagined happenings from the near or distant past. And if the older singers or storytellers of the *clann Chalum Ruaidh*, the *seanaichies*, as they were called, happened to be present they would "remember" events from a Scotland which they had never seen, or see our future in the shadows of the flickering flames.

In the winter, when my brothers went to bed, they seldom took off their clothes but often added extra old overcoats to the makeshift coverings of their beds, sometimes adding the robes and blankets which they used for their sleighs and their horses as well. In the morning the heads of the nails in the half-finished bedrooms would be white with frost, and the frost on the windowpanes would have to be scraped away with fingernails or melted by the warmth of breath before the outside world could be seen in its icy stillness. The water supply, which stood in two buckets on the table and which had been drawn from the ice-covered outside well, would be converted back to ice by the morning, and my brothers would smash the surface with hammers to get enough water for their tea. And after the fire had been lit, the buckets would be placed near the stove or even upon it, and after a while the ice on the bottom and around the sides of the bucket would thaw until it was possible to lift the inside circle of ice out of the bucket and place it, standing, in a dishpan. The circle would be of translucent crystal, like the perfect product turned out of the mould, bearing all the indentations and contours of the bucket which had shaped it, and with small bits of grass and leaves and sometimes tiny berries frozen within its shimmering transparency. Later, as the kitchen warmed, the ice would melt and, still later, the leaves and small berries would float unceremoniously in the tepid water and be lifted out by dippers or spoons or by the blades of knives as my brothers clutched their steaming tea. They seemed to have great difficulty in keeping intact cups within their house, or perhaps they were never really there to begin with. In any case they drank their tea from cups which had no handles or from jam jars or from the tops of thermos bottles.

I think of all this now much as I think I marvelled at it then. Marvelling, somehow, that they could live such different lives than I, while still somehow belonging to me, as I and my sister belonged to them. For at times they seemed almost more like our distant uncles than like our actual brothers. And they never paid attention to the regulations that governed our lives. Never paid attention to Canada's Food Guide or to brushing their teeth before and after meals or to changing into clean pyjamas before going to bed. And at their house the bathroom was a bucket.

In those early years my sister and I were given advantages which my grandparents had been unable to give their own children. There was space enough for each of us to have individual rooms, which was a luxury my grandparents' own children had not had. And my grandmother indulged her feminine fantasies in the clothes she purchased for my sister and in the elaborate doilies and afghans and bedspreads she crocheted and knitted and quilted for her bedroom. Grateful for "the chance" which had freed her from slapping her washing on the rocks and grateful too for the gift of time which she had not had much of when she was raising her own children. "We have a lot to be thankful for," she often said, "even though we have had our losses."

Throughout our formative years, my sister and I lived under the ambiguous circumstances of being the "lucky, unlucky" children, and of regarding our grandparents as our parents because they were closest to us in that role, while still yearning for the drowned idealized people who had gone into the sea.

Some weeks ago, my eye fell upon an article in one of those magazines you sometimes see in the waiting rooms of the orthodontist's office. It was called "Rearing the Modern Child," and one of the subheadings was entitled "Grandparents." The modern parent must sometimes be wary of grandparents, the article warned, for grandparents have a tendency to be overindulgent and sometimes to act irresponsibly. "They often act this way," the article stated, "because they know the child will eventually go to its own home and they will not be responsible for its behaviour in that area."

The article pointed out that grandparents are generally more indulgent with their grandchildren than they were with their own children, "because modern psychological theory indicates that they do not love them quite so much."

"You are lucky that you can live here all the time," said our enraged cousin, the red-haired Alexander MacDonald who lived some fifteen miles away in the country and was visiting us on a particular afternoon. "Just because your parents died."

We were all very young then, perhaps seven or eight, and my

sister and I had laughed at him for spilling his tea into his saucer to cool it before drinking it from the same saucer. Later, in my room, he had punched me in the nose and I had hit him in return, and then we had fallen upon one another. As we wrestled back and forth across the room, he said, "They're my grandparents too, you know." He was stronger than I was and I can still feel the callouses on his small hands as they grappled about my face and neck. "No, they're not," I gasped, perhaps because I felt I was losing the physical battle or because of who knew what psychological theory. And then Grandpa was in the room. "Here, here," he said. "What is going on in here?" and he grasped us both by our upper arms and lifted us off the floor so that our small angry feet kicked vainly in the useless air, even as we felt our arms and shoulders growing numb within his powerful hands.

"He says you're not my grandfather, only his," said the sobbing red-haired Alexander MacDonald.

"Of course, I'm yours," said Grandpa, setting us both down and motioning us towards neutral corners as the referee in a boxing match does. "Of course, I'm yours," he said, going to stand in the corner of the red-haired Alexander MacDonald, as my sister and I both felt a slight twinge of betrayal. And turning and pointing to me with his huge forefinger, he said, "Don't you ever say that again. Ever."

"They're just lucky," said Alexander MacDonald, perhaps because he perceived the advantage of having the referee in his corner, "just lucky because their parents are dead."

"And don't you," said Grandpa, suddenly reversing the direction of his finger until it was under the trembling nose of Alexander MacDonald, "ever say that again, either. Never."

Later, much subdued in the kitchen, Alexander MacDonald sat beside his father, who patted him on the knee but also smiled across at me. His father continued to talk to Grandpa in a mixture of English and Gaelic as Grandpa slid the bottles of beer across the table in his direction. It seemed strange that such a big man could be the father of Alexander MacDonald, while, at the same time, being the son or "boy" of Grandpa. But there was no doubt that he was, especially when you saw the way that Grandpa patted him on the shoulder when he rose to leave. "Take care," said Grandpa. "Everything will be all right."

"Yes," said Grandma, "*Beannachd leibh*, good luck."

"I will return it as soon as I can," he said, standing framed in the doorway before going out into the suddenly descended night.

"It is all right," said Grandma. "No hurry."

"Yes," agreed Grandpa. "No rush, and take care of yourself," and then he patted him on the shoulder once again.

I think now, years later, that he had probably been borrowing money from them so that he might get over some seasonal crisis or other. Or perhaps it was something else. But at that time I thought, in the security of my childish selfishness, it was unfair that Alexander MacDonald should have such a big, strong father *and* a grandfather as well. And it was also unfair that this same big man should have *his* father to pat him on the shoulder and tell him to "take care" and "everything will be all right," while I and my sister, in our smallness, did not have one at all.

"I will not have any more of that performance," said Grandma with icy efficiency after the door had closed. Both my sister and I then realized that she had been talking to Grandpa.

"Saying that you are our only grandchildren. There are enough problems in the world without fighting with your own blood."

"Oh, they won't do it any more," said Grandpa. "We all lose our tempers from time to time. I believe I'll have another beer. We're not here for a long time but for a good time."

10

Now, in the sky, on the high-rise horizon, seagulls appear caught in the glint of the September sun, and beneath them, but invisible to me, is the white activity of Toronto harbour. Farther south, in the country from which I have come, and to which I will return, the fruit and vegetable pickers bend and stretch wearily. The sweat trickles down the crevices of the weekend pickers and blotches their clothes. The children become grumpy and stage brief sit-down strikes, oblivious to the speeches of their parents who tell them of the money they are saving or of how good the produce will taste in winter. Sometimes the parents criticize them harshly, telling them they are lazy, or uttering speeches, beginning, "When I was a child . . ." The children look at their hands and are fascinated by the earth beneath their fingernails and mildly fearful of the beginning hangnails and the unfamiliar scratches. "I think I've got a thorn in my finger," they say. "What time is it now?" "Haven't we got enough?" "If I promise not to eat any of this stuff in the winter can I stop picking now?" "My thumb is bleeding. I can see my own blood." "I wish I had something to drink."

In other fields the imported pickers move with quiet speed. Sometimes they look towards the sun to gauge the time, and sometimes they stand straight and place their hands to the smalls of their backs but never for long. Their eyes scan the rows and the branches and the full and the empty baskets. They are counting all the time and doing primitive arithmetic within their heads. They do not sweat, and their children do not complain. When the sun goes down, this Saturday evening, the field owner may sell them cases of beer purchased from the local beer store or some of the men may find their way to certain taverns. The strictly religious and the most fearful will not go. Those who do go sit by themselves and talk in their own languages and some add up present and future totals on cigarette packages. Many of them are imagining themselves back home, as they sit nervously tearing the beer labels off their bottles or drumming their blunt brown fingers on the uneven surfaces of the crowded tables, slopped with beer.

I do not know what to buy for my brother or for myself. What to buy for the men who have everything or nothing.

"It doesn't make much difference," he said. "It doesn't make much difference." Pick your own.

II *B*y the time my sister and I were entering our teenaged years, a lot had happened to our older brothers. A lot, I suppose, had happened to us all. A lot of it quietly, coming like the growth of hair in new places for some, while the hair of others was receding or thinning or changing colour. Change without sound, yet change nonetheless, and change that was important, although sometimes invisible as well as silent. As quiet as the cancer cells which multiply within the body or the teeth within the imperfect jaw which "drift" towards the spaces vacated by their fellows. As quiet as the ice which wears and rots beneath its white deceptive surface or the sperm which journeys towards the womb and reaches its destination without a single sound – after the screams of orgasm are no more.

When my sister and I were smaller, we visited our brothers with all of the excitement of children going to visit grandparents who happened to live in the country. We did not go there for Thanksgiving or for Christmas, it is true, but we went when we were offered rides or when we could convince Grandma that we would be careful and not get in our brothers' way. We explored what seemed to be the surfaces of their lives, although we did not think of it that way. We were fascinated by all of the differences. By the animals which crowded around their house and even came inside if they got the chance. Lambs and calves and hens which would walk into the kitchen if the door was left open. Horses which would press their noses to the window, as if to see what was going on inside. Flies and sometimes wasps and hornets which buzzed in through cracks or tattered screens or opened doors. Cats with kittens in the upstairs bedrooms. And the ubiquitous *Calum Ruadh* dogs, lying like rugs beneath the table or following behind whatever humans seemed to catch their fancy.

If we were there in the windy days of fall, and if the wind were off the sea, we would run down to the *Calum Ruadh*'s Point and engage in contests to see who could remain standing in the wind's force the longest. If we faced the sea, the wind would blow our breath back within us as the spray from the water on the rocks rose and covered us and *Calum Ruadh*'s gravestone with glistening drops, and we would have to avert our heads and gasp for air or throw ourselves on our stomachs and breathe with our mouths pressed against the flattened grass or the cranberry vines or the creeping tendrils of wet moss. If the wind were off the land, we would not be allowed to go, for fear that a sudden gust might lift and carry us over the point and dash us down to the shining boulders or out to fall into the wind-whipped sea, which was always brown and angry in its state of agitation.

After such storms, the face of the cliff would be changed, although ever so slightly. Bits of rock would have fallen because of the waves' pounding, and small sections of the seams of clay and shale would also have been washed into the sea. Only the hardest promontories of pure stone seemed to remain constant, but if one looked closely one could see changes in them also. A new smoothness born of a new wearing, or small pockmarks on new surfaces where previously there were none. The cliff was moving inland, slowly but steadily, while *Calum Ruadh*'s grave seemed to be moving out towards its edge.

Gradually, it seemed, my sister went less frequently to the house of our older brothers. It is always hard to notice change when you are in its midst, especially as a child. Perhaps in the same way that one does not notice the change the sea inflicts upon the cliff until the morning following the storm. In retrospect, it seems the change was as much due to their perception of her and her own changes as to any other factor. A certain uneasiness at the development of her own small femininity in the midst of their masculine lives. Almost as if they became more unsure as we all grew older. As if their lives and the environment surrounding it were good enough for them but not for her.

Perhaps they were embarrassed by the fact that the bathroom was a bucket or sometimes not even that; that in the hot summer nights, after drinking beer, they would raise their upstairs windows and urinate down the outside clapboard walls of their silent house, the steam rising upwards to meet them from the dark. Embarrassed by the fact that they slept with loaded rifles under their beds, and on nights when the moon shone with its full brightness, they would kneel or crouch by their opened windows, straining to sight the antlers of the deer who moved across the silent fields towards their beleaguered garden. They would lean forward from their windows, straining to see along the blue-grey barrels of their rifles which glinted in the moonlight, straining to get the antlered head in line with the rifle's sights by the light of *Lochran àigh nam bochd*, the Gaelic phrase for the moon, "the lamp of the poor."

And if the shot were true, they would race down the stairs, fastening their trousers as they ran, and gather their long-bladed knives from the waiting kitchen table. Out in the field, lit by the "lamp of the poor," they would cut the throat of the still-thrashing deer so that the blood would run free and not taint or ruin the valuable meat. They would work quickly and efficiently, disembowelling and skinning and cutting the carcass into quarters, their knives flashing in and out of the body's cavities, severing the grey ropes of the intestines and separating the still-shuddering redness of the heart. Later they would pack the meat within buckets and lower it into the well as a means of basic refrigeration, pulling it up by wet ropes when it was needed, but ever aware that it would not last for very long.

My brothers were embarrassed, in my sister's presence, by the silver-grey rooster energetically servicing the members of his harem, pressing their beaks towards the dust, it seemed, whether they liked it or not, and by the slavering, moaning bull mounting the cow as she offered herself to him in the yard.

And they were embarrassed at mealtimes, embarrassed by the cups without handles and by the fact that they sometimes ate standing up, spearing the half-boiled potatoes out of the bubbling pot upon the stove and sometimes peeling them with the same knives they used to bleed the deer's throat or to cut the rope and twine of their fishing gear. Embarrassed by the flies and by the dishes waiting too long in the dishpan to be washed.

One day, at noon, my small sister said, "Don't you have a tablecloth here?" and again, "Don't you have any napkins?" I remember the eyes of the youngest of my older brothers clouding over at her questions as if he were saying to himself, "If mother were here now, she would know what to do." Feeling inadequate, perhaps, in what he perceived as a feminine situation and perhaps remembering his mother in a way in which my sister and I did not. Remembering her interest in order and cleanliness. "You are the only person I know who goes around looking in other people's ears," he had said grumpily to her that morning before they set off across the ice and when she was making her final inspection. More final, it turned out, than was then realized, for she was never again to look into the cavities of the ears of anyone.

Because there was no wharf on the shore off which my brothers fished, their boat had to be dragged onto the rocks above the high-water mark when the day was done. It also had to be pushed into the water when the day began, and sometimes they would be up to their knees or even their waists before the boat would have enough water to float free of the strand without grounding its prow upon the rocky bottom. After the final shove, they would clamber over the bow or even the sides, if the boat had begun to turn, and they would grasp the oars and pole or row themselves out farther until it was safe to kick their engine into life. Eventually they built themselves a primitive skidway of creosoted timber, which they coated with grease and which made both the launching and the landing considerably easier. On the shore, beside the skidway, they kept a horse collar and a set of harnesses and a whipple tree and a chain. And each morning, when they set out, they took with them a can of oats with a tightly secured lid which they placed within the bow of the boat.

When their day on the water was done and as they approached the shore, my oldest brother, Calum, would stand forward in the bow and, placing the fingers of his right hand within his mouth, emit two piercing whistles. And the mare, Christy, although often grazing almost a mile away with the other horses, would raise her head and toss her mane and come galloping down towards the shore, sending the small rocks and flecks of turf flying before her eager hooves.

And after the engine was shut off, and as the boat glided silently towards the land, its wake spreading out in a widening V behind it, she would wait, nickering and tossing her head and lifting her front hooves impatiently in the water curling upon the shore. "Ah, Christy," he would say, "*M'eudail bheag,*" and he would jump over the bow and come towards her, holding the oats before him like an ancient trader proffering goods to the individual who waited upon the land. And as she nuzzled the oats, he would pat her neck and croon into her mane, a mixture of Gaelic and English syllables – almost as if he were courting and she were the object of his strong affections. And then he would put the collar on her neck, followed by the harness, and hook the chain into the steel ring which he had drilled into the boat's prow. And, again, responding to his whistle, she would leap forward and, in a scrabble of flying rocks, haul the boat up the greased skidway and to the safety which lay beyond the water's reach. And then he would pull the harness off and pat her some more while she rubbed her strong head up and down against his chest, and then she would go off to join her fellows while he and his brothers walked towards home.

And I remember a day when I had accompanied them on the water and everything had seemed to go wrong. It had been cold and raining and the engine seemed to sputter and cough because of what was perceived as water in the gas and the carburetor had to be checked and the gas lines blown free while the boat rocked randomly at the mercy of the waves. The buoys were adrift and the ropes seemed to become fouled and tangled with a perverse spirit all their own. And the left side of Calum's face was swollen and throbbing because of the broken and infected molar which had been pulsating there for days. It was a Saturday morning and I had received a ride to their house on Friday evening and had begged to go with them in the boat on the following morning. They had not been expecting me and were reluctant to take me because of the unpleasant weather but uneasy too about leaving me in their house alone. I had finally been allowed to accompany them and my responsibility was to take the oats for Christy. Now as the boat finally neared the shore I realized I had forgotten it. We had been rushed in the morning and everyone had been so occupied with the day's problems that its absence had gone unnoticed. I did not say anything. It had been a miserable day and I longed for the comfort of my grandparents' house and my microscope and my stamp collection and the radio and the possibility of playing chess with my sister. I had made more than one mistake, it seemed, but I still did not say anything.

As the boat approached the shore, the engine which had been so troublesome all day was shut off and Calum went to the prow and uttered two shrill whistles. We could not see any horses, but assumed they were standing in the trees as they sometimes did to take shelter from the rain. He whistled again and then she appeared, silhouetted in the rain high above the *Calum Ruadh*'s Point. And then she came galloping down to meet us. Once, her hind legs slipped sideways on the rain-drenched footing, leaving a brown skidmark on the wet greenness of the grass, but she recovered quickly and came hurtling headlong down towards us.

"Where's the goddamn oats?" he said as he prepared to go over the side to meet her. My omission was suddenly noticeable to all.

"Jesus Christ," he said. "As if there hasn't been enough wrong with this goddamn day, and now this." And he seized me by the front of my jacket and lifted me with my feet dangling above the side of the boat as I looked into his enraged and swollen face. I had the temporary sensation that he might fling me overboard.

"Put him down," said my other brothers in chorus even as I said, "But it's okay. She comes anyway."

"It's *not* okay," he shouted, shaking me so that my teeth rattled. "She comes because it's part of the bargain. She depends on us to do the right thing." And then he more or less let me fall into the bottom of the boat. And it was difficult to know whether I had been rejected or released.

"Jesus Christ," he said, putting his hand to his jaw. "This is killing me." And then he reached forward to the box of tools he had been using too much all morning in an attempt to solve the engine's problems. Taking the grease-stained and gasoline-smelling pliers in his right hand, he thrust them into his mouth and twisted even as he pulled. There was the sharpened shudder one associates with the fingernail upon the blackboard except it was more screamingly intense. And perhaps it was caused by the steel on the tooth but more likely by the tooth grinding on the bone of its foundation. Twice he twisted and jerked his head sideways even as he leaned it in the opposite direction and the blood and pus began to run down the contours of his jaw and down his neck to vanish within the hair upon his chest. But in spite of the strength of his hand, the loosened and bloodied tooth held firm within its place.

By this time the boat was drifting sideways towards the rocky shore where Christy waited impatiently, tossing her head in the falling rain and nickering for our landing. We had to shake ourselves like people coming out of a mesmerizing trance to reach for the oars and to redirect our bow towards the land. Calum went over the side, although he had no oats, and Christy came down to meet him and nuzzled his extended palm, which was all he had to offer. And he patted her neck and crooned to her as always, even as he wiped his bloodied hands on her wet and glistening mane. And then he harnessed her as usual. But instead of hooking the chain into the boat's ring he asked for a length of rope which he fastened to its end. And to the other end of the rope he fastened a length of light but tensile line and, climbing back into the boat, tied the line somehow around his tooth.

"Hold me down," he said to his brothers. And when Christy heard the whistle, she bunched her shoulders and sprang forward as she was used to, without knowing she was tied to a man instead of to a boat. When her weight hit him, his head and the upper part of his body snapped forward but his brothers had braced their feet and set their shoulders and they held him firm as the yellowed infected tooth flew out and over the bow and rolled at the end of its line like a white and yellow seashell in the waters of the shore. It seemed very flimsy now in proportion to the pain that it had cost, and Christy stopped and looked over her shoulder the way she did when the chain had not been hooked properly to the boat's ring or a piece of her harness had become disconnected or broken. She had felt little or no weight at all.

"Thank Christ," he said, reaching over the side and scooping up handfuls of salt water which he splashed into his bleeding mouth, rinsing and spitting and coughing. "I was not angry at you, *'ille bhig ruaidh*," he said, turning to me. "It was my tooth that was bothering me." There was a cut on his lower lip where the line had sliced through at the zinging moment of tautness. It seemed to bleed with a bright clear redness all its own.

12

On Monday morning my office will be filled, as it was on Friday, with those who want to be more beautiful. Some are children whose parents have made their appointments for them. Some are referrals made by friends and colleagues who practise the more basic forms of dentistry. Others have sought me out from considerable distances in the hope that I might give them what they want and think they need.

There are some who would wish to alter their jawlines so that they might look more like current pop stars. Sometimes they bring pictures of what they would hope to be along with them. Shyly they bring the pictures forth from within their purses or from the inside pockets of their expensive jackets.

"You really do not need this," I say to some of them. "Think of the future. If this were to happen, you might find out it is not really what you want at all." I look at them carefully, as might the doctor advising the young man against a vasectomy. Quietly we talk about the consequences and the expectations.

In some cases we talk more basically about the impacted wisdom tooth, the mesiodens and the supernumerary teeth of children. I give them leaflets with titles such as "What May Happen After the Removal of an Impacted Tooth" or "Advice Following Oral Surgery." The leaflets contain headings such as *Pain, Swallowing, Swelling*, along with advice on medication:

To reduce the density of pain, you must take the medication which is prescribed. Follow the instructions exactly. Do not wait for the pain to become too severe before taking the prescribed tablets; otherwise it may become more difficult to control. Should the pain become too intense please notify this office immediately.

Or:

Do not rinse the mouth until the following morning and then only gently. Rinsing too early and/or too frequently may prevent clotting and also healing. When rinsing use warm salt water which will help to flush out food particles lodged in the operated area. (Half a teaspoonful of salt in a glass of lukewarm water.) If in doubt do not hesitate to call this office.

Or (under the heading *Complications Which May Occur*):

Sometimes the hole left behind after the molar's removal may remain for some time. Gradually it should fill in with bone and new tissue. Sometimes, as healing advances, small sharp splinters may work up through the tissue and be a source of discomfort and unexpected pain. Gradually, though, they should disappear. If in doubt do not hesitate to call this office.

Here in the September sun, on my reluctant way to purchase the alcohol which my eldest brother may or may not need, the newspapers rise on gusts of wind before my feet. Sometimes the sheets flap open and float like the roofs of pagodas revealing the different languages of their origin. The people jostle and bump momentarily on the way to their private destinations. The pigeons walk and flap, rising sometimes almost in concert with the newspapers. They cast their bright eyes everywhere and seem never to be surprised. One alights before me, but upon landing tilts sideways. I notice that its right foot is a pink and crumpled ball almost like a knob, and that it is crippled upon the sidewalk. When it rises in the wind, the defect is not noticeable and it seems to flap and fly like all the others. It rises above the greyness of the buildings, circles, and returns.

13 As my brothers grew older, they moved out more from their home and land. They became more rest-less, perhaps, the way all young men do. Indirectly we heard of their involvement in fights as they travelled what seemed like long distances over the winding roads of night: going to dances, going to play hockey, going sometimes merely "to see what was going on" ten or twenty or thirty or forty miles away. Sometimes Calum and my brothers were "saved" from their impetuosity by the members of *clann Chalum Ruaidh* who rallied to their aid in the distant darkness, and sometimes they themselves went to the aid of casual cousins and the various causes they espoused. Travelling in their patched-up and wired-together cars and being frequently stopped by the RCMP for driving without a headlight, driving without a tail light, driving without a muffler, driving without proper registration, driving on expired licence plates, driving under the influence of alcohol.

Old men and old women would tell my grandparents such third- or fourth-hand information while sitting in the kitchen drinking tea or perhaps some of Grandpa's freely offered beer.

"I hope no harm will come to them," Grandma would say, looking out her window towards the ocean which had swal-lowed up "the children" who were the parents of the young men under discussion. And again, "If only they had come to live with us, but they were too old to be children and still too young to be like men."

"They are still only being young," Grandpa would say, rising optimistically from his chair at the kitchen table. "I was young once myself," he would say, winking at Grandma, "perhaps you remember."

"Oh yes," Grandma would say, "we were all young once. This, though, is different."

Sometimes, at night, when I walked home from my other grandfather's (after I had taken to going there to listen to him talk about his views on Highland history or to be tutored in chess), I would see my brothers rolling through the streets in whichever of the battered, rusted, reconstructed cars they were using at the time. In memory, it seems always to be winter, although I know it was not so. Yet they seem to ride most consistently through streets of muffled snow; to glide almost quietly, in spite of their imperfectly tuned engine, through the snow beneath the balding tires and through the flakes that slanted down, yellow and golden before their headlights.

Sometimes they would stop and talk, rolling down the windows but keeping the engine running. The falling snow would melt upon the heated hood and the windshield wipers would squeak back and forth describing arcs which cleansed imperfectly. The rumbling, coughing exhaust system held up by haywire would melt the snow on the street beneath it, turning it first to a carbon black before it vanished in an ever-widening and imperfectly jagged circle. Sometimes they would reach for bottles of beer beneath the seat, opening the bottles with their teeth and spitting the caps through the opened windows and down the side of the car and into the snow. They would ask me how things were going and about my sister, who was also theirs, and sometimes they would offer me money, although they knew I did not need it. And then they would move off into adventures which, it seemed, were very different from mine. For by that time I was beginning to play "organized hockey" and was interested in my stamp collection and the "modern" music on the radio and the chessboard and the microscope which my other grandfather had given me for Christmas.

Sometimes, in the morning of the later summer months, Grandpa would find inside his porch, placed there beyond the door which he always left open, roasts from the deer which had been shot beneath "the lamp of the poor," and sometimes gallon jugs of clear white moonshine. Grandma was more skeptical than usual of the moonshine, saying, "You never know what might be in it," although Grandpa would maintain, "They would not bring it if there was anything wrong with it."

"I hope they are not making that stuff themselves," said my other grandfather. "Nothing good ever came of it." And then he would add, with a shudder as he watched Grandpa emptying his glass, "How can you drink that stuff? Once when I was a young man, I was at a Saturday-night dance at a country schoolhouse. And out behind the building, where we had gone to urinate, someone offered me a drink from a jug. It was dark and on my second swallow I felt something going down my throat and then something like legs against my lips and teeth. They were huge dead June bugs – the kind that bang against the screen door in the summer. I spit the one out of my mouth, but I had already swallowed the other and then I started to vomit and I remember holding my legs apart, like a horse when he urinates, so I would not vomit on my new shoes and on my pants which I had spent the early evening ironing. Whoever had run off the shine from the still must have done so in the dark and did not know that the June bugs had fallen into it. It cured me forever."

"Oh well," said Grandpa. "They were probably pretty well pickled by the time they got to you. You can't worry about everything."

I think now, on this Toronto afternoon, of the different men who became my grandfathers even as they were many other things as well. I think of how Grandpa would go forth on such a mission as this of mine with boyish enthusiasm and of how he would return with his arms full of beer and wine; how he would step briskly up the dirty stairs and along the corridor lit by the forty-watt bulb, moving past the moans from behind the closed doors and through the stench of vomit and urine while seeming oblivious to it all. And of how he would enter the door and hope to sing his Gaelic songs and tell his jokes and his mildly off-colour stories, slapping his hand on his huge knee, while dispensing and trusting in his own form of medication. And of how my other grandfather's pace would be even slower than mine, if he would go at all. And of how he would recoil and purse his lips and try to think of other solutions. Of how he might fix or mend or balance, wrinkling his forehead as he might do when confronted with filling out Grandpa's income tax return, trying to make sense of the scribbled bits of information and the crumpled balls of paper which were supposed to serve as receipts and messages from the past.

One spring when he had completed Grandpa's tax return, and after he had properly affixed his signature, and stroked his t's with his careful fountain pen and replaced the cover on the ink bottle and was ready for Grandpa's question, which was always "Do I get anything back?" he went over the form with me, pointing out how easy it really was if all the information were correct. Grandpa had lost interest in the project almost immediately upon entering the door, preferring to console himself with the available whisky and choosing to regard the whole process as a mystery not worth solving, brightening only when it was time to ask his question. When he was told he would get money back, although only a modest amount, he slapped Grandfather on the shoulder and said, "My hope is constant in thee, Clan Donald," which is what Robert the Bruce was supposed to have said to the MacDonalds at the Battle of Bannockburn in 1314.

"When the MacDonalds came back from the Battle of Killiecrankie," said my grandfather thoughtfully, leaping ahead more than three and a half centuries in historical time, "it was in the fall of 1689. They had been away since May and in that time some of their children had been born and some of their parents had died. Their barley and oats had ripened, and they were already late for the season's harvest."

"But they had won," said Grandpa, who, with spirits raised because of his promised tax refund, had seated himself at the table and poured himself another glass of whisky.

"Yes, they had won," said Grandfather. "They had won the battle in the old way, but they had also lost a lot. They had lost the exciting young man who was their leader and their inspiration and who, somehow, gave them a belief in their cause. They carried his body from the field in their bloodied plaids and buried him in the churchyard. Perhaps it was the beginning of the end, for afterwards it was not the same – although they remained and fought for a man they did not much care for, after others who began with them had gone home."

"Loyal as hell," said Grandpa appreciatively.

"Yes, loyal to a cause which was becoming daily more muddled and which was to cost them dearly in the end," said Grandfather reflectively. "Trying to hold their place. They lost a lot of men," he added seriously. "A lot at Killiecrankie and more at Dunkeld after the major battle."

"They were brave as hell," said Grandpa with enthusiasm.

"Yes," said Grandfather, "but I think they were also afraid."

"Never," said Grandpa, half rising tipsily from his chair, as if he would defend the honour of all the MacDonalds in the world. "Never was a MacDonald afraid."

"I see them sometimes," said my grandfather, looking at the table and seeming to see his vision rise from the envelope containing Grandpa's tax return. "I see them sometimes coming home across the wildness of Rannoch Moor in the splendour of the autumn sun. I imagine them coming with their horses and their banners and their plaids tossed arrogantly over their shoulders. Coming with their broadswords and their claymores and their bull-hide targes decorated with designs of brass.

Singing the choruses of their rousing songs, while the sun gleams off the shining of their weapons and the black and the redness of their hair."

"Great," said Grandpa, slapping his knee, as if he were watching a favourite television show or sitting in a theatre watching a movie.

"But sometimes," said Grandfather, smiling almost half apologetically as if he might be spoiling Grandpa's picture, "I imagine them thinking of the dead they left behind. Of the hundreds of bodies at the pass of Killiecrankie, even if they won, and of those left behind in the streets of Dunkeld. Of those who sought refuge in the houses and were burned alive when the houses were set aflame. I think of them carrying home their wounded, draped over the horses' backs or on stretchers which were only plaids clutched in white-knuckled fists. Of the one-legged men with their arms thrown over their comrades' shoulders, trying to hop back the long miles they had walked or run across in the months of spring. Trying to get back to Glengarry or Glencoe or Moidart or wherever they came from. Of the men with bleeding stumps where their hands used to be, or of those bleeding between the legs – ruined in *that* way," he said quietly, looking at Grandpa. "Those who, if they ever got back, would never leave again. And of those who did not get back, although they had made it through the battle, but could not make it over the long, mountainous walk back home and were buried instead beneath cairns of stones in the rocky or the boggy earth, depending upon when and where they died. Never to get back in time for themselves or for those who waited for them."

"Like your own father," said Grandpa helpfully, by this time trying to make connections.

"When I think of them in this way," said Grandfather, who had hesitated only momentarily, "I think of their thoughts in a different manner. Coming back the way they or their fathers had come some forty years before. They and their fathers coming back in 1645 over the mountains. Fighting then for the Royalist cause or their own individuality. Led by Montrose and the poet Iain Lom across the high corries in late January and early February. Licking the oatmeal out of their palms, lapping the blood and gnawing the raw meat of the slaughtered winter deer because they were afraid of the betrayal of fires. When I think of them coming down bare-legged through the blizzards, with the sleet and ice in the black and redness of their hair, I think of them saying 'Well, this better be worth it. Somehow.' And here they are again, forty years later, coming back with the ambiguous thoughts of Killiecrankie.

"When I think of them in this way," said Grandfather quietly and almost embarrassed because he seldom spoke for so long, "the sun does not shine in the fall on Rannoch Moor, but instead it is raining. Their feet within their brogues slip on the edges of the bog and they are tired and hungry. The rain runs down their necks and in rivulets from their hair, and falls from their eyelashes and their noses. They curse at the treacherous footing and when their larger weapons grow too heavy, they throw them away into the heather."

"Well, we have to be going now," said Grandpa, rising from his chair and seeming almost self-conscious because of the serious turn of the conversation. "But I will have one for the road."

"Help yourself," said Grandfather with a smile. "Take care. *Beannachd leibh*."

On the way home through the darkened spring streets, Grandpa and I walked side by side, although sometimes his body lurched against mine. At a secluded spot, he stopped to urinate and said to me over his shoulder, "I liked the first picture best, didn't you? The one about the MacDonalds coming home in the sun?" I did not know what to say, so only made a noncommittal sound which I hoped carried over the steaming hiss of his water. From the ponds beside the sea the frogs were in full chorus, singing forth the songs of their courtship, and out on the island, the light my parents once kept flashed its regulated warning, and far along the coast we could see the lights from the houses of *clann Chalum Ruaidh*, with those of my brothers bright among them.

When we arrived home, Grandpa said, "Well, I'm getting money back after all." He had regained his old enthusiasm, and made the announcement as if he had filled out the form himself.

"God bless that man," said Grandma. "All he has done for us all."

"I told him," said Grandpa. "I said, 'My hope is constant in thee, Clan Donald.' "

"Yes, indeed it is," said Grandma. "He is a fine, good, lonely man who has lived a life without a father and without a wife and these last years without his only daughter. He has only these grandchildren," she said, looking at me and my sister, who was doing her homework at the table. "Somehow, I wish they could be closer to him."

"Oh, they are close enough," said Grandpa. "They are young and he is serious. We can't all be the same. But of course it's just not age. He is just a bit older than we are, but he is different from you and me." Then he added with a twinkle, "I bet you'd rather be married to me than to him?"

"Of course I'd rather be married to you," said Grandma, as if she had said it all before. "I never wanted to be married to anyone else. But you know what I mean. Our house is always full of people. You have your friends and your beer and your songs, and although you are thoughtful and kind, you have a good time."

"I think of him sometimes," said Grandpa, as if he were summing it all up for the evening, "the way I think of Robert Stanfield. He might not be the kind of man you'd invite to sing and dance and do imitations at your party, but he is a good man nonetheless. I believe I'll have a beer," he said "to celebrate my tax refund."

I 4   *T*wo years ago on a sunny afternoon, I sat and listened to my sister, within the walls of her modernistic house, located high upon one of the more prestigious ridges of the new and hopeful Calgary. In the luxury of her understated living room we held the heavy crystal glasses filled with the amber liquid or placed them carefully on the leather-embossed coasters. In the bathrooms, discreetly located in angled alcoves, the toilets made no sound when they were flushed. The rushing waters all were stilled.

She had gone with her husband, the petroleum engineer named Pankovich, to the oil city of Aberdeen, she said. And one day when he was out on the North Sea she had rented a car and driven across the comparatively narrow but deceptive width of Scotland, below the Cairngorm mountains and through the pass of Killiecrankie. Because of the roads she had driven south, although her eventual destination was north, and she had skirted the edge of Rannoch Moor and told me that there she had remembered a T. S. Eliot poem about the moor that began "Here the crow starves." Then she entered the stillness of Glencoe, where the MacDonalds were massacred in their beds early on the morning of February 13, 1692, by the government troops they had fed and sheltered for two weeks. Their tall and gigantic leader, "Mac Ian," rising from his bed to answer the five a.m. knock upon his door while the blizzard raged outside. Offering his hospitable glass of whisky, even as he turned his back to pull on his trousers, only to have the bullet smash into the back of his head, causing him to pitch forward across his wife within their still-warm bed; his once-red hair, which had lightened with his advanced age, reverting suddenly back to the even brighter redness of his blood while the soldiers fell upon his wife and gnawed the rings from her fingers with their teeth.

"Scarcely a trace any more," said my sister, "except the river and the mountains and the stones and their memories."

And she had gone north to the place called Fort William, *an Gearasdan*, which was originally built to control those people whom Dr. Johnson described as "savage clans and roving barbarians" – although he had not minded accepting their hospitality. And then she had gone west a few miles to the high cemetery of *Cille Choraill*, where she stood, she said, with the wind in her hair, beside the Celtic cross of *Iain Lom, bard na ceappach*, the fierce poet of the high corries and the long march through the winter's snows.

"The cross faces the mountains that he loved," she said. "It is the way he wanted to be buried – and the place."

"I guess he never had any doubts," she continued. "You know, about loyalty and who and what he really loved and who he really hated. Never doubted the value of his verses, never doubted the worth of his poems nor the worth of the blood upon his hands. Never wavered in the intensity of what he cared for."

"No," I said, "I guess he didn't. Or so they used to say."

"Do you remember," she asked, "when Grandpa would drink his whisky and how he would start to cry when he told the story about the dog going back across the ice to the island? Of how he let her go because she broke his heart. And of how she was shot by the man who didn't know."

"Yes," I said, "shot by the man who grabbed her by the hind legs and threw her into the sea."

"Oh, I think of that so many, many times. It was as if she had what the churches call a 'strong faith,' you know. That she waited and waited for them, thinking that they would come back, long after everyone else had given up hope. Thinking that they would come back and she would be waiting for them."

"My hope is constant in thee, Clan Donald," I said, regretting it almost immediately.

"Oh, don't mock," she said.

"I wasn't really," I said. "I was just thinking of another occasion."

"Well, I just think of her there, caring so much and dying for the island and for them. Trying to hold their place until they got back. She thought the island was theirs. Our parents and hers."

"Yes," I said, betrayed back by my own memories. "Grandpa used to say, 'Poor *cú*.' She was descended from the dog from Scotland, the one who swam after them in the boat in the 1700s and would have drowned if they had not cared for her the way she cared for them. Giving it everything she had."

"Yes," said my sister. "It was *in* those dogs to care too much and to try too hard. Oh," she said, raising her hands towards her hair, "here am I, a grown woman, spending my time worrying about the decisions made by a dog."

"No," I said, reaching for her hand across the table, the way we used to do as children, "you are doing more than that. You know you are doing more than that."

In the modernistic house in Calgary, we held hands across the table the way we used to do as children. Held hands the way we used to do on the Sunday afternoons after we had finished tracing our wistful fingers over the faces of our vanished parents: the faces looking up towards us from the photograph album spread out upon the table.

"Did you know," she said after a while, "that Glencoe means Glen *Cú*, the Dog's Glen, after mythological hounds that once were supposed to have run there?"

"Yes, I guess it makes sense when you think about it," I said, "although I didn't know about the mythological part. It seems somehow that I remember hearing it meant the Glen of Weeping."

"That was Macaulay," she said, "the historian. He just made it up after the event. The people gave it the other name years before they had any cause for weeping."

"Is that the Macaulay who wrote 'Horatio at the Bridge'" I asked, trying hard to remember the poems of distant high school.

"Yes," she said. "The same one. He was one of those people who went through history picking and choosing and embellishing." She paused. "Still, I guess when you look at it now, one meaning can be true and the other can be accurate."

The Alberta sun came through the window, infusing the amber liquid and the heavy crystal glasses with particles of light. We took the glasses in our hands and moved them in clockwise circles. The door opened and her children, arriving home from school, came into the room.

"Is there anything to eat?" they asked, "We're starved." The light reflected off the black and the redness of their hair.

15 Now across the canyons of Toronto streets, I hear the voices of the protestors, the chants and songs and slogans of their beliefs, and the equally strong voices of those opposed to them. "No cruise here," they say. "A strong defence is not an offence." "Say no to nuclear war." "If it's not worth fighting for. . . ." The sun hangs hot and high and golden, seeming to be above it all.

Once, on such a golden September afternoon, I was visiting my brothers, and the time now seems very long ago. It was a Sunday and one of those hot, calm days when there was not a ripple of wind and the ocean was so still it seemed almost like a painting. We were in the kitchen and had just finished eating when my oldest brother went to the window, "Look," he said excitedly, "the blackfish, the pilot whales."

Out of the stillness of the calm, blue ocean, they rose and rolled in glistening elegance. One after the other their black, arching backs broke the flatness of the sea, sending geysers of white water before them as they shattered the glass–like surface, the still, blue water being transformed into jets and fountains of streaming white – almost as if it were another element. There were, perhaps, twenty in all, although it was difficult to count them as they appeared and disappeared, now here and now there

in the waters off the *Calum Ruadh*'s Point. All of us put everything aside and hurried the three quarters of a mile down to the
shore to watch them. Standing on the extreme edge of the point,
we shouted to them and offered our applause as they spouted and
sported and turned and flipped, so near and yet so far in the
splendour of their exuberant happiness.

Sometimes, said my brothers, the blackfish would follow their
boat, and they loved applause and appreciated singing. If they
vanished beneath the surface, my brothers would clap their
hands in rhythmic unison like fans at a sporting event, and soon
they would break the surface, sometimes so close to the boat as
to be almost dangerous, drawn by the sound and the perceived
good fellowship. They would leap and arch and then vanish
again, although my brothers knew they were never far away but
seemed like children involved in games of hide and seek, hoping
to startle and surprise by their unexpected nearness. Sometimes
when they were invisible my brothers would sing songs to them
in either English or Gaelic and place small bets as to which set of
lyrics would bring them whooshing to the surface, cavorting in
their giant grace around the rocking boat.

But on this Sunday we were not in a boat, so we sang and
shouted to them from the farthest extension of our land that
reached out to the sea. For almost two hours we shouted and
waved and sang and applauded to their magnificent response.
Sometimes they came quite close to the shore, as if they were
trying to hear what we were saying or else trying to show
themselves off to a greater advantage. As they spouted and
splashed we sang and shouted, yet as the sun moved on, we

seemed to tire of the game sooner than they did and directed our steps inland, although still turning to shout and wave in a series of last-time farewells.

Later in the early evening, I went down to the shore to bring home my brothers' milk cows and discovered one of the whales washed up on the rocks near the slip where my brothers drew their boat. I saw the crowds of crows and smaller predatory birds rising from the shore as I approached and it was not until I had taken farther steps that I recognized what must have been for them a great bonanza delivered by the sea.

The tide was out and he lay in his gigantic length upon the rocks, while the sea which was his element of grace lapped quietly some yards beyond him. Already the birds had pecked out his eyes and begun their work on his anus and reproductive system. There was a jagged tear about five feet in length which ran from his throat through his stomach and down into his abdomen, and some of his internal organs had spilled out upon the rocks. Already the heat of the still-present sun had begun to have its effect, and soon the odour would be pronounced. Out of the water, he was no longer black and glistening but dull and brown in the beginning stench of death.

I went home and told my brothers, and later they came down and we all looked upon him. We decided that he had not realized that the tide was falling and that in the afternoon's high spirits he had come too close to the shore and in one of his undulating dives he had found not the expected depth of water but instead the submerged and jagged reef which had slashed his soft underbelly and left him disembowelled and unable to rise again. We thought of ourselves as deceptive male sirens who had lured him to his death, although we did not phrase our thoughts in such language at the time. My brothers, who were aware of practicality even in the face of death, feared that his presence and the resulting odour would interfere with the working of their boat. They feared he was too big to be towed back out to sea, even if they were able to fasten grappling hooks to him and pull him off the rocks with their boat at full throttle. The afternoon had ended differently than we had expected.

That night there came a great storm from off the sea. We heard the wind and the pellets of rain upon the windows as we lay within our beds and my brothers rose in great agitation, fearing that their drawn-up boat was not sufficiently out of the way of the mounting waves. All of us ran down to the sea in the dark, taking with us storm lanterns and flashlights and summoning the ever-faithful Christy. The waves were booming and high and it was almost impossible to stand on the wetness of the drenched and glistening boulders, and overhead there was no sign of the "lamp of the poor." Even Christy was afraid as the high surf broke about her knees and her hooves slipped on the wet rocks she could not see. Calum grasped the cheek straps of her bridle in both his hands and we could hear him singing in Gaelic, loudly and clearly at the side of her head, in an attempt to steady and calm her, much as a parent might sing to a frightened child. Calum's steady voice rose above the roar of the sea and she followed him as did we all, although the water swirled about our knees. We were able to hook the chain to the boat's ring and to steady and balance the boat itself and to direct Christy inland and upward to the higher levels of the *Calum Ruadh*'s Point. On her final lunge, a gigantic wave smashed into the boat's stern, lifting it forward with tremendous momentum, even as Christy scrambled upwards to the point. The wave which would have destroyed the boat if it had been fastened to its moorings became almost the agent of its deliverance since it seemed now high enough to be relatively safe. We flopped on our backs in exhaustion upon the wet moss and cranberry vines, knowing that the boat was high and beyond the ocean's force for the duration of the night. In the darkness and excitement we had not paid any attention to the whale.

In the morning the storm's rage was spent and, although the ocean rolled in a surly fashion, its temporary tantrum seemed to be over. We went down to the shore and the boat was safe and dry and none the worse for the night's adventures. There was no sign of the whale and we were all relieved, assuming that the force of the waves had taken it back out to sea. But then we found, in a cluster of glistening boulders, its internal organs, trapped by the boulders which the waves had rolled upon them, yet still fluctuating to the sea. The grey intestines coiled and sloshed, as did the liver and the stomach and the great, gigantic heart.

Hundreds of yards inland, we later found the body itself, disguised beneath a small mountain of brown and tangled seaweed adorned with scattered stones and sticks of broken driftwood. The sea had taken the body in instead of out, and it stayed there for more than a year until only its bones were visible to the eye.

In the room my brother waits, seeing, perhaps through the window of his imagination, the leaping sporting blackfish at play in the waters of the September sun. "Take your time," he said. "I am not going anywhere."

16 *In* the southland of Ontario, the contract pickers bend and reach within their circle of the sun and calculate quietly the gains and losses of their day and of their season. The weekend pickers are preparing to go home, and even farther south my own children play their beeping computer games within their shaded and muffled rec room. The patients who will fill my waiting room on Monday are getting through their weekend as well. The children, perhaps, trying not to think about Monday while actually thinking about it too much. The adults, always hopeful of beauty, are resigning themselves to the price they must pay. I am in the business of "improving on God," as Grandma might say, and in the affluence of this part of North America both I and my patients have done pretty well.

When I was a student at the university in Halifax, and studying dentistry in the early stages, my professor invited me one evening to have a beer with him. We went to the tavern beneath the big hotel and he said, "You are capable of making a lot of money in this field, but you will never do it in the Maritimes. There is not a population here which cares enough about its teeth. Over 60 per cent of the people never go to a dentist until it is too late and most of the male population, anyway, are candidates for false teeth before they reach their twenties. They prefer to pull them rather than fix them. It's almost as if they *want* to. Only Quebec and the aboriginal population have statistics that are as bad," he said. "And Newfoundland. I never know whether to include it as part of the Maritimes or not."

He was not a native of the Atlantic area, although he had been living in Halifax for some time because he liked the university and the city and the people.

I was young then and did not know what to say, listening to words of prophecy from the mouth of the great man with perfectly capped teeth. I was nervous in his presence and did not have enough money to buy my share of the beer. And I did not want to drink it, anyway, as I was afraid it would make me sleepy and I wanted to study for my exams. For I knew I had a chance for the various awards and scholarships and medals which might launch me on the way he was indicating.

But he did not mind when I switched to Coke and rolled the ice cubes circularly within the glass even as they melted to the touch of my warm and perspiring hands. I had never met anyone quite like him before and was suspicious of what he might want, and fearful that I might make some mental or verbal error which might jeopardize our tenuous student-professor relationship. As I drank more and more Coke and he more and more beer, I became increasingly edgy, feeling the caffeine filling my veins and imagining the pupils of my eyes dilating. His speech became more and more slurred and sometimes his reaching hand came down beside the glass instead of grasping it and sometimes he knocked it over, causing little waves of beer to slosh across the table, even as we moved discreetly away, both of us pretending that it had not happened. It seemed that a chasm gradually widened between us because of our drinking progress. As if one of us were on the shore and the other on a departing boat bound towards the open sea. Our voices becoming unintelligible to each other because of our different circumstances.

Yet it seemed he was sincerely interested in his profession and in me as part of it, and it seemed also, perhaps, that he was lonely in his way.

"Where did you say you came from?" he said, bending forward from the waist until his nose almost touched the glasses on the table – like one of those trick birds who dip their beaks forward in novelty-shop windows.

"Oh," I said, startled by the simplicity or complexity of the question. "From Cape Breton."

"Never been there," he said. "Should I?"

"What?" I said.

"Go there?" he said. "Should I go there?"

"I don't know," I said, scurrying around inside my mind for some kind of suitable answer.

"Are your family dentists? Is your father a dentist?" he asked, still bobbing forward and backwards from the waist with measured regularity.

"No," I said. "They're not. He's not."

"Oh," he said. "Most people who go into this profession come from dental families. But I suppose you've got to start somewhere. Look," he said, leaning forward and grasping my shoulder firmly in his wet hand. "You've got to make teeth *better*, not just pull the fuckers out."

That spring, at my graduation, the sun shone and the trees and flowers were in leaf and blossom as we paraded through our paces and received our awards and rewards, as the case might be. I had gone home two days earlier to drive the car which the father of the red-haired Alexander MacDonald had kindly offered to us for the graduation. Grandpa and Grandma came and my other grandfather as well, and also the parents of the red-haired Alexander MacDonald.

The afternoon before the graduation and after we were settled in our rooms, my grandfather said, "Show me where the library is, I want to look for something." Grandpa said, "Are there any good taverns around here?" and Grandma and the others went off to buy presents for those they had left behind only hours before. My sister was graduating at the same time in distant Alberta, which seemed so far away that no one could attend – although we sent identical telegrams. And those of *clann Chalum Ruaidh* who followed my brothers, including the red-haired Alexander MacDonald, were near Ontario's Elliot Lake, where they had been for nearly a month. There they were sinking shafts and developing drifts for Renco Development – rediscovering the uranium they had originally discovered some ten years earlier, now that the prices and markets made it once again worthwhile. Their telegrams came too, in a mixture of Gaelic and English accompanied by a cheque for five hundred dollars.

Before going to Elliot Lake, they had been at home for a short time on their return from Peru, that country uncertain of its borders. And they had spent a brief afternoon visiting me in Halifax on their way to Ontario. High in the mountains of Peru, where they had been sinking shafts, they told me the air was so thin that, at first, they suffered from *soroche*, the altitude sickness. Later, they said, they became more used to the height. Peru was strikingly beautiful, they said, although the people were poor and the political struggles intense. It was in the year before the military coup and they were warned to stay out of any political involvement and to keep to themselves and to do their work. And they were told, also, that if they should happen to run over an animal or even a person on the twisting mountain roads or in the single-street villages (speeding to their work in the mountains' early-morning darkness) that they should not stop, for fear that they might be hacked to death. Instead they should continue to the next village and notify the authorities there, or those in Cerro de Pasco. Even at that time, it was a country of *los desaparecidos*, "the disappeared," and many of the people were living as exiles within their own country. The national anthem, said my brothers, was *Somos libres, somos lo siempre.* We are free, let us always be so.

The day of the graduation, as I said, was sunny and golden, just the way such days are supposed to be. "Good for you," said Grandpa as I stood in my mortar board and gown, clutching my various diplomas and awards and the offer of a summer Research Fellowship, while Grandma snapped the pictures. "Good for you, *'ille bhig ruaidh.* This means you will never have to work again." What he meant was that I would not spend my life pulling the end of the bucksaw or pushing the boat off the *Calum Ruadh*'s Point in freezing water up to my waist. "Jesus, though," he added, "thirty-two teeth. Think if you had to be responsible for running a whole hospital."

On the way home on that hot afternoon and early evening we were all taken with the changes in our lives and with our near and distant pasts.

"It is true," said my grandfather after we had been travelling for about an hour. "I found it in the library in Halifax."

"What?" asked Grandpa.

"Wolfe and the Highlanders at Quebec, on the Plains of Abraham. He was just using them against the French. He was suspicious of them and probably would have been satisfied if the French had killed them all. Just using them for his own goals, for as long as they might last."

"But," said Grandpa, "didn't you tell me once that it was a French-speaking MacDonald who got them past the sentries? And that he was first up the cliff with the other Highlanders, that they pulled themselves up by grasping the roots of the twisted trees? Didn't you tell me that?"

"Yes," said my grandfather. "*First up the cliff*. Wolfe was still below in the boat. Think about it."

"They were first because they were the best," said Grandpa stoutly. "I think of them as winning Canada for *us*. They learned that at Culloden."

"At Culloden they were on the *other side*," said Grandfather in near exasperation. "MacDonald fought *against* Wolfe. Then he went to Paris. That's where he learned his French. Then he was given a pardon so that he could fight *for* the British Army. He fought against Wolfe at Culloden and then fought for him years later at Quebec. Perhaps you can't blame Wolfe for being suspicious under the circumstances. He had a memory like other men. Still MacDonald died fighting *for* the British Army, not *against* it. And one doesn't like to think of people giving their best, even their lives, under deceptive circumstances."

"No one knows all the thoughts of those men," said Grandpa philosophically.

"No," said Grandfather, "but some men do leave records of their thoughts. Wolfe referred to the Highlanders as his secret enemy and once, speaking of recruiting them as soldiers in a letter to his friend Captain Rickson, he made the cynical comment, 'No great mischief if they fall.'"

"Speaking of wars," said Grandma, who had remained silent throughout the conversation, "I got this letter from my sister in San Francisco the morning we left. But in all the excitement I forgot about it."

Taking a letter from her purse, she began to read:

"Dear Catherine and Alexander:

Received your last letter and, as usual, we were very glad to get it. We were glad to learn that you were keeping well and looking forward to your trip to Halifax to attend Alexander's graduation (or *gille beag ruadh*, as you have always called him). Very pleased also that his sister Catherine is graduating in Alberta. It is too bad that you could not attend her graduation as well, but we cannot be in two places at the one time, as we all know. Those children must be a source of great satisfaction to you both.

I am sure you were glad to see the other boys as well on their return from Peru. It is too bad that they could not stop off in San Francisco to see us, but we understand the complications of air tickets and immigration and all the rest of it. Maybe sometime. I hope they are doing well in Ontario. Speaking of Ontario, our own grandson Alexander has received his draft notice, which means that they want him for Vietnam. He does not want to go and now we don't want him to go either. We supported the war under that *nice* President Kennedy, but it seems different now. Calum says he does not trust Lyndon Johnson's eyes and that we at home here are not being told the truth and that the people over there (Vietnam) only want their own country for themselves. Anyway, there is a great deal of confusion over the war here now and many protests as you probably know from the newspapers and television and many of our young people are going to Canada.

If you could give us the address of your boys in Ontario and write to them, maybe they would help him. 'Blood is thicker than water,' as the old saying goes and you know we would do the same for you.

Both of us are keeping well, although we are not getting any younger. I must close this now and make a cup of tea. It is too bad that you could not be here to join us. Calum says that if you were here we would have something stronger than tea. He says that in retirement he is going to start to make homebrew in the basement, so I guess the old habits die hard.

All our love and *Beannachd leibh*,

    Your fond brother and sister,

    Calum and Sarah."

"Write them and tell them, 'Yes,'" said Grandpa without a moment's hesitation. "The boys will do it. They will help him there in Ontario. *Gille beag ruadh* here will tell them" he said, tapping me on the shoulder. "We have given you the best life we could. From the day you came to spend the night with us when you were three right through until now."

"Yes," said Grandma, "I will write to them as soon as I get home. And you can write to your brothers in Ontario. They are our grandchildren too, but you are our own *gille beag ruadh*."

The sun continued to hang and burn in the sky as we travelled homeward through Pictou County. Near the Pictou County line my uncle tapped my shoulder and pointed out the window.

"There's Barney's River," he said. "In 1938 your father and I came to work in the woods here. There were other people from the *clann Chalum Ruaidh* working in the camp and they sent word that there was work, but to bring our own axes as those in the camp were not sharpened well enough. It was in December and when we got off the train at Barney's River Station it was night and the snow was deep and I still remember how cold it was.

"The camp was about twelve miles in there," he said, gesturing with his hand at the receding hardwood hills, "and we started to walk in, hoping that we were following the right trail. It was one of those nights which was so cold that you could hear the trees exploding with the frost. Splitting open with a sound like gunshots. But we could see our way because of the whiteness of the snow and the full moon, the *Lochran àigh nam bochd*, 'the lamp of the poor.' Sometimes we would sing songs to keep ourselves company and regulate our walking to keep time with the songs, like in a march. And then we came over a hill and there was the camp beneath us. I remember that there were moose in the yard, looking for bits of hay around the doors of the barn where the horses were kept. When we came down, they just looked at us and hardly moved at all. They were more hungry than they were afraid. We opened the barn door and threw them some hay, threw it out on the snow, and then we went to sleep on the hay in the barn ourselves. It was warm because of the heat given off by the horses and we could hear the horses' movements, their stompings and turnings and the rubbing of their necks on the mangers, even while we were asleep.

"We started work the next morning and we stayed until the end of March, until it was time to get ready for fishing. Going to work with the stars in the sky and coming back under the stars as well – cutting the stands of hardwood for a dollar a day."

He paused and smiled briefly. "After we received our pay and before we returned to Cape Breton we went on the train to Truro. The streets were still covered with snow. There were no public taverns in Truro at the time, so we bought a little bottle for ourselves. We did not know where to drink it, so we went down a side street. There was a house with an outside staircase leading to the second floor. We went under the staircase to have our drink. Just as we were putting the bottle to our lips a woman came out on the upstairs landing and saw us standing beneath her. 'Get out of there,' she shouted 'or I will call the police right this minute!'

Your father said "*Pog mo thon*," assuming she would not know Gaelic.

'Oh, you dears,' she said. 'Come in and have supper.' She was part of *Clann Chalum Ruaidh*, and was both surprised and over-joyed to hear someone speaking Gaelic in Truro – regardless of what was actually said. When her husband came home he was as nice as could be, and we stayed for supper and then went to bed. I remember how white and clean the sheets were after what we were used to in the lumber camps. For years afterwards we used to send them a Christmas card, but then one year the card was returned. I guess they must have moved. Your father used to say 'It's not very often, you can say "kiss my rear end," and get a splendid supper and a bed with clean sheets in return.'

"Another time," he said, "we were in a lumber camp that was filled with rats. Before going to bed we used to take two or three loaves of bread and throw chunks of the bread on the floor, so the rats would not try to eat us in our beds.

"You know," he said, stopping suddenly and placing his hand upon my shoulder as I drove, "I missed and still miss your father a great deal. I was with him longer than he was able to be with you, and Grandpa and Grandma here knew him in still a different way. Perhaps," he said after a pause, "it's just the same sadness in different packages."

"Oh well," said Grandma, "we should be grateful for what we've had. Some people never see their parents at all, and some men do not even know that they have children in the world."

"I have never gotten over that," said my grandfather quietly. "Not knowing whether my father ever knew that he might be responsible for me, or someone like me. I think it would have made a difference."

"What could the man do?" said Grandpa. "He was young and it was not his fault that he was killed. He did not plan on things turning out the way they did. If he didn't know about your life he didn't know about his own death either – unless perhaps he saw it coming, and by then it was too late."

"Once when I was a child," said my grandfather, "I was being teased by the other children and I went to ask my mother a question. I don't even know what the question was and probably didn't then. Something inarticulate about the circumstances of my conception and why I was different. She slapped me so hard that she knocked me almost halfway across the room. 'Don't ever ask me anything like that again!' she said. 'Don't you see that I have enough trouble with you as it is?' So that was the end of that conversation – if you could call it that. She became a bitter woman, my mother, and perhaps you cannot blame her. She didn't have an easy life."

"No, she didn't" said Grandma. "Under the circumstances she probably did the best she could."

"Perhaps. I have always missed not having a picture of him," said my grandfather. "An image of him in my mind. I am of the age now when I might well be a great-grandfather myself, but I am still looking for him. When I shave in the morning, even this past morning in Halifax, I look into the mirror and try to find him in my face, in my eyebrows or in the slant of my jaw or in my cheekbones – but then we all look quite a bit alike. But the one time in my life that I was drunk, I saw him in the mirror. I went to the sink to splash water on my face and when I looked up into the mirror he was standing there behind me. He had reddish hair and a reddish moustache and he was younger than I was at the time. Strange to see your father as younger than you are yourself. I turned around as quickly as I could, but I slipped on the water on the floor and fell and hit my head. When I got up I was still groggy and he was gone. It so unnerved me that I was never drunk again, but I have worn this moustache ever since." He paused and touched the moustache with his right hand.

"And one other time, the night after my wife died, he came where I was sleeping and it was probably a dream. He came and stood beside the bed and he had on long woollen underwear, like Stanfields, the kind you would wear in a lumber camp in the winter. And he bent down and put his hand upon my shoulder. 'Look after the little girl,' he said, 'and each of you will then be less alone.' "

The sun shone down upon the moving car, but the hottest part of the day was over. We were all silent for a while as the miles slipped past us and beneath us. And then we began to climb the Havre Boucher hill and the signs began to announce our closeness to Cape Breton. But before the climb and the signs we could see Cape Breton lying blue and green across the water before us and to our left.

"No more sad stories," said Grandpa. "Let's sing some songs."

And then we all began to sing:

"Chi mi bhuam, fada bhuam,
Chi mi bhuam, ri muir lain;
Chi mi Ceap Breatuinn mo luaidh
Fada bhuam thar an t-sail."

shouting out the names of the places as far as we could see them strung out along the coast; trying to change what was perhaps intended as a lament into a song of happiness and joy at our own homecoming.

Whenever our voices wavered or hesitated at the beginning of a new verse, we would turn to my grandfather and he would lead us clearly and without ever faltering. Again, as with his playing of the violin, it came almost as a renewed surprise – the fact that he was seldom associated with singing but still could do it so well.

"You never make a mistake," said Grandma to him after the song was done.

"I try hard not to," he said. "I try to do the best I can."

We crossed the Canso Causeway. When the front wheels of the car touched Cape Breton, Grandpa said, "Thank Christ to be home again. Nothing bad can happen to us now."

We still had an hour's drive or perhaps more along the coast, but it was obvious that Grandpa already considered himself in "God's country," or "our own country," as he called it. Reaching into his inside coat pocket, he pulled out a bottle of whisky he had apparently purchased in Halifax and, rolling down the half-open window, he wound up like a baseball pitcher and threw the cork as far as he could out into the waving grass beyond the road.

"We will damn well *have* to drink all of this now," he said, raising the bottle triumphantly above his head. "When I was a young man," he continued enthusiastically, buoyed up by his own good spirits, "when we would come home in the spring from working in the woods, I would get a hard-on as soon as my feet touched the ground of Cape Breton. Yes sir, it would snap right up to attention at the front of my pants. I couldn't hold it down. We had buttons on our trousers then," he added helpfully. "It was before they began to use zippers."

"Hush," said Grandma, nudging him in the ribs with her elbow, as if he had gone too far even for her.

"Okay," he said. "Let's sing some more songs. Would anyone like a drink?"

"Let's sing," said my grandfather. "Anything would be better than this."

And so we sang as I drove my uncle's car along the winding road beside the sea and towards the setting sun. We sang "*Fail-ill-o Agus Ho Ro Eile*," "*Mo Nighean Dubh*," "*O Chruinneag*," "*An T'altan Dubh*," "*Mo Run Geal Dileas*," and "*O Siud An Taobh A Ghabhainn*." We sang all the old songs, the songs that people working together used to sing to make a heavy task lighter.

And as we drove by the houses of "our own country," Grandpa would identify or shout to his relatives as they stood beside their doors or walked about their yards or worked at the various tasks of early evening.

"There's *Aonghas Ruadh*," he would say. "There's *Mairi*." "There's *Gilleasbuig*." "There's *Domhnull Ruadh*." "Honk the horn."

And I would honk the horn at his bidding and the people would wave back, recognizing the car and its occupants as it rolled along beside the sea. Sometimes when I would honk the horn, Grandpa would wave his whisky bottle out the window as if to emphasize the fact that he was having such a good time.

"Don't be such a fool," said my grandfather, who looked as if he wished he were somewhere else, "or the police will arrest us all."

And we drove and waved and sang our songs and the sun glinted off my uncle's car and touched the various colours of our hair and tinted the flat calm ocean and outlined the island off which my brother and parents had drowned, it seemed, so many years ago.

17 *W*hen we arrived home, we went first to drop off my grandfather at his house. "Come inside for a minute," he said. "I have something to give you." From inside his closet he took two carefully wrapped presents.

"Open them," he said.

One was a hand-carved chess set which must have taken him a very long time to complete; the scrolls and curves of the individual pieces delicately and intricately seeming to move through the burnished wood. The other was a hand-carved plaque bearing the coat of arms and the motto of the MacDonalds. "My hope is constant in thee," said the carefully raised and out-lined letters.

"I made these for your sister as well," he said shyly. "I sent them in the mail to Alberta about two weeks ago. I wanted to be sure that they would get there in time."

"Thank you very much," I said. "Thank you very much."

I tried to imagine all the care that had gone into them – all the painstaking detail accomplished by his mind and hands and the fine-tempered tools that my sister and I, as children, used to leave out in the rain.

"Thank you very much," I said again. "Thank you very much."

As we drove towards home we waved again to the people on the streets, but it seemed they only half-raised their hands and looked at us too intently. When we drove into the yard there was a knot of people gathered about the doorstep and there was also smoke from the chimney. Someone who knew the house had raised the back window and gone in and started a fire and opened the doors from the inside.

The red-haired Alexander MacDonald had been killed that afternoon, the people said. The ore bucket had hit him in the shaft's bottom and he had died instantly. My brothers had phoned. They were coming home with the body.

It was so sudden and so unexpected that there seemed no place to turn. Nothing to grasp nor to hold. It seemed so complex – that while I was going forth into a world of perfect teeth, his unanticipated death was waiting for him in a hole in the ground outside of Elliot Lake. And that even as I drove his parents' car, and as we sang our songs, he was dying far away on the edge of the Canadian Shield. I thought of how we had fought as children and of how I had laughed at him for drinking his tea from his saucer. And I could feel his small but determined calloused hands on the back of my neck in the moment before Grandpa had interrupted us. And I thought of how we thought we had known who the lucky ones were.

"A lot has happened to us on this day," said Grandma as she put her arms around the mother of the red-haired Alexander MacDonald. It was the first time I ever thought of my grandmother as old, seeing her there with the strain of the long day and the hot drive etched upon her face.

"A lot has happened to us on this day," she said, "but we will have to face this. We will have to be strong. We can't dissolve like a spoonful of sugar in a glass of water."

"I bought him a shirt in Halifax," my aunt said quietly. "A MacDonald plaid shirt. I was going to wrap it for him tonight."

"Goddamn it," said Grandpa, who was rapidly becoming sober under the impact of the news. "Goddamn it," he said and, "Goddamn it once again."

18 The remains of the red-haired Alexander MacDonald came from Sudbury to the airport at Sydney in one of those plastic bags the airlines use for ferrying the dead. The members of the *clann Chalum Ruaidh* who had been with him accompanied him home on his last and final journey, and I was asked by his father to meet the plane at Sydney. I went by myself so that there would be more room in the car for those who would be arriving.

It seemed a strange and solitary hundred-mile journey, following the winding road and climbing and descending the mountains in the same car that had been so crowded going to and coming from my graduation in Halifax. The slight odour of some of Grandpa's spilled whisky still hovered about the car's interior, and the radio played erratically as stations faded in and out because of the elevation and depths of the mountains and valleys and the sometimes dominant presence of the overhanging out-crops of rock. The radio gave the weather forecast and played the Scottish violin selections and announced the death and the funeral arrangements of the red-haired Alexander MacDonald. The time was early afternoon.

When the *clann Chalum Ruaidh*, led by my oldest brother, poured off the plane in Sydney, most of them were already far advanced in drink. Many of them were angry, and spoke in a mixture of English and Gaelic. The management of Renco Development was on a tight schedule and had objected to so many men wanting to leave for the funeral.

"It was only one man," the management said. "The rest of you are still able to work. The job has to go forward."

But the job had not gone forward at all, for all of them had quit. They had come out of the bunkhouses and up out of the drifts and the shaft's bottom and some had flung their gear into the bush at the headframe's site, the wrenches, still in the miner's belts, clanging onto the stone of the hardened Canadian Shield. Some of them had collected their pay before they left, while others had not bothered.

Now they milled about the baggage carousel dispensing bits of information. "It was an accident," some said, while others were not so sure. The hoistman had mixed up his signals and had sent the ore bucket hurtling down the shaft when he was sup-posed to be raising it. The red-haired Alexander MacDonald, thinking the bucket was going up, had moved into the sump to clean it and was trapped in the bottom. He had probably not even seen the bucket whistling down upon him. No one could be sure. Everyone had ideas. The main thing was that the red head of Alexander MacDonald was forever separated from his body and would not be reunited unless at the time of some future resurrection. For some reason I found myself thinking of "Mac Ian," the leader of the MacDonalds of Glencoe, falling forward across his bed on February 13, 1692. Propelled forward and downward by the unseen and unexpected force at the back of his head. The redness of his hair dyed forever brighter by the crimson of his blood.

The luggage began to roll onto the baggage carousel, revolving and twisting on the way to its owners, who leaned forward from their waists with outstretched hands.

Because I had only the one car, and because so many people had come, the *clann Chalum Ruaidh* rented other cars and we set out in our convoy of confused and exhausted grief with my oldest brother leading the way. Perhaps Calum was too tired or too taken over by grief or too angry at his loss or too inebriated or too eager to get home. Perhaps a combination of all these factors led my brother to drive too fast on the highway leading home. Almost immediately his rental car began to pull away from the rest of us and by the time we saw the Seal Island Bridge and the waters of Bras d'Or it had already climbed Kelly's Mountain on the other side and vanished from our view.

Later, beyond the mountain's top and on a barren and desolate stretch of road, we saw the flashing red light of an RCMP cruiser ahead of us. It was pulled to the side of the road, but when we came abreast of it there was no evidence of any officers, although one of the cruiser's doors was open. Some ten or fifteen miles farther, when the road straightened somewhat, we could see my brother's car again in the distance ahead of us.

And then after another ten miles or so on the brow of a high hill we saw more flashing lights and what seemed like a hastily constructed police barricade thrown up across the road some miles ahead of us. My brother's car was descending the winding road ahead of us and we saw it glinting in the sun before it vanished into the valley. We watched for it to emerge from the valley floor and begin its ascent towards the flashing lights, but it never appeared. When we came to the valley floor ourselves there was still no sign of it, but on a secluded stretch of flatness there was a dirt road that veered to the left and seemed to vanish almost immediately into the overhanging trees at the base of the mountain. The road was invisible from our previous vantage point and also invisible to those who waited at the barricade ahead and above and around the bend. When we came to the road the dust was still hanging in the air and we could see the disturbed stones caused by the recent passage of the tires. We continued up and around the bend, and the police officers at the barricade waved us through.

When we arrived at my grandparents' house the yard and roadway were full of cars, most of them belonging to the *clann Chalum Ruaidh* who had come to offer condolences and to welcome the living who had accompanied the dead. About a half-hour later the missing rental car rolled into the yard. It was covered with dust and splattered mud from the mountain roads and streams. My second brother was at the wheel and Calum was asleep in the front passenger seat. His right hand was closed into a fist, and the knuckles were bruised and swollen.

Apparently their car had been pulled over and my brother had gotten out and walked back towards the police cruiser. The officer had stepped out of his car and they met at the roadside in the space behind the rental car and in front of the police cruiser. No one had heard the details of the conversation, although they heard the voices rising in anger, and then my brother had turned away to walk back towards his own car. The officer had struck Calum from behind with something – a billy club or a flashlight – and his head had flopped forward, but he had regained his balance and, in turning, struck the officer in the mouth, knocking him over the bank and down into the roadside ditch.

Calum still lay sleeping in the front seat, and there was some fear that he might have been more seriously injured than was first realized. Clots and scales of blackened dried blood lay caked and matted in his hair and plastered along the back of his neck. We attempted to wake him and half carried and dragged him into Grandma's kitchen, where she waved away Grandpa's whisky and tried to ply him with cups of hot tea. The thin scar line on his lower lip turned white and purple by degrees.

Later in the afternoon three RCMP squad cars with lights flashing arrived at my grandparents' house. They had probably recognized the car's licence plates or gained information from the rental agency or the other police detachment. Obviously we were not very hard to find.

By this time my brother had recuperated somewhat and his eyes began to flash with anger as he pushed his chair back from the table.

"You," said Grandpa, "go right upstairs to bed." He said it with an authority he did not often show, and I was reminded of the time he had separated the red-haired Alexander MacDonald and myself and held us firmly at arm's length while our small indignant feet kicked at the air. Calum looked at him in amazement and I was struck by the fact that not many people in recent years had told him what to do. Perhaps not since the death of my parents had he been the child who hears and accepts the authority of others, perhaps with resentment but not unmixed with a certain sense of relief and complex gratitude. His feet sounded on the stairway above us and we could hear him falling heavily upon the bed.

"The rest of us," said Grandpa, "will go outside."

There were probably thirty or forty of us standing on the lawn outside of Grandpa's house looking at the three police cruisers with their flashing roof lights and the six officers standing nervously before them. The *Calum Ruadh* dogs cocked their ears and moved erratically through the crowd, as if sensing a great event was about to unfold within their lives.

"We've come for MacDonald," said the officer in charge. There was a ripple of laughter through the crowd and various shouts of "Right here." "Over here." All of the officers were from outside the local area and it probably had not entered their minds that almost all of us were named MacDonald. Nobody moved except for the shuffling of feet. The red roof lights revolved in the afternoon sun and even the dogs were temporarily quiet.

Then the door banged and Grandma came out, drying her hands on her apron.

"This is ridiculous," she said, moving through the crowd that parted before her like the water in front of a boat's prow.

"This family has suffered a death," she said to the officer, "and we would appreciate it if you would leave us alone during our period of mourning."

The officer took off his hat as she spoke to him and then withdrew a few steps and beckoned his men around him. After a brief conversation he nodded to Grandma and then all of them got into their cars and drove away, turning off their revolving lights as they departed. Everyone was relieved, although we all stood rooted to our spots for a few seconds. Then the dogs began to stir and romp and we all went forward into a life of movement.

The wake of the red-haired Alexander MacDonald began the next day at noon. His body was transferred by the undertaker from the plastic bag to the casket of oak which was set upon its trestles. The casket was closed because he was no longer recognizable to those who once knew and loved him. Instead his picture was placed upon the casket's surface, the picture taken at his high-school graduation. His red hair was carefully combed and his dark eyes looked hopefully into the camera. There was a boutonnière in his lapel. Beside the picture there was a small stone chip from the original *Calum Ruadh* boulder. About the casket were the ferns and rushes from the *Calum Ruadh* land. It was still too early for the summer roses, the pink and blue lupins, the yellow buttercups or the purple irises with their splashed white centres. Still too early for the delicate pink morning glories growing from their tendrils among the rocks beside the sea. Growing low and close among the rocks and seeming to derive their sustenance from an invisible source, yet quick to die if plucked and removed.

On the third day and just before the funeral procession began, a letter came from the red-haired Alexander Macdonald addressed to his parents. It had been mailed on the morning of his death, before he had gone to work his final shift. It did not contain a great deal of information, only general comments about how well they were getting along and a cheque for two hundred and forty-five dollars. Both of his parents burst into tears, as if it were, somehow, the final straw. But then they embraced one another and composed themselves and went forth to what they saw as their immediate responsibilities.

On the day that we had fought as children, I remembered, his father seemed to have come to borrow money from Grandpa and Grandma. And I remembered how I had thought that the world had seemed unfair to me in terms of who had fathers and who did not. And that it had seemed unfair to him as well. Fathers helping sons and sons helping fathers in the mysteries of ability and time.

The funeral procession to the white country church stretched out for over a mile and the RCMP cruisers with their flashing lights sealed off the access roads as we passed through. We looked straight ahead, as did the officers, and neither of us acknowledged the other.

The interior of the church was packed with people, with some standing outside on the steps. The piper and the violinist and the singers waited for their time of contribution.

My other grandfather, "the man who could be counted on to be always in control," went to the lectern to give the first reading. He was meticulously dressed, with his gold watch-chain stretched across his vest and his highly polished shoes glinting in the light. His neat red moustache was carefully trimmed and his fingernails immaculately clean.

He turned the pages of the Bible and began: "A reading from the letter of Paul to the Romans: 'The life and death of each of us has its influence on others.'"

Then he stopped and seemed to reconsider, turning back towards the Old Testament. He began again: "A reading from the book of Wisdom: 'The virtuous man, though he die before his time, will find rest. Length of days is not what makes age honourable, nor number of years the true measure of life; Understanding, this is man's grey hairs. . . .'"

I had heard him read before, carefully selecting the texts to suit the occasion. Once, as a child, I had heard him read from the Book of Revelation. It was a description of the coming of the New Jerusalem and the attendant preparations and miraculous happenings. One line, above all others, had remained most force-fully in my mind. It was "And the sea gave up all the dead who were in it."

After my grandfather had finished the reading, the service proceeded in accordance with our customs. The violinist played "Niel Gow's Lament" and "*Mo Dhachaidh*" ("My Home"). And outside the church the piper played "Dark Island" before the coffin of the red-haired Alexander MacDonald was lowered into the grave by the hands of the men who had worked with him underground.

19 After the funeral we went back to my grandparents' home, and later in the afternoon a long-distance call came from Toronto. It was a person-to-person call for my oldest brother and it was from the management of Renco Development, in fact from the superintendent of operations, the man who had sent the shaft crew to Peru. When he began to speak, Calum held up his hand for silence and the hubbub of conversation was stilled. The man spoke very loudly, as if the volume of his voice might transcend the distance of a large half-continent, and those of us who sat within the room could hear him clearly.

"Look," he urged, "I'm very sorry about what happened up north. Sorry about the death and sorry about the hassle. It was all a mistake. The management up there doesn't know you people the way I do. They should have just let you go to the funeral. If anything like that ever happens again, phone me directly. Phone me right away. I understand. You people have been working for me for a long time."

There was a silence.

"Are you still there?" he asked.

"Yes," said Calum, "I'm still here."

"Well," he said. "Listen. We want you back. *I* want you back. There is no problem. Just say you'll come."

"I don't know," said my brother, casting his eyes about the room. He looked very tired and the thread-like scar stood out whitely on his lip. He moved his head with difficulty and held it at a slanted angle, indicating that his neck was still causing him pain. "I don't know," he said. "Maybe we'll just stay home for a while."

"Listen," said the insistent superintendent. "We'll raise your bonus by one-third. I guarantee it. Haven't I always kept my word to you people?"

"Oh, it's not the money," said Calum.

"Haven't I always kept my word?" repeated the voice. "Haven't I always kept my word?"

"Yes," said my brother.

"Well, give me yours. Just tell me you'll come with the same number of men. Give me a date. The end of the week? The beginning of next week? We'll send cars to meet you at Sudbury. Give me your word, and I'll know I can depend on you."

As the superintendent spoke, my brother's eyes made contact with the eyes of the others in the room. He raised his eyebrows in the form of a question as he held the receiver in his hand. And he seemed imperceptibly to nod his head even as his eyebrows asked the question.

As his eyes moved from face to face, his men nodded slightly.

"Are you still there?" asked the superintendent once more.

"Yes," he said, "still here."

"Well, just give me your word."

"Okay," he said. "We'll come."

"Great," said the relieved superintendent. "I knew I could count on you. And with the same number of men?"

My brother looked at me and I, in turn, looked at the faces of my grandparents and at the parents of the red-haired Alexander MacDonald. I nodded my head slightly.

"Yes," he said into the telephone's receiver. "With the same number of men. We'll be there."

That afternoon my brother took three loaves of bread and two boxes of sugar cubes and went down to the land beneath the *Calum Ruadh*'s Point. Past the house where he used to live and which was now even more worn by time and weather. Down to the rocky shore where the pilot whale had foundered and where some of the creosoted timbers of his skidway still remained. It was, as I said, in the time of spring graduations, when the summer had not yet come into its full splendour and the grass, though not lush, was new and green. He stood on the timbers of the skidway and on the boulders of the shore in the expensive shoes he had worn to the funeral, and he looked up towards the trees of the *Calum Ruadh*'s Point. It was a hot afternoon and only the forms of the horses could be seen standing in the trees to take shelter from the flies. But when he placed his fingers within his mouth and emitted the two sharp whistles, the response was immediate. There was motion among the trees and the horses, and she came galloping down towards the shore, sending the small rocks and flecks of turf flying before her eager hooves. "Ah, Christy" he said, "*m'eudail bheag*," as she thrust her head into his chest. She had grown grey about the eyes and muzzle, and a slight film was beginning to appear in her left eye. All afternoon he lay on the warm grass offering her the bread and sugar cubes while she nuzzled his face and his twisted neck, placing her great hooves carefully about the outline of his body. Some of the younger horses who had once been her colts looked on with something like amazement at the behaviour of their mother. He sang to her in Gaelic, perhaps as he had at the time of the great storm when we had needed her strength, and she had needed his faith and calming confidence in order to go on. All day they stayed together on the green grass, giving and taking to and from each other.

Before we left, my aunt gave me the gift she had purchased for her son. "Take this and *wear* it," she said, passing me the shirt. "Don't leave it in the box. Will you do that?"

"Yes," I said, "I'll do that. Thank you very much."

20 *W*hen we arrived in Sudbury it was late afternoon approaching evening and the cars from Renco Development were there to meet us as promised. We started out driving westward on Highway 17, past Whitefish, and McKerrow, and the road to Espanola. Past Webbwood and Massey and Spanish and Serpent River. Some ten years earlier my brothers had come to the area as young miners in the first heyday of the region's uranium boom. The boom had turned into a glut and many of the prospective headframes had been abandoned. Now with the promise of a contract to deliver 52 million pounds to the Japanese over the next decade they were

back, rediscovering what they had already found. It was, as the man from Renco Development said, "all systems go."

When we turned off Highway 17, the long spring day had become early night. The roads changed surfaces, the pavement giving way to what seemed like hastily laid-down asphalt, and later to gravel which had been covered with a solution to keep down the dust. Sometimes the solution smelled like oil and at other times like salt through the opened windows of the cars. Still later the solution vanished and there was only the smell of the dust and the sound of the stones thrown up by the tires against the bodies of the cars. Occasionally the cars "bottomed" on ridges of rock jutting up from the middle of the road and the oil pans and mufflers jarred and scraped against the exposed stone. On either side of the hastily constructed road lay the trees which had been bulldozed out of the way, their long yellow and white roots nakedly exposed, with strands of moss and disturbed muskeg still hanging from them. The roots looked like diseased and badly pulled teeth. Wrecked and abandoned cars had been pushed to the roadside's edge and, once, on coming around a turn, our headlights picked up the eyes of a gigantic moose standing beside the front end of a smashed Buick. The red eyes of the moose glowed out of the darkness and into our lights like burning intense coals while the dead lamps of the Buick's headlights and the silver of the grille's chrome flashed bright and shining for only an instant. The moose did not move from its stand beside the road, where it seemed to be guarding the remains of what had obviously once been a high-powered and expensive car.

When we got to the camp near the headframe's site, we were

issued blankets and sheets and assigned temporary rooms. The rooms were in hastily constructed huts made mostly of plywood. There were four bunks in each room, two upper and two lower. We flipped coins to decide who would get the lower bunks. In the morning, we were told, the rooms might be reassigned. There were some rooms that contained only two bunks instead of four, but right now all of them were occupied. It might take a little time.

The superintendent came in and shook hands with my brother and clapped him heartily on the shoulder. Apparently he was the man in charge when the red-haired Alexander MacDonald had been killed and the one who had said, "It was only one man," and, "The job has to go forward." As he spoke to my brother he counted us with his eyes.

Out in the night the lights of the headframe glowed and we could hear the sound of the hoist and the singing cables and sometimes even the signals as the giant ore bucket thundered up and down the darkened shaft. The French Canadians were working the night shift, and we would begin in the morning. Now that Renco Development had "the same number of men," there was some discussion as to whether three eight-hour shifts or two twelve-hour shifts would be more effective. If it were the latter, one crew would begin at seven a.m. and the other at seven in the evening. If we wished to substitute for one another it would be okay and we could roughly keep our own time. Much would depend on the quality of the rock.

Early the next morning my brothers and the other members of *clann Chalum Ruaidh* began to assemble their underground gear. Some of the belts and the wrenches they had thrown into the bush at the headframe's site had been retrieved and saved by men who thought the original owners might be back. Some of their gear they recognized as being worn by other men. Some of it was returned; some of it was not. When you throw things away, I suppose, you never can be sure that they will ever be yours again. My second brother recognized his miner's belt on another man and pointed out his initials scratched with a nail on the belt's inside. But the man said he had bought it from one of the French Canadians and would only sell it for twice its original price. He agreed, though, to lend it to my brother for a day as he was coming off his shift and my brother was going on. And so the summer began.

21 In addition to the frenzied activity beneath the headframes of the region there was also a great deal of action on the surface of the land itself. Roads were being constructed and crews of labourers hacked and slashed at the forest and blasted at the surface rock in an attempt to establish footings for the foundations of new buildings. Trucks groaned in and out with lumber and revolving cement mixers. Hammers banged and saws of various kinds whined and shrieked, each saw having its own sound, like the motors of

individual cars. Heavy earth-moving equipment rumbled constantly and shrill whistles pierced the air, announcing the immi-
nent blasts and warning those nearby to take cover.

Financial transactions were conducted at the bank, which
was in a hastily erected trailer, and the armoured cars clanked
in, bringing the money to meet the various payrolls and also to
take the money out. Many of the construction and cement
crews were Italian or Portuguese, while some were German.
Almost all of the men from a small village in the south of
Ireland were there and, from our own region, the always cheerful Newfoundlanders. For a while all of us ate in a common
dining hall and when the whistle would blow announcing
noon, the construction crews would drop whatever they were
doing and run to be near the front of the jostling line, throwing their hard hats in the air and leaping over whatever obstacles might be in their way. Within the dining hall the ethnic
groups sat by themselves, each group speaking its own language, leaning forward intensely amidst gesticulating hands.
Because we worked underground, those of us on the surface at
midday were not as frantically influenced by the noon whistle,
having at that point of the day more time than those who were
limited by the boundaries of twelve and one. We would come
later or perhaps earlier, slightly before the havoc-creating blast
of the anticipated whistle. Taking our trays, we too would go
to certain areas, like students who always choose specific seats
in the classroom although such seats are never formally assigned.
We would pass by the various groups bound for our own region
of the country while voices from the small intense divisions of

Europe rose around us. Sometimes as we passed by certain voices would quietly attempt to identify us. "Those are the Highlanders," they would say, "from Cape Breton. They stay mostly to themselves."

It is hard to know why, in such circumstances, we spoke Gaelic more and more. Perhaps by being surrounded by other individual groups we felt our lives more intensely through what we perceived as "our own language." Sometimes we would talk to the Irish, comparing phrases and expressions. There was a determined effort in Ireland, they said, to preserve Gaelic or "Irish." "It was the language spoken in the garden of Eden," they said. "It was the language that God used when speaking to the angels." We could understand each other reasonably well if we spoke slowly and carefully. "Why not?" said one of them. "After all, we are but different branches of the same tree."

As the days of summer lengthened, our own work became more desperately intense. After the shafts were sunk to the required depths the drifts were driven in the direction of the ore. *Clann Chalum Ruaidh* leaned into the jacklegs at the rock face, the hammering of the wet revolving bits changing the stone into dribbles of grey water which trickled from the holes like constant streams of watery semen or liquid, weak cement. The snaking yellow airhoses trailed behind the jacklegs and the men leaning into them. If the rock were "hard," a shift's "round" might progress only eight feet, but if the rock were "soft," twelve-foot steels were often used to drill the deeper holes. When the holes were drilled they would be loaded and wired with dynamite, the slender, dangerous sticks tamped in with long wooden poles and connected to each other with the fragile, delicate blasting wire. It was important that the centre of the face explode first and that the succeeding blasts be directed towards the blown-out centre. The dynamite in the holes at the bottom of the face, in the "lifters," would have to lift the rock towards the empty centre while that in the holes at the face's top would be helped by gravity. The skill was in knowing not only how many holes to drill but how deeply they should be drilled, and in calculating the rock's resistance to the dynamite's force. If the blast was not clean and the rock was not blown away evenly and to the required depth, all the work of the shift would be largely wasted, and much of it would have to be begun again. Only it would be more difficult because of the unevenness of the face, the dislocated piles of rubble, and the fear of concealed and unexploded dynamite or non-ignited blasting caps.

When the face was wired we would withdraw from it, walking back out the drift or tunnel we had earlier already created towards the station and trailing the detonating wire behind us. When the handle of the plunger was pressed down we would listen to the sequential explosion of the charges. Counting them on our fingers one by one, telling by the sound the effectiveness of each. Worried and fearful of "blowouts," which meant that the dynamite, instead of shattering the rock around it, would merely shoot back out of the hole in which it had been tamped. When there was a blowout the charge would "pop" instead of explode and, on hearing it, we would curse or shake our heads or drive one fist into the palm of the other hand and wonder what went wrong. By the time the last charge had exploded, the acrid smell of the powder from the first would be wafting towards us, accompanied by its yellow sulphurous cloud.

Often we would ring for the cage and the hoistman would take us to the surface so that we could breathe.

It was always something of a surprise to come to the surface and to be reacquainted with the changes of weather and of time. Sometimes it would be four in the morning and the night would be giving way to dawn, and the stars would appear to be going out like quietly snuffed candles as the sky began to redden with the promise of the sun. Sometimes the moon would gleam whitely above us and my brothers would say, "*Chointhe, lochran aigh nam bochd,*" "Look, the lamp of the poor." And sometimes at the appearance of the new moon Calum would bow or almost curtsy in the old way and repeat the verses taught to him by the old *Calum Ruadh* men of the country:

"In holy name of the Father One
And in the holy name of the Son
In holy name of the spirit Dove
The holy three of Mercy above.

Glory forever to thee so bright
Thou moon so white of this very night;
Thouself forever thou dost endure
As the glorious lantern of the poor."

Sometimes he would repeat them in English or switch to the original Gaelic:

"*Gloir dhuit féin gu bràth,
A ghealch gheal, a nochd;*

Is tu féin gu bràth
Lochran àigh nam bochd."

In the country of the *clann Chalum Ruaidh* the moon governed the weather and the planting of potatoes and the butchering of animals and, perhaps, the conception and birth of children. "The moon will change tonight," Grandma would say to the overdue, anxious expectant women who were her daughters and daughters-in-law. "After supper we will take a walk, and if God is with us the baby will be born tonight." And even as I think and tell this now, the moon-affected waters are exerting their pressure by the *Calum Ruadh's* Point. Within the circle of the sun the tides are rising and falling, thrusting and pulling and bringing to bear their quiet but relentless force under the guidance of the moon.

At other times when we would come up from the shaft the sun would be blazing. We would shut off our miner's lamps almost in embarrassment and drape the rubber cords around our necks, even as we blinked our eyes in an attempt to accustom ourselves to the fierceness of the sun. We would take off our miner's hats and our oilskin rubber coats and throw them on the ground. And we would unfasten the braces from the bibs of the rubber oilers which covered our more conventional clothes and let them dangle below our waists down to our knees. We would take off our rubber gloves, sometimes pulling the fingers inside out to give them some chance to dry, or else we would merely shake the water droplets out of them. The gloves would smell from the stench of human perspiration – like socks that had been worn too long. Regardless of the hardness of our hands, our fingers were always pink and crinkled from the heat and moisture of the gloves. They would appear almost like someone else's fingers at first, or like the hands of women who spend too much time in the dishpan, or the hands of small children who are left too long in their baths. When they were exposed to the air they would assume their normal colour and texture once again. The wet grey muck that clung to our steel-ribbed rubber boots would dry in the sun and be converted to finely powdered grey dust.

Sometimes when we came to the surface it would be raining and this too would be a surprise. Or the wind would be blowing, causing the still-standing trees to moan and sigh as their moving limbs rubbed against each other.

Underground, beneath the earth's surface, the weather was always the same. The sun never shone and there was no reflection from the moon. There was no wind, except the slight whisper of the air forced down the shaft to keep us alive, and there was no rain, although the trickle and tinkle of water sounded everywhere. Besides the water there were no natural sounds other than those of our own voices. Only the humming of the air compressors and the generators and the sound of moving and revolving steel hammering and grinding into stone. It was easy to lose track of time and space because life underground dictated, for us, what happened on the surface.

One summer, my oldest brother told me, *clann Chalum Ruaidh* worked at Keno Hill in the Yukon. They would awaken from their off-shift sleep at four o'clock and the sun would be shining through their bunkhouse windows. Sometimes they would tack their shirts over the inside of the windows to keep out the sun so that they might sleep better, but when they awakened and looked at their watches they would at first be uncertain as to whether it was four in the afternoon or in the morning. They would lie quietly for a while and think about themselves and where they had been before they went to sleep and what was expected of them during the coming day or night. Sometimes they would get up and take down the tacked-up shirts and look at the position of the sun as it hung in the sky. Looking at the sun to give them information or to reconfirm what they thought they believed. Uncertain of time, just as those who travel a great deal are often uncertain on awakening as to place. As the frequent traveller awakens to the strange but familiar decor of yet another hotel room. "Where am I?" he may think for a moment, as his eyes rove over the pulled beige drapes and the bolted-down brown television set and the cream-coloured card announcing room service. "Oh," he will say, after the moment has passed, "it is all right. I am okay. I am in Toronto, or Cleveland, or Biloxi, Mississippi."

When our shifts were over we would trudge wearily to the wash house, or "the dry," as it was called. We would check in our miner's lamps to the old man with the missing fingers and silicosis who could no longer work underground, and he would place them on the charger so that they would be ready for our next shifts. We would take off our rubber oilers and then our steel-toed rubber boots and our perspiration-soaked woollen socks. And then our flannel shirts and whatever we chose to wear as trousers. Some of us would take off our tattered grey undershirts and our shorts. My brothers, however, wore the long combination suits of woollen underwear. The underwear prevented chafing, they said, and absorbed both the underground water which fell upon them and the perspiration produced by their own bodies. Sometimes they would take the long suits of woollen underwear in their hands and wring them out, the splashing water forming grey, expanding puddles beneath their pink and wrinkled feet. We would go then and stand for a long time beneath the hot jets of water in the huge communal shower, clearing our throats and spitting out the gobs of phlegm, grey with silica, and lathering ourselves with the strong antiseptic yellow soap.

We would wash away the acrid sulphur smell of the blasting powder and look with a kind of wonder at the changes which had taken place upon our bodies during the past eight or twelve hours. There would be new lumps and swellings and fresh cuts and contusions. Sometimes on the backs of our necks there would be small cuts caused by chips of flying stone. And when we removed our hands from lathering our necks there would be tiny trickles of blood mingled with the soapy water which coursed between our fingers. And our necks would sting from the action of the strong soap within small wounds we could not see. Sometimes tiny particles of dust would enter our pores, which opened in the heat and moisture of our work, and later small infections would set in, resulting in eruptions not unlike the salt-water boils which rose on my brothers' wrists during the years they fished off the *Calum Ruadh*'s Point. The eruptions rose most frequently under our arms and in the area of our groins and, later, in the privacy of our rooms, we would lance them with needles and squeeze out the pulsating poison. Before the lancing we would hold the points of the needles over the flame from a cigarette lighter to prevent further infection from establishing itself.

After our showers we would retrace our route to the bench and baskets which contained our clothes. We would leave our individual wet footprints on the grey cement floor, where they would remain in their uniqueness for only the briefest of moments before evaporating in the gusts of heat. From the lowered wire baskets we would select our "street clothes," although we knew that outside there were no streets. And then we would hoist our work clothes on their pulleys up to the roof of the building where they would revolve and dry until we came for them again. We would run combs through the black or redness of our hair and then take our empty lunch cans and go out either into the darkness or the day. If it were day the black-flies would form around us in clouds: entering our nostrils, our ears and the corners of our eyes. They attacked the red-haired people most viciously of all, and even those who were not regular smokers sometimes puffed on cigarettes so that the smoke might keep the flies at bay.

We lived in special bunkhouses provided for us by Renco Development and, given the camp's condition, our housing was relatively elite. Many of the construction workers slept in large open bunkhouses with twenty or thirty beds pressed too closely together. Men worried about where to leave their wallets while they worked and complained about the petty thievery of shaving cream and razor blades and undistinguished socks. Many of the men kept calendars above their bunks and at the end of each shift crossed off the date of the day that was done. Some of them had futuristic specific dates circled or boxed, often with a word or phrase beneath: "Freedom" or "Gone" or "Last Day" written in English; or words of equivalent meaning in the various languages of Europe. If and when the authors made it to the specific date, they would whoop and shout and throw their hard hats into the bush. Some of them would spray-paint obscenities on the rocks of the Canadian Shield – directing their remarks towards exploitative companies or disliked foremen or unappreciated cooks.

They would go with their earnings to the lives envisioned beyond the circled or boxed dates. To Toronto or Portugal or southern Italy. To get married, or to take a course, or to start a business, or to buy a car. Some few would get no farther than Espanola or Spanish or Sudbury and would return days or weeks later, wan and depressed, having lost their money in poker games or to conniving pimps, or to muggers in men's washrooms, or to investments in short-lived expensive cars, smashed and abandoned and forever beyond repair. They would return wan and depressed, hoping that no one would associate them with the obscenities of what seemed like another time. Hoping for another opportunity and the chance to begin another calendar. Making private vows and resolutions.

The *clann Chalum Ruaidh* worked in a different manner. As specialized drift and development miners, we worked on a series of short contracts with Renco Development. Although we were paid a fixed hourly wage, the various bonus clauses were what really interested us financially. We were paid by our footage and by how rapidly we progressed to the black uranium ore which waited for Renco Development and for us behind and beyond the walls of stone. In some ways we were like sports teams buoyed forward and upward by private agreements and bonuses based upon our own production. We worked mainly for ourselves, our victories and losses calculated within our individual and collective minds, and our knowledge of individual and collective contributions a shared and basic knowledge.

When we were not working or sleeping we played the records of the Cape Breton violin which accompanied my brothers everywhere. Sometimes my brothers played their battered violin themselves. And sometimes we hummed or sang the old Gaelic songs. And when we talked, often in Gaelic, it was mostly of the past and of the distant landscape which was our home. The future was uncertain and, for us, it did not have to do with where we were. The death of the red-haired Alexander MacDonald hung heavily on all of us, emphasizing the danger and transience of our lives. Already there was talk of the new townsite that would develop, and of where houses and hockey rinks and schools might stand. And simultaneously there were conversations as to where our branch of *clann Chalum Ruaidh* might go when the sinking of the shafts and the driving to the ore were completed tasks. One week Renco Development flew Calum to Squamish, British Columbia, to set up a blast at a rock face. The company paid him upward of fifteen hundred dollars to set up a blast that lasted only seconds, but which was so fine and delicately expensive that it was felt that only he could engineer it. Perhaps when dental school rolled around for me in the fall the others would go to Squamish. Perhaps they would go back to South America or South Africa. Vaguely people looked at their passports to check expiry dates. Perhaps they would go home.

Sometimes those of us who were off during the days or early evenings would sit on benches outside our bunkhouse doors. We would engage in desultory games of horseshoes or talk with the Irish and the Newfoundlanders. Many of them were older married men with families who, on paydays, lined up at the small temporary bank to purchase money orders or international bank draughts to send to their distant loved ones. Sometimes they would sit on the benches unconsciously rubbing themselves between their legs. "In Ireland," said the red-haired Irishman, "I have a home but I have no money. Here I have lots of money but I have no home." We raised our eyebrows in unison to indicate that we understood.

Sometimes when we passed the bunkhouses of the French Canadians, we could hear them singing and playing their own music through the partially opened windows. Many of their violin jigs and reels were like our own, although played at a faster tempo. We could hear them slapping their feet on the plywood floors and clapping their hands together or upon their thighs without ever missing a beat. Sometimes we could hear them "playing the spoons" in accompaniment to their music, the rhythmic clicking of the spoons, pilfered from the dining hall, changing in texture as they snapped off the hand, the thigh, the knee, the elbow, or the shoulder, in time with "*Les Souliers Rouges*," "*Tadoussac*," or "*Le Reel St. Jean*." We never entered their bunkhouses, as they never entered ours. It would have been like going into the dressing room of the opposing team.

In South Africa, my brothers said, the Zulus always sang. They sang mythic songs and tribal songs and work songs with choruses of wordless but rhythmic sounds and syllables. In the season of migration to the mines, they came in singing convoys from their homelands. Strong, arrogant young men singing songs about the lengths of their penises and the many women they intended to impregnate in some distant but uncertain future. Coming for money and bravado to the heat of the underground, and the quarrels and knife fights of the miners' compounds.

22 Outside the camp gates and beyond the posts of the security guards, there existed another world.

No one was legally allowed within the camp gates unless an identification card or badge number could be produced, indicating the company of employment. To the security guards in their small plywood huts, there came a constant stream of people with a variety of petitions and requests. Some were looking for work and had driven in over the rough and rocky roads encouraged only by the possibilities of speculation. Others had hitchhiked in and stood with their backpacks at their feet, the sweat-blotched outlines of the packs still visible on their shirts. Others were looking for real or invented relatives: brothers, cousins, boyfriends, men who had not paid their child support. Some were there to collect debts. Some were looking only for a meal. "No," said the security guards over and over again. "No badge number, no entry." "No, I don't have a master list of everyone who works here." "No, I don't know if anyone is hiring now. You'll have to go back to Sudbury and register there at the Unemployment Office." "No, I don't know any tall dark man with a missing finger and a scar running down his cheek." "No, I don't recall anybody by that name." "No, you can't go in just to have a look around." "No, there is no need to leave a message here, because I can't deliver it." "No, I told you the same thing yesterday." "No, I can't let you in even if you give me twenty dollars."

Farther outside the camp gates a primitive parking lot had been hastily bulldozed out of the bush. Amidst the overturned boulders and the uprooted stumps waited the automobiles of the few employees who considered it worthwhile to own them, as well as the cars of uncertain visitors. At the edge of the parking lot and strewn along the roadside were other smashed and abandoned vehicles which had been bulldozed to one side or the other. Most of these had been stripped of their licence plates by former owners who wished to avoid detection, and many of them now served as temporary shelters or primitive places of commerce. Out of the abandoned cars and those of the visitors came individuals who offered products and services for sale. Pedlars sold work shirts and gloves for prices lower than those of the commissary within the gates. There were men with trays of rings and watches, and others with pornographic pictures and various sexual gadgets. The nervous, suspicious bootleggers were always there, constantly looking over their shoulders as they offered cases of warm beer they had secreted among the tree stumps, or jugs of wine or bottles of liquor at twice the legal price. In some of the cars sat young native girls from the reservations who had come looking for money and perhaps adventure and excitement. Sometimes they sat on the hoods of the cars in the hot summer sun, sitting on blankets spread to absorb the hood metal's heat. Sometimes they leaned sideways, combing and brushing their long black hair in the reflection of twisted side-mirrors or cracked or splintered windshields, pursing their lips as they applied their blood-red lipstick and concentrating fiercely as they lacquered and buffed their long and pointed scarlet nails. Offering one another sticks of gum, or crumpled cigarettes, or drinks of warm wine from opaque paper cups. Trying to pick up the country western stations on their tinny portable radios; turning the radios one way and then another in an attempt to lure the music in and over the static-producing rocks of the Canadian Shield.

If one walked in the area of such cars at night one could hear the moans and groans as well as the snatches of muffled conversations. Sometimes the oral sounds were diminished by the creaking of the shifting springs beneath the soiled upholstery.

One morning Calum and I went for a walk outside the camp gates. We had just come off our night shift and eaten our breakfast and although we were tired the sun hung in the sky like a molten ball forecasting the coming heat and the difficulty of sleep for our weary bodies. We decided to postpone the effort of sleep and walked out of the gates, over the small grey stones of the crushed still gravel, and towards the direction of the parking lot. And then we could hear the sound of the fiddle hanging or beckoning us in the promised heat of the day. We looked at each other, recognizing the tune of "MacNab's Hornpipe," which was a classic piece at the Cape Breton square dances. The music was coming from one of the abandoned cars and as we were drawn in its direction we focused upon what had once been an elegant dark-blue Crown Victoria with its grille now smashed and its hood buckled back so that it looked like the peaked roof of a house. It sat on its wheel rims, as someone had removed the tires and also, it appeared, its trunk lid. Most of the glass from the windshield and the windows was broken and only the jagged edges remained, seeming, even in the summer's heat, like the beginning slivers of ice at the edge of an autumn pond.

Through the broken front window we could see the form of a small man hunched forward in the passenger seat. He moved his whole body as he played, and his right foot tapped out the beat on the floor mat of the car even as the bow flew over the four taut strings. Although it was still early in the morning, beads of perspiration were already beginning to form on his upper lip and his forehead. He looked up at us through the broken glass of the window and smiled. "*Cousin agam fhein,*" he said in a mixture of English and Gaelic, looking directly at my shirt although not quite into my eyes. He wore a soiled red baseball cap which read "Last Stop Hotel" above the sketch of a gigantic fish leaping towards a lure. He was a James Bay Cree, he said, and his grandfather or his great-grandfather, he was not sure which, had been a man from Scotland who had plied the trade routes of the north in the years when fur was king. This was the man's fiddle, he said, offering us the battered instrument. He told us that his own name was James MacDonald and he had recognized the tartan on the shirt of the red-haired Alexander MacDonald, which I had been wearing at the time. The English/Gaelic phrase meant "cousin of my own."

"What do you call that tune you were playing?" asked my brother as he turned the fiddle within his hands.

"I call it 'Crossing the Minch,'" he said and nodded towards the fiddle. "That's the name that came down with it."

"Come with us," said my brother, "and we will get you something to eat."

At the security gates Calum said, "*Cousin agam fhein*," and gestured towards James MacDonald. And then in response to the guard's puzzlement he added, "He's with us."

My brother and the guard looked into one another's eyes for an instant. And then the guard, who was nearing the end of his shift and did not want to be involved in a confrontation, waved us through.

We took James MacDonald to our bunkhouse and someone went to the cookhouse and brought back a basket of food. Mounds of bacon and toast, and hard-boiled eggs wrapped in a napkin, and stacks of hotcakes, and a thermos of coffee. He was ravenous and seemed to eat almost one-third of his fragile weight at a single sitting. And then he took his fiddle and went outside and sat on one of the benches.

He was, as Calum said, "a wonderful player" and my brothers brought out their own fiddle and took turns playing with him. And then out of the bunkhouses of the French Canadians came their leader, big Fern Picard, with some of his men. They watched us for a moment from a distance, and then went inside and returned with their own fiddles and their spoons. Two of them brought harmonicas and one of them a button accordion. They sat on the benches beside us, which we had never seen them do before, and joined in the music. After a while one of them got up and went into his bunkhouse, where he ripped two sheets of plywood off the wall and brought them out to the sundrenched benches.

"For *la Bastringue*," he said. "*La danse d'étapes.*"

He slid one sheet under the feet of the French musicians and as he did so they lifted their legs but remained seated and continued to play without missing a note, and when the wood was in place their feet came down in perfect unison. The toes of their shoes struck the wood as one, and then the sound of leather on wood became one with the music. The staccato rhythm of the percussion blended with the clacking of the spoons and echoed and amplified the soaring sound of the more conventional instruments.

"*Le gigeur,*" said the man who had brought the plywood, nodding in the direction of his nearest fiddler. The man smiled and nodded his head slightly to the left, without raising his chin, which was tucked tightly into the angled base of his violin. As his fingers and feet flew and as he moved to and with the music, only the area around his waist remained still. I noticed that he was wearing one of my brothers' belts.

The sun moved higher and heatedly across the sky, yet no one seemed to think of sleep. It was as if we had missed the train to sleep and there was nothing we could do about it in our present state.

The music dipped and soared and the leather-soled shoes snapped against the reverberating wood. Sometimes a fiddler would announce the name of a tune and the others would nod in recognition and join him in "The Crooked Stovepipe" or "Deeside" or "Saint Anne's Reel," "The Farmer's Daughter" or "*Brandy Canadien.*" At other times the titles seemed lost or perhaps never known, although the tunes themselves would be recognizable after the first few bars. "Ah yes," the fiddlers would nod in recognition, "A ha," "*Mais oui,*" and they would join one another in the common fabric of the music. Gradually the titles from the different languages seemed to fade away almost entirely, and the music was largely unannounced or identified merely as "*la bastringue;*" "an old hornpipe," "*la guigue*"; "a wedding reel"; "*un reel sans nom.*"

"Sometimes," said James MacDonald after finishing a tune which everyone knew by sound though not by name, "it is like a man have a son and he is far away and does not give the son a name." He paused. "But the son is there anyways," he added shyly, as though embarrassed by the fact that he had said so much.

The music continued and its tempo seemed to rise. Someone dragged the second sheet of plywood into the dusty square in front of the musicians and tried to arrange it evenly as a primitive platform for stepdancing. It was difficult because of the ribs of rock which protruded through the scanty soil. Small stones were placed under the wood at strategic corners in an attempt to construct a level surface. The dancers took turns, although sometimes two men would attempt to share the quivering wooden rectangle. Some danced in the "old" way with their torsos straight and their arms held stiffly by their sides. Others moved their whole bodies.

"We need some beer," someone said.

A hat was placed by the dancer's platform and soon it was filled with money. Someone placed a stone on top of the money so it would not blow away, although there did not seem to be any breeze. Later, the hat and money vanished and still later the cases of warm beer appeared, purchased from the nervous bootleggers in the parking lot and smuggled somehow past or around the security guard's post. Some opened the beer with bottle openers attached to key chains, others with the blades of pocket knives, others with their teeth, spitting the caps before them onto the dusty rock. The perspiration beaded on the foreheads of the musicians and the dancers and formed dark circles beneath their arms.

"What the hell are you guys doing?" said the superintendent as he unexpectedly appeared from around the corner of one of the bunkhouses.

The fiddlers fell silent and the dancing feet stilled. The silence seemed even more profound in the absence of the music.

"Who the hell are you?" he said, stepping in front of James MacDonald, who averted his eyes and began to put away his fiddle.

"How did you get in here?" he asked, this time more forcefully while towering over the small man who was still seated on the bench. James MacDonald shrugged his shoulders in a noncommittal fashion and turned the palms of his hands upward to complete the gesture.

"He's with us," said my brother, stepping forward from the small knot of men which had gathered at one side.

"*Cousin agam fhein,*" said someone from the crowd and there was a nervous ripple of laughter.

The superintendent turned sharply in the direction of the voice. He was a man who understood neither French nor Gaelic nor Cree and he did not like hearing phrases in languages he did not understand.

"Get him out of here," he said, turning back to my brother and indicating James MacDonald with his foot. They looked at one another for what seemed like a long time.

"And get the beer out of here too," he said more quietly and averting his gaze. "You know it's illegal within the camp gates. I'll expect you all on your shifts tonight."

He turned on his heel and walked away.

The musicians began to gather up their instruments. Someone threw a beer bottle into the bush and we waited until we heard its distant explosion on an unseen rock. The man who had brought the plywood sheets carried a case of beer into his bunkhouse and left the wood behind. James MacDonald said something to himself in Cree and smiled resignedly, as if he had seen it all before.

"Never mind him," said my brother to James MacDonald. "You don't have to go if you don't want to. You can stay with us as long as you like."

That night we went to work with the sound of the music still in our ears. For the first hour we were quiet and almost light-headed because of all the beer and the fact we had not eaten or slept all day. And the air seemed fouler than usual and the stench of the powder stronger. Later the pounding of the steel drill bits into the stone contributed to our mild nausea and seemed to evoke a similar pounding within our heads. Our underwear was drenched with sweat and we rummaged in our lunch cans for oranges to ease our dehydration.

When we came to the surface in the morning the music seemed to have happened a long time ago. We stood under the showers as the water lashed down upon us. The hair on our bodies flattened against our skins, all of it lying in the same direction. Far away when the wind and the sea blew across the *Calum Ruadh*'s Point the grass lay flat upon the flesh of earth, clinging by its roots in water and in wind and rising again when the storm subsided. When we left the wash house we realized that it had rained heavily during the night and as we approached the bunkhouses we noticed the two sheets of plywood from the previous day. They were muddied and dirty and seemed already to be warping due to the pressure of the rain. The French Canadians took one sheet and we the other, and we threw them into the bush behind our dwellings.

James MacDonald was asleep with all his clothes on in Calum's bed. The cap which read "Last Stop Hotel" was on the floor beside him. My brother crawled into the bed of one of our cousins who had gone to his shift as we were coming off ours.

James MacDonald remained with us for two days. He had no money and asked for work. My brother took him with us on two shifts and paid him in cash at the end of each. We all contributed some kind of underground clothing, although it was difficult to find garments and footwear to fit his small stature. He was deadly frightened of the underground and could not adjust to the confined spaces and the darkness, and the stench of powder, and the assault of noise. And he was not strong enough to do even

the lightest tasks, and mucking machines and the loud and unexpected noises caused him to jump and cower against the walls of
stone. Once, on one of his rounds the superintendent noticed
him but did not say anything. We were making good progress at
the time and our footage was ahead of schedule. One early afternoon when we awoke from our post-shift sleep, we realized that
both James MacDonald and his fiddle were gone.

"He was not made to do this anyway" said my brother after
the realization had settled in. "He's better off away from the
underground." Two weeks later someone told us we were
wanted at the camp gates. One of the native girls was there and
led us to the shell of the once-elegant Crown Victoria. Lying on
the seat was a haunch of moosemeat carefully wrapped in cheesecloth, although the blood was seeping through. Pinned to the
cheesecloth was the torn sheet from a calendar. "Thanks," read
the single word printed in pencil, and then there was a picture of
a fiddle and a sketch of a gigantic fish leaping towards a lure.

23 Once, said my sister in Calgary, she was in the oil
city of Aberdeen with her husband, the petroleum
engineer named Pankovich. They had been to a
splendid dinner at one of the grand hotels and were in the
company of oil executives and their wives from Houston and
Denver. They had eaten too much and drunk too much and

wobbled their way through parodies of Scottish dancing. Later as they ascended the stairs to their room, she met a young woman, perhaps it was one of the maids, she could not be sure, who brushed against her and murmured something to her in Gaelic. When the phrase registered, she looked around, but the woman was gone.

Later, as she slept, she was strangely awakened and there was the form of a woman standing by her bedside. She sat up and the form moved to the foot of the bed and seemed to beckon to her. She dug her elbow into her husband's back but could not awaken him. The room was in semi-darkness, but because it was summer and Aberdeen so far north it was brighter than one might expect. She looked more closely, straining her eyes. The form moved towards the door and then seemed to vanish. She got up slowly and walked towards the door herself. She tried it cautiously, but it was locked. She opened the door and looked down the hall. Halfway down there was a man in a kilt, sleeping on the floor with his room key still clutched in his hand. She went back into her room and pulled open the drapes. She looked out the window. It was quite bright, but the street was deserted. The only sound came from the gulls hanging in the air. She went to the hallway once again. The man was gone. It was four a.m.

When her husband awakened she asked him if he recalled the woman who brushed by them on the stairs. He said he didn't remember. He was going out to look at the oil towers in the North Sea, he said. He would be gone for two days.

At breakfast she looked for both the young woman and the man in the kilt but could not find either.

"Why don't you rent a car," said her husband, "and take a drive? Go wherever you want."

It was late in the day when she entered what she knew had been called the "rough bounds" of Moidart. Entered what the visiting scholar called "these horrid parts." Passed the rhododendrons and the fassfern, went to look for Castle Tirim, the castle destroyed according to the prophecy, and walked across to see its remains at low tide. Could hardly get back to her car in time, she said, because the tide began to rise. Had to take off her shoes and hold them in her hand. Her skirt was wet and dripping. Got into her car and drove along the narrow winding tracks, watchful for the sheep and mindful to pull over to one side at the sight of rare approaching vehicles. Went to another spot near the sea and walked along the rocks looking at the seaweed and a pair of splashing seals. Listened to the crying of the gulls. Saw the form of an older woman approaching her, carrying a bag in her hand. Later she learned the bag contained winkles, which the woman had been gathering at low tide.

And then, she said, she met the woman face to face, and they looked into each other's eyes.

"You are from here," said the woman.

"No," said my sister, "I'm from Canada."

"That may be," said the woman. "But you are really from here. You have just been away for a while."

She walked with the woman to the low stone house and three brown and white dogs ran to meet them, running low to the ground with their ears flattened against their heads.

"They won't bother you," said the woman. "They will recognize you by your smell."

The dogs licked her hand and wagged their tails.

"This woman is from Canada," said my sister's guide to an old man who sat on a wooden chair inside the house. "But she is really from here. She has just been away for a while."

Although it was summer the inside of the stone house was cold and damp. "It reminded me of the cellars at home," my sister said.

"Oh," said the old man and my sister could not judge his degree of comprehension. He had on a soiled tartan shirt covered with a black sweater and wore a cloth cap. His eyes seemed rheumy and she thought he might be hard of hearing and that, perhaps, his mind wandered.

"*Co tha seo?*" he said, looking at her more closely.

"*Clann Chalum Ruaidh,*" she said

"Ha," he said, continuing his gaze.

"Wait here," said the woman, and she went out, leaving them together.

"Did you come far?" he said.

"From Canada," she said, again uncertain of his degree of comprehension.

"Ha," he said, "the land of trees. A lot of the people went there on the ships. And some to America. And some to Australia, the country back of the sun. Almost all gone now," he said, looking out of the window. "They are the lucky ones," he added, as if talking to himself, "the ones who went to Canada."

"Tell me," he said, looking closely at her once again, "Is it true that in Canada the houses are made of wood?"

"Yes," she said. "Some of them."

"Oh," he said. "But wouldn't such houses be cold? Wouldn't they rot?"

"No. Well, I don't know. Maybe some of them in time."

"What a strange thing," he said. "I often wondered about it. Houses made of wood."

There was a pause.

"The prince was here, you know," he said suddenly.

"The prince?" she said.

"Yes, the prince. Bonnie .Prince Charlie. Right at this very spot. He came from France in the summer of 1745 to fight for Scotland's crown. We were always close to France," he added dreamily, looking out the window again. "It was called 'the auld alliance.' "

"Oh yes," said my sister. "I've heard."

"He was only twenty-five," he said, suddenly becoming animated by the story. "Although he was our prince, he was raised in France and spoke mainly French, while we spoke Gaelic. Almost a thousand men went with him from here. The *Bratach Ban*, the white and crimson banner, was blessed at Glenfinnan by MacDonald. Most of the men went from here by boat, although some walked.

"We could have won" he said excitedly, "if the boats had come from France. We could have won if the rest of the country had joined with us. It was worth fighting for, our own land and our own people, and our own way of being."

He had become so excited by his story that he leaned forward, from the waist, in my sister's direction and his large hands which grasped his knees turned white along the ridges of his knuckles.

"The prince had red hair," he said, suddenly changing his mind and lowering his voice in a quiet conspiracy. "And was said to be very fond of girls. Some of us," he whispered, "may be descendants of the prince."

The door opened and the older woman came in accompanied by a number of people of different ages.

"Some of them," my sister recalled to me, "had red hair and some had hair as black or blacker than my own. All of them had the same eyes. It was like being in Grandpa and Grandma's kitchen." I sat back as my sister continued with her story:

The older woman said to the group she had brought in, "This is the woman I told you about." Then she spoke to them in Gaelic and they all nodded their heads. I nodded back and it was a few seconds before I realized that she had spoken in Gaelic and that I had understood her. It seemed I had been away from the language for such a long, long time.

They were all shy at first and then a woman about my own age said, "You have come a long way and your skirt is still wet from the water."

"Yes," I said.

"But it is all right," she added. "You are here now. We will get you some dry clothes. One has to be careful of the water."

She said everything in Gaelic, and then I began to speak to her and to them in Gaelic as well. I don't even remember what I said, the actual words or the phrases. It was just like it poured out of me, like some subterranean river that had been running deep within me and suddenly burst forth. And then they all began to speak at once, leaning towards me as if they were trying to pick up a distant but familiar radio signal even as they spoke. We spoke without stopping for about five minutes, although it might have been for a longer or shorter time. I don't know. And I don't even know what we said. The words themselves being more important than what they conveyed, if you know what I mean. And then all of us began to cry. All of us sobbing, either standing or sitting on our chairs in Moidart.

"It is as if you had never left," said the old man. "Yes," said the others all at once, "as if you had never left."

Suddenly we were all shy again. Wiping our eyes self-consciously. It was like the period following passion. As if we had had this furious onslaught and now we might suddenly and involuntarily drop into a collective nap.

"Would you like some tea?" said the woman I had met on the beach, rousing herself from her chair.

"Yes, that would be nice."

"Or perhaps a dram?" she added.

"Yes," I said. "That would be nice also."

"Wait here," she said, "and I will get it and some dry clothing as well."

She went through a door into an adjoining room.

"Do they still have the red hair?" asked the woman when she returned.

"Yes, some of them do."

"Aha," said the old man from his chair.

"And the twins?"

"Yes, I am a twin myself."

"Oh? Another girl?"

"No, a brother. He has red hair."

"Oh," they said, "a *gille beag ruadh?*"

"Yes," I said, "a *gille beag ruadh*. That's what they called him. When he started school he didn't know his given name."

"Thanks a lot," I said to my sister in her modernistic house in Calgary.

"Oh, don't be silly," she said. "You weren't an orthodontist then, charging thousands for a set of braces. You were only a little boy."

"And the dog?" said the older woman. "All of the older people used to talk about the dog. I remember my grandparents saying that they had been told about the dog by previous generations. How she had jumped into the ocean and swam after the boat when it was leaving for America. The people who were left behind had gone up to the highest hill to wave goodbye and they could see the dog's head carving a V through the ocean, swimming and swimming after the departing boat and after a while her head was just a speck and they could hear *Calum Ruadh* shouting and cursing at her, could hear his voice coming across the flatness of the ocean, shouting, 'Go back, go back, you fool, go home. Go back, go back, you're going to drown.'"

"And then I suppose," said the older woman, "he realized she would never go back. That she would try to swim to America. Or she would die in making the effort. And the people standing on the cliff, waving their bonnets or bright items of clothing in final farewell, heard his voice change. Heard it crack with emotion as he began to shout, 'Come on. Come on, little dog, you can make it. Here! Here! Don't give up! You can make it! Come on! I am here waiting for you.'

"And the people on the cliff said they could see the speck of her head rise out of the ocean in response to his positive shouts. As if he gave her hope. And the V quickened and widened as she tried harder and harder. The man leaning over the side of the boat and banging the palm of his hand on its wooden side to offer encouragement and then reaching down to lift her from the water. That is the last picture anyone here ever had of that family," said the woman. "After that, it was just waving from the cliffs until the ship itself became a tiny speck on the ocean, no bigger than the dog's head had earlier been."

"Yes," said the old man, nodding in the direction of the brown and white dogs, which lay like rugs beneath the table and the chairs in the stone house in Moidart. "It was in those dogs to care too much and to try too hard."

And my sister agreed and told them the story: "One of them was with my parents when they drowned. And she later died herself, on the island. Died from caring too much and trying too hard."

"How did your parents drown?" asked the people in unison. "We are sorry. Where was this island?"

"Oh, I forgot you didn't know," said my sister. "I feel somehow that I have known you all my life and that you should know everything about me. I will tell you later."

"It is good that you feel that way," said the woman with a smile, offering her a glass. "You are home now."

"Did you know," asked my sister in her modernistic house in Calgary, "that after they landed, *Calum Ruadh* stabbed a man in Pictou?"

"No," I said. "I don't think I ever heard that. Only that he was depressed."

"Well, he did" she said. "Grandfather told me. Do you know why he stabbed the man?"

"No," I said.

"For kicking his dog," she said quietly, looking directly into my eyes while drumming her fingers on the expensive table.

"His dog was heavy with pups and the man kicked her in the stomach."

We went outside the house and looked down from the prestigious ridge. It was in the late afternoon and in the distance we could see the cars streaming east along the Trans-Canada Highway. Coming from Banff and the B.C. border. The sun glinted off their metallic rooftops and seemed to bounce in shafts of reflected golden light back towards the direction of the sky.

24 Now in the Toronto streets the sun hangs high above the smog while the people jostle and bump on the way to their individual destinations. Some carry string bags filled with produce from their own original regions of the world. The barbecuing ducks rotate slowly behind the window glass and the disembowelled piglets hang from the steel hooks driven through their legs. Their small determined teeth are clamped fiercely shut in death and their pink and purple gums are visible behind their silent and retracted lips.

In southwestern Ontario the pickers move across the flat hot fields or reach into the branches of the laden trees. The children of the families from the local towns and cities are even more weary now, and close to open rebellion. They long for their rec rooms and their video games and iced drinks and for long tele-phone conversations with their friends in which they can express the anguish of their pain. Their parents are by this time hot and tired and irritably exasperated by what they perceive as the non-cooperative attitude of the young. Now they no longer cajole but openly threaten. Angry fathers in their sweat-drenched under-shirts, with their huge hands quivering at their sides, take giant steps across the green rows to confront the reluctant harvesters. "Why are you too lazy to pick the food you're going to eat?" some will ask. "If you don't smarten up you'll be grounded. You'll have to stay in your room for two weeks." Soon such families will drive home in sullen silence, glumly looking out the windows at the fields and the orchards and the pickers left behind.

The Jamaicans and the Mexican Mennonites and the French Canadians move with dexterity and quiet speed. Their strong sure fingers close and release automatically even as their eyes are planning the next deft move. They do not bruise the fruit and their feet do not trample the branches or the vines. And they will not die from heart attacks between the green and flowering rows. They will work until the sun descends and then retire to their largely all-male quarters. Many are in Canada on agricultural work permits and when the season is done they must make the long journey back to their homes.

Some are on "nine-month" contracts allowing them to stay in Canada for a maximum of nine continuous months. If they stay longer they become eligible for Canada's social assistance and health programs. No one wishes them to become eligible for such programs except themselves. Sometimes, if they are in demand, they will leave the country for only a few days and then re-enter to begin another nine-month stay, or until they are no longer needed. Some have been following this pattern for decades while their children are continents and oceans away. They do not see their children or talk to them very often. Neither they nor their children ever visit the orthodontist. In the small houses in which they temporarily live they sit, at the end of the day, in their undershirts and on the edges of their steel-rimmed beds. The slowly revolving fans stir the humid air as those who are literate read their letters from home. Those who are less fortunate ask their friends to read and also to write for them. Sometimes they lie on top of their beds with their hands clasped beneath their heads and stare up at the chipboard ceiling. Sometimes they listen to music on cassettes, the rhythm and the dialect and the language often being foreign and indiscernible to those who pass by on the larger highways. Photographs sit on orange crates or the scarred night tables. On Monday morning when I smilingly greet my first patient, the small houses will be empty and the men will, already, have spent long hours in the sun.

With no need for dexterity or speed I will pick and choose whatever liquors are before me, and perhaps it is not important. What is important is that I will return.

25 In the heat of that summer our underground footage moved forward rapidly. We struck an area of a soft rock which yielded easily to our bits and to our powder and we began to run ahead of schedule. The time lost due to the death of the red-haired Alexander MacDonald was rapidly made up and Renco Development was more than satisfied. There was a suggestion that perhaps we were being paid too highly, especially since we had encountered the "soft rock." Still, we pointed out that an agreement was an agreement and perhaps "hard rock" and hard times lay ahead for all of us, as they did for all those who worked within the rock-bound confines of

the mine. Calum did the negotiations for all of us and no one wished to argue with him or be an obstacle in his path.

After the departure of James MacDonald our music seemed to wilt within the summer's heat and the French Canadians did not seem to play that much either. They withdrew more into the privacy of their own bunkhouses, as did we, and we viewed each other through eyes tinged with suspicion. Among ourselves the idea persisted that the French-Canadian hoistman on duty at the time had *known* that Alexander MacDonald was at the shaft's bottom when he sent the ore bucket whistling down, that he had *not* been mistaken and confused his signals. We heard also that Fern Picard had approached Renco Development the day following Alexander MacDonald's death with the proposition that he could bring in another crew of his own relatives from Temiskaming to replace *clann Chalum Ruaidh* in the shaft's bottom. We heard, as well, that he and his men were aware of the private offer made by phone to us and that they were displeased because of the suspicion that we were being paid at a higher rate than they. We viewed them, as they did us, with a certain wariness; always on the lookout for the real or imagined slight or advantage; being like rival hockey teams, waiting for the right time to question stick measurements or illegal equipment; biding our time and keeping our eyes open. Still the work went on as we alternated our lives between the cool and dripping wetness underground and the stifling fly-infested heat on the summer surface.

Sometimes I thought of the life that could have been mine had I remained in Halifax and accepted the summer research grant I had refused in order to come out here. It was true that in

Halifax there was a very different kind of life, a life that included movie theatres and music and the possibilities to be found in libraries and laboratories. At times I missed, or imagined that I missed, the theatres and the restaurants which I hardly ever frequented or the discussions with classmates on the subjects of the day. There was a life, I knew, which was not so totally masculine nor dominated by the singleness of one profession.

Sometimes my thoughts drifted to the small rented room and my Halifax boarding house. There I imagined my middle-aged landlady stifling in her own heat, fanning her face with the newspaper while sitting on her wooden chair with her stockings rolled down beneath her knees. Relieved yet bored by the absence of her transient students, having no belongings to rifle through while they were gone and no one to listen to her rules regarding the radio, and the houselights, and the closing of doors and the shovelling of her walk in winter. Sometimes I imagined my white-coated supervisors and colleagues moving on their soft-soled shoes across the polished floors of the air-conditioned labs, monitoring their trays of cultures and peering into their microscopes and sometimes encountering the flickers of boredom flashed back into their eyes from the fluorescent glare of washroom mirrors.

I was also aware of a certain guilt concerning the death of the red-haired Alexander MacDonald, although I was not sure if the guilt really was or should have been mine. But there was a vague uneasiness associated with the circumstances and the timing of it all. I told myself that he had gone into the mine after high school because he was not academically inclined. But I knew also that he had done so, at least in part, to help the members of his family who had been haunted, through no fault of their own, by the echoes of a kind of regional, generational poverty which whispered and sighed with the insistence of the unseen wind. I realized that Alexander MacDonald had partially paid for the car which ferried me home from my splendid graduation, and I realized that the opportunity to thank him and make amends was now no longer there. I had often recreated the scene in which he had called me "lucky" because my parents had lost their lives, and the feeling of the callouses on his small, determined, hardworking hands seemed permanently bonded to the rising hair on the back of my neck. The touch of his small hands, it seemed, would now and forever be mine, although I told myself that his passing had affected others much more profoundly, and I had best not consider myself so precious.

26 *I*n the lulls between shifts my brothers often spoke of the landscape of their youth and their later young manhood. Far away on the edge of the Canadian Shield they recreated images of seasons and time separate from them by great distances of physical and mental geography. They remembered with great clarity their early lives upon the island: the clouds of gulls rising from the cliffs and the colony of seals at the island's northern end. If one swam in summer, they said, you had to be careful of the male or bull seals; sometimes

they would attack you, thinking you were intruding on their territory or threatening the members of their harem who lay basking on the rocks in the summer sun. And they spoke often of the miraculous fresh water well which burst from the rocks at the ocean's edge.

"Do you remember the well, *'ille bhig ruaidh?*" they asked.

"No, I don't," I said, "only what I have been told of it."

The well was nourished by an underground spring and its water was particularly sweet. It was frequented by humans and animals as well, and visitors from the mainland would take bottles of it back with them, thinking of it as a tonic or a particular refreshment. "Grandpa used to take bottles of it with him," said my brothers, "he thought it fuelled sexual desire and was also a cure for arthritis."

I remember he used to call it "arthur-it is." When the sea was agitated by storm, or even sometimes at high tide, the well would be submerged. It would become invisible to the eye beneath the pounding surf, and those who anticipated the vagaries of the sea would hasten to scoop pails of fresh water and "save" them in a series of wooden barrels and puncheons secured to the rock above the high-water mark. In the full fury of storm it would seem as if the well had no existence, and even after the waves receded, its water would be salty and unfit to drink. But in a matter of hours it would "clear itself," as they said. "We used to watch the animals," said my brothers. "They would stand around it and when they began to drink, we knew the water was okay for us. For a long time there was fear that a severe storm might totally destroy it or reroute the water vein, but it never happened.

It was always there in the calm following the storm. And even there when it seemed to be overwhelmed."

"Once, in March," said my second brother, "Grandpa came across the ice with a load of hay. We were running short and we had no way of shoeing our horses so they could walk upon the ice. He borrowed a team of horses and had them shod with 'ice-corks' in their shoes and came across. He had ropes with rocks on each end strapped across the load so the hay would not blow away, and the brown dog was with him. The mother or grandmother of the one who was shot by the man who came from Pictou.

"He had fortified himself with two or three bottles of rum to 'protect' him from the cold, as he said. We could see him approaching the island, the dog running ahead of him, and then the team of horses pulling the sleigh. The horses were brown with white stars on their foreheads, one was the mother or grandmother of Christy and the other was one of her colts. I remember our father saying, 'Look how in step they are. They raise and set their feet in perfect unison. They have the same rhythm. If you were to buy another horse and pair it with one of them, they could not pull the load in the same way, because they would always be slightly out of step. They are like dancers or singers from the same family. They are always perfectly in tune. And in time. And have a harmony all of their own.

"The horses moved forward," my brother continued, "confident in the sharp corks upon their shoes which bit into the ice and gave them a purchase on the slippery surface. In spite of the cold they were sweating from the heaviness of their load, and the white froth beneath their collars emphasized the hoary white-ness of their coats as their perspiration froze upon them. Frost upon frost moving across the whiteness of the ice.

"As they approached we could hear Grandpa singing Gaelic songs to himself out on the ice. We knew he was slightly inebri-ated because he was singing some of the verses out of sequence and repeating others which he had just finished. We went down to the edge of the ice to guide him ashore. After we had unloaded the hay and stabled the horses and had something to eat, Grandpa lay down for a nap, but then he got up and said he was going back. He had slept longer than he intended and dark-ness was not far away. Everyone wanted him to stay for the night, but he said he was planning to play cards with his friends later on, and that the horses would be eager to get home, and without the load behind them they would make the crossing rapidly. After he left our father said, 'It is difficult for a man ever to give advice to his father. Even if you try to think of him as just another man he is still your father and you are his child, regardless of how old you have become.'

On the return journey Grandpa apparently fell asleep, com-forted by the warmth of his winter robes and his rum and trust-ing to his horses and his dog. When the sleigh stopped he assumed he was in the yard of the horses' owner and leaped out of the sleigh and began unharnessing them. It was then that he noticed the dark water slashing before him. The ice had "opened" and the dog had stopped and then the horses. Darkness had fallen and his fingers were too numb to reharness the horses and he knew he would have difficulty getting them to turn back towards the island so he finished unharnessing them and let them go.

He turned back himself to walk towards the island's guiding lights, hoping that the open water was now behind him instead of in front. Later in the darkness he came scrambling up the rocks of the island's shore, apparently still in possession of one of his rum bottles. He had not had a light with him on the sleigh and no one on the island or on the mainland was aware of what had happened. His ears and his cheeks, along with his fingers and toes, were badly frostbitten and we heard later that he confided to our father in Gaelic, "I think I froze my dick, but don't say anything in front of your wife and young children."

They bathed most of Grandpa's extremities first with snow and later with cloths soaked in lukewarm water. Said my second brother, "You could see the ice crystals glittering in his frozen ears as they gradually thawed."

Later he sat with his feet in a dishpan of warm water and with his hands wrapped in wet warm towels.

Later that night, said my brother, the dog and the horses arrived home on the mainland. They had picked their way across the ice, perhaps jumping or swimming across any narrow leads that opened up in the ice before them. The people in the house were playing cards when they heard the dog barking and jumping at the lighted window and heard the scrunch of the horses' hooves upon the snow and then saw the huge brown heads of the horses against the window's frosted panes. In extremely cold weather, horses that were outside would be drawn towards the orange glow of the light beckoning from behind the windows. It seemed to symbolize, for them, an image of warmth and hopeful salvation, perhaps like that offered by the lighthouse on the island. If someone did not rush outside to respond to their mute request, there was a danger that the pressure of their heads against the panes would break the glass and the warmth that had attracted them would escape into the frigid air.

Before the people went outside they feared there had been a tremendous accident, but when they saw that the horses were unharnessed they reasoned that they had "escaped" from the island because they wanted to be at their own home. There was no telephone to the island and no way to make contact, so the people stabled the horses and waited for morning.

In the morning the sleigh was visible out on the ice where Grandpa had left it. People from both the mainland and the island could see it clearly through their binoculars. There was no longer any open water before it and it was as if the ice had "healed" during the night and the open wound was no longer visible. Later in the afternoon the sun shone and our father walked across the ice from the island and was met by the men from the mainland. They used the sleigh as a meeting point, all of them carrying picks and poles and testing the ice before them. The mainland men were told what had happened and were assured that Grandpa was all right. The water and slush had been frozen to the sleigh's runners and the sleigh was solidly embedded, but after testing the ice around it, the men decided to pick the runners free. Later they came with the nervous horses approaching the sleigh from the direction opposite to that of the recently opened channel, well aware that what supported a man might not support a horse. The ice "held" and they were able to get the sleigh ashore safely. Because it was March and because of what had happened no one wanted to risk horses on the ice again. Because Grandpa's feet had been frostbitten he could not walk very well for a while and stayed on the island for a number of weeks. His frostbitten ears turned black and then a kind of purple, yielding to pink as the colour and circulation returned to normal.

Grandfather crossed over a couple of days after the accident. He took two of his younger relatives with him and they all wore "creepers," which were somewhat similar to the "corks" on the bottom of the horses' shoes. They were attached to the footwear in a manner similar to the horses, and gripped the surface of the late ice. Grandpa kept them hanging on a nail within his porch. The men carried ice poles and coils of rope and a portable light, although the sun was shining. "You never can be too careful out on the ice," said Grandfather. They also took some clothes for Grandpa and a bottle of whisky and a note from Grandma, "Bless his dear heart," she said to them before they left.

After they arrived on the island, Grandpa asked Grandfather to go with him into one of the bedrooms at the top of the stairs. They were both older men of roughly the same age and had been together for a long time and shared a sense of intimacy. The different cadences of their voices drifted down the stairs as they shifted from Gaelic to English and then back again.

"Froze your dick?" said Grandfather in exasperation. "It sounds to me like you froze your brain. What kind of old fool are you? Out on the ice, drunk and by yourself in the dark without a light. You might easily have drowned. You should have thought of what you were doing."

After Grandpa had fallen asleep, lulled by the warmth of the whisky, Grandfather spoke to the rest of us gathered in the kitchen. "I talked to Grandma before I came over," he said, "and she misses him terribly. You ought to know that he spent two days borrowing that sleigh and getting those horses shod and purchasing and loading that hay. He paid for the hay with money from his own pocket. He knew you were in trouble out here as far as your animals were concerned and if someone did not come across your animals might starve. He was in the business of salvation." Grandfather paused. "He might not approach life the same way I do," he said, "but as your grandma says, 'He has a heart as big as the ocean.' I believe that, and none of you should ever forget it."

The ice apparently broke quickly that spring and it was possible to launch a boat and get Grandpa home safely. His hands and feet had healed and the embarrassment of his black and purple ears was no more. When he was leaving our father inquired discreetly about his "other business."

"Oh, it will be all right," he said with a smile. "I will have a warm place to put it when I get home." Grandma was overjoyed to see him. She had purchased a large bottle of rum for him and decorated it with a ribbon and placed it on the kitchen table. As they embraced, Grandpa's eyes filled with tears. "God bless your dear heart," said Grandma. "It is so good to have you home."

In the time following Grandpa's "almost accident," there was little said about it, perhaps because it seemed embarrassing and might have been avoided. Once, though, when Grandpa had had too much to drink, he was overheard talking to Grandfather. "Do you remember the way it looked?" he asked cheerily.

"No," said Grandfather grumpily, "I don't. Let's change the subject."

"Okay," said Grandpa agreeably, "but, by golly, let me tell you that night out on the ice it was hard in a way you'd never want it to be."

"You wouldn't remember any of this, *'ille bhig ruaidh,*" said my oldest brother. "At that time you and your sister were only infants, sleeping in baskets by the stove."

"I guess that's right," I said. "It was before our time to remember."

"It is peculiar what you do remember," said my second brother. "In hindsight I often think of what our father said when Grandpa started across that evening with the horses, about how it is difficult ever to give advice to your father because somehow you are always his child regardless of your age. At that time," he continued, "we would sometimes question our parents' decisions and wish we could be free of all their advice, and then one day we had more freedom than any of us could have wanted. There really was no one to tell us to wash our faces or change our underwear or socks or to tell us when to get up or when to go to bed or if and when we should go to school. I have often thought of our mother's remarks about my ears on that final day, of how I was annoyed that she wanted my ears to be clean while all I wanted was to be free."

"For some years there in the old house we really did do almost anything we wanted apart from the necessities needed for staying alive," said my third brother. "Sometimes girls would come to visit us and they would say, 'Isn't this great to be in a house with no parents nosing around,' but after a while, even they would begin to look at their watches and speak of deadlines and boundaries that spoke to them but not to us."

"It is curious," said my second brother, "how Grandpa was saved from the ice in March and yet was perceived as a careless man, while our parents who tried to do everything right went down without salvation. Grandpa could have been lost as well and then things would have been quite a bit different – especially for you, *'ille bhig ruaidh*. Do you ever think of that?"

"Yes I do," I said. "Quite a bit."

"He never mentioned his own close call after the loss of Colin and our parents. I guess he considered it trivial by comparison," said Calum. We were sitting on benches outside our bunkhouse when this conversation occurred. It was late in the afternoon and the sun was in decline. Fern Picard walked by and we thought we heard him say, "Fuck you," but we could not be certain. We went inside to get ready for the evening shift.

27 *A*bove the Toronto street the sun moves on its appointed journey. Lost in my own thoughts I have not noticed that it has achieved its zenith and now, in this country, beyond the towers and the expensive restaurants and the Supreme Court of Ontario, it begins its descent towards the west. Still it is very hot and, perhaps because of the heat, I

decide to buy beer because it will last longer and because the alcoholic content is submerged within its liquid volume.

The beer store is fashioned with items of commercial happiness. It seems at first glance like a cheery clothing store for those who are under the age of twenty-five. Brightly coloured shirts and caps and jackets and tank tops proclaim the jolly goodwill of their distant manufacturers. There are coolers and icepacks and thermoses; all of them dedicated to summer fun although it is already September. The companies are reluctant to relinquish the joy of summer. The handsome young man who waits upon me whistles as he works. When I ask for two cases of twelve he is temporarily taken aback because I do not mention a specific brand. He gestures towards the array of bottles and cans displayed above the conveyor. "Pick your own," he says. When I assure him that it doesn't matter he regains his smiling composure and rolls the cardboard cartons lightheartedly towards me. I place my money on the plastic tray. Everything in the beer store exudes happiness and goodwill. It is as if the store is imitating the relentless TV commercials, and obviously both the commercials and the store itself are born of similar agencies. I do not think the agencies would recruit my blood-stained brother sitting on the edge of his bed in his underwear as an example of one of their happy consumers.

As I leave through the automatic doors, a shaking old man in a winter overcoat asks me if he might "borrow" a cigarette. I give him the change from the plastic tray. The ever-alert and pleasant young employee comes to the door and tells the old man to move along. He no longer seems quite so upbeat. The old man shuffles away. The young man returns to his oasis of happiness.

The street is more congested now and I keep my beer cases close to my knees to avoid contact with my fellow pedestrians. I have ordered two cases of twelve rather than one of twenty-four because they are easier to carry, but now I can feel the cardboard handles of the cases digging into the tenderness of my hands. My hands have grown soft from the years of exploring the insides of other people's mouths. Since the AIDS scare we have all taken to wearing latex gloves. When the gloves are peeled off I see my hands with their damp pink wrinkles as they were so many decades ago when released from the stench of my miner's gloves.

In the years when my brothers lived in the old *Calum Ruadh* house and before they went to the mines, their hands were so calloused that they could hardly close them. In the evenings by the light of the oil lamp they would cut off the hardened dead skin with their knives or with razor blades. The discarded remnants of dead skin would lie on the oilcloth of their tabletop like the curled yellow parings from old fingernails. My brothers would open and close their hands to ascertain movement and feeling. Where the dead skin had been cut away, the flesh was first white and then pink when it came in contact with the deepened pulsing of their blood. On the next morning when their hands gripped the axes or chains or the ropes from their lobster traps, the callouses would begin to build again. My brothers were always careful not to cut so deeply as to cause their blood to flow.

When I leave the street and ascend the stairs once more the atmosphere no longer seems surprising or shocking. Familiarity establishes itself rapidly. "You will get used to almost anything," Grandma used to say, "except a nail in your shoe."

The door is open and he has splashed some water on his face and his undulating white hair. He seems to have been pacing across the small room. The water droplets glisten on the whiteness of his hair. "Ah," he says, "you are back. That did not take very long. I see you brought beer. It will last a long time. Any port in a storm."

He reaches for the nearest case and rips open the cardboard top with his huge hands, which are steadier now after his consumption of the brandy. I notice that the brandy is almost gone; perhaps two inches of it remains in the heel of the bottle. The brandy is like a transfusion and one can almost see it flowing through him. It reddens his face and highlights the crosswork of tiny damaged purple veins high above his cheekbones and beneath his eyes. The huge veins on the backs of his hands have become distended as the fluid pulses through them.

As he removes the beer bottle he twists off the cap in a single motion. No need to open it with one's teeth any more. He throws the cap towards the wastebasket, but he misses and it lands with a small clatter upon the floor. He offers the bottle to me. "Not now," I say. "Maybe I'll have one later. I have to drive back. We have to go out to dinner tonight."

He smiles and then gulps from the bottle. Then he moves towards the brandy bottle and swallows the remainder of its contents.

"Now that I have the beer," he says, "there is no need to save this."

He drinks more beer to ease the burning sensation of the brandy. The beer bottle is now either half full or half empty, depending on one's point of view.

"It's a nice day on the *Calum Ruadh*'s Point today," he says, moving towards the window. "I listen to the national weather forecast every morning to check on the Cape Breton weather. I did it even when I was in Kingston. Even when we were in the mine and the actual weather didn't matter for our work, it was still an interest. I guess we were so close to it for so long, always thinking of tides and storms and weather for hay and the winds that might damage the boat or bring the mackerel or herring. And of course the shifting and changes of the ice," he adds after a pause, directing his glance through the grimy, sun-shot window. The dust motes flutter in the rays of the sun. He wipes the back of his hand across his mouth.

"Remember when we lived in the old house and we would go outside right before going to bed to check the weather for the next day? To feel for moisture in the air and dew on the grass, to check the direction of the wind and to listen to the sound of the ocean and to look at the stars and the moon? Do you remember?"

"Yes, I remember."

He turns from the window to face me. "Poor Grandpa," he says, "he had an old joke about an older couple who go outside before bedtime to check on the weather but also to relieve themselves. The woman makes a comment about the moon, but the man thinks she is referring to his penis. He says something like, 'Don't worry, it's low now but it always rises during the night,' or 'Later when its darker it will rise up higher,' something like that. Do you remember? Did he ever tell you that?"

"No," I say, "he didn't tell me that."

"Oh well," he says, "perhaps at the time he thought you were too young. The past is not the same for everyone, but it catches up with you. I was thinking the other day of how the exhaust from our old cars used to be visible in the coldness of the winter air. Often we had smooth tires and we would have to gun the cars to get them up the icy inclines, but when we came to intersections we would have to stop and then the blue whiteness of the exhaust would overtake us. We could see it and smell it. We thought we had left it behind us somewhere back on the road, but when we slowed down it seemed to overtake and surround us. I guess we were not going fast or far enough. Funny to think of that in the hot weather," he adds. "Maybe we always think of the season we're not in."

"Yes, maybe we do."

I reach for a bottle of beer, not because I particularly want it but because it seems unsociable and almost patronizing to watch him drink so rapidly by himself. Later I will have to drive for close to four hours to join my wife and my colleagues for an almost compulsory dinner.

"Did I tell you that I saw your old friend Marcel Gingras a few months ago? I was walking along the sidewalk and I saw three cars coming towards me. They were Cadillacs or Lincolns, big expensive cars, filled with men and the windows were rolled down and their tattooed arms were hanging over the side. I almost knew who they were before I recognized them because they drove in that same kind of arrogant fashion, staying close together and straddling two lanes on the streetcar tracks. I recognized their licence plates, *Je me souviens*, at about the same time I noticed their driving.

"Marcel pulled his car up on the sidewalk as soon as he saw me and the others did the same. He was wearing a flowered shirt open almost to his belt, and sunglasses, and he had a gold chain around his neck and several large rings on his fingers. He had had his hair styled. It was long and wavy. Remember he used to always have a brush cut?"

"Yes," I said, "I remember."

"He put his car in park but didn't shut the motor off and almost jumped onto the sidewalk where I was. It happened so fast that although I thought I recognized them as a group I wasn't sure of him as an individual. I was carrying a bottle of cheap cooking sherry in a bag because it was all I could afford and I remember thinking, 'Well, if I have to defend myself with this, I won't miss the contents.' I grasped the bottle by the neck but then he was upon me and put his arms around me in a hug.

"'*Bonjour*,'" he said, 'I recognized you by your walk.' He introduced me to the other men in the cars. 'This is *Calum Mor*,' he said. 'Long time ago when we first came with Fern Picard, this was the best miner we ever saw.'

"The men in the cars nodded their heads and held out their hands. They were all basically French-speaking, although two of them were MacKenzies, descendants of Wolfe's soldiers from the Plains of Abraham. We talked for a while. They had heard that there was work driving a railroad tunnel from Sarnia under the river to the American side. Or that there was a tunnel near St. Louis and work near Boston. 'Better money in the U.S.,' said Marcel, rubbing his thumb against the first two fingers of his right hand in the old gesture. 'Lots of people from Cape Breton in Massachusetts, in Waltham. We've been there before. Come with us.'

" 'No,' I said, 'I don't think so. I couldn't pass the X-ray.' They all laughed and Marcel asked about you – 'the book one,' they used to call you. I told them what you did and he said he remembered that you were good at school. I gave him your number. Did he ever call you?"

"No, he didn't."

"Anyway, we talked for a while. Traffic was building up behind them and people were getting annoyed. A policeman came along. At first he was impressed by their cars and thought I was merely an old alcoholic bothering the well-to-do. Then he noticed their licence plates.

" 'You can't block traffic like this on the street and on the sidewalk,' he said. '*Je ne parle pas l'anglais*,' said Marcel. The policeman turned to me. 'I was just trying to give them directions,' I said.

"They put their cars in gear and began to drive off. The MacKenzies waved from the the back seat of the last car and Marcel put his hand out the window and waved. I remember the sun glinting off his rings.

"The policeman said to me, 'You better get home with your wine. What would you know about French?' "

"I think I've told you that before," said my brother. "It was unusual just to meet them like that."

"Yes, you have told me," I say. "It was unusual. Marcel wanted to learn English more than anything in the world, he once told me. He offered me money to teach him. He thought it would guarantee him a job in Sudbury. Perhaps with Inco or one of the big companies."

The sun has moved across the sky so that its light no longer penetrates directly into the room. I nervously peel the label off my beer bottle. My brother staggers towards the sink, unzipping his trousers as he goes. Although he is still clear in his speech, his movements are erratic and he no longer cares about real or imagined niceties. Grandpa used to say, "It's a great thing, drinking beer. It cleans out your system and it comes out of you the same colour as it goes in." I am not sure how he would react to this present scene, or if his goodwill would extend this far.

"Once, before everything happened," Grandma once said to my twin sister and me, "we were all sitting around the table. It was years before you two or Colin were born. Grandpa had his beer bottle on the table and Calum was perhaps four or five. As he passed it the sun came through the window in a certain way that reflected off the glass and he saw his little boy's reflection thrown back towards him. 'Oh,' Calum said, 'I see myself in that beer bottle. It's really me. It's like I'm in there.'

"He was so excited that I never forgot it. Later I saw him looking at the bottle, but the light had changed and he couldn't find himself again. It seemed almost like a prophecy of what was to happen later. He was such a dear little boy."

"I have to go now," I say, rising from my chair as Calum turns from the sink, the dark wet blotches visible on the front of his trousers and his zipper still undone. "But I will be back if not next week, the week after. I will leave you some money if you wish, to tide you over until Monday."

"Oh, I think I'll be all right," he says. "No need of that."

I reach into my pocket and feel for the crumpled roll of bills dampened by my own perspiration. I place the money on the table and try to avoid looking at it or counting it because it seems, somehow, so condescending.

"Take care," I say. "*Beannachd leibh.*" He approaches me and takes my right hand in his and places his left hand upon my shoulder. He is now swaying slightly and because he is still a big man his weight causes me to shift my own feet in an attempt to achieve balance.

"My hope is constant in thee, Clan Donald," he says with a smile. We lean into one another like two tired boxers in the middle of the ring. Each giving and seeking the support of the other.

He turns towards the window and I leave and close the door.

My exit from the city of Toronto seems fairly simple. The protestors and their opponents have apparently gone home. The traffic is heavy but not oppressive. Because it is late Saturday afternoon the ordinary commercial traffic of the weekdays is stilled and to the north of the city the major arteries reflect the comparative calm of the mid weekend. The desperate impatience of Friday and Sunday evenings is either past or yet to come, and the overloaded trailers and swaying boats seem to have attained their autumn destinations. People are trying to make the summer last as long as they are able.

Through his sun-smudged window perhaps my brother sees Cape Breton's high hardwood hills. There the colours have already come to the leaves, and slashes of red and gold glow within the greenery and beneath the morning's mist. The fat deer move among the rotting, windfallen apples and the mackerel school towards the wind. At night one can hear the sound of the ocean as it nudges the land. Almost as if it is insistently pushing the land farther back. The sound is not of storm but rather one of patient persistence and it is not at all audible in the summer months. Yet now it is as rhythmical as the pulsing of the blood in its governance by the moon.

The "lamp of the poor" is hardly visible in urban southwestern Ontario, although there are many poor who move disjointedly beneath it. And the stars are seldom clearly seen above the pollution of prosperity.

28 "*W*hen I take transatlantic flights at night," said my twin sister, once, in Calgary, "I look at the brightness of the stars and the constancy of the moon and, coming back, I always try to look down on the ocean. I think of Catherine MacPherson, our great-great-great-grandmother, sewn in a canvas bag and thrown overboard, never able to arrive at the new land nor get back to the old. I wonder what her thoughts were before she died, leaving everything she knew to be with the man who had married her sister. I often wonder if her Gaelic thoughts were somehow different because of her language, but I guess you think and dream in whatever language you are given."

"In the bunkhouses of the mining and construction camps," I said, recalling an old image, "late at night you could hear the men dreaming in all their different languages. Sometimes they would shout phrases in Portuguese or Italian or Polish or Hungarian or whatever might be their language of origin. Shouts of encouragement or warning or fear or sometimes softer expressions of affection or of love. No one would know what they were saying except those with some kind of shared background. We used to dream ourselves, the older ones among us in Gaelic, and the French Canadians had their own dreams as well. And in South Africa, our brothers said, the Zulus also spoke at night."

"Remember," asked my sister, "how Grandpa and Grandma used to dream, sometimes in English and sometimes in Gaelic, but towards the end their dreams were almost totally in Gaelic? It was as if they went back to the days when they were younger. As if it had always been the language of their hearts. Sometimes I think I dream in Gaelic myself but somehow I'm never sure. When I awake I am never quite certain, although the words seem still to be coursing through me. I ask Mike if he hears me talking in my sleep and he says he never does, but then he sleeps so soundly.

"There is a passage by Margaret Laurence in *The Diviners* where Morag talks about lost languages lurking inside the ventricles of the heart. I return to that passage a lot and when I touch the book it flies open to that page, page 244." I smiled at my sister.

"When I first came west to study drama," she continued, "my professor told me I would have to get rid of my accent unless I wanted to spend all my career in the role of an Irish maid. I didn't even know I had an accent. I thought everyone spoke as I did. Do you ever think about that, about the way you speak, about the language of the heart and the language of the head?"

"No," I said, "in my world nothing like that matters. It is almost as if we are beyond language."

"Perhaps you are," she said. "Perhaps that is part of the reason why people in your profession have such a high rate of suicide. Do you know that you have one of the highest suicide rates?"

"Yes, I know that."

"You have to be careful," she said, with a flash of concern.

"Oh, I'm careful."

She sighed. "Sometimes I am at Pearson airport between flights, and if I have time, I walk down to the departure gates for the East Coast flights. The gates always seem to be the farthest away and I cannot do it unless I have a lot of time. I have no real reason for going except that I want to be in the presence of those people. To listen to their accents and to share in their excitement. Sometimes there are business executives as well, but you can always recognize them because they sit apart and are not emotionally involved. I am always moved by those middle-aged Newfoundlanders from Fort McMurray trying to tell their children that Newfoundland is a place to be proud of, rather than ashamed of, and trying to justify their accents and the manner in which they speak. Does this seem silly to you?"

"No," I said. "It doesn't seem silly at all."

"Once, I was at the Halifax gate and a woman said to me, 'Isn't it great to be going home?' I was startled because maybe I thought I looked like one of those executives, but I guess I didn't. She asked me where I was from and before I could think, I said, 'Glenfinnan.'

"'Oh,' she said. 'My husband is from there. It's a very beautiful spot. There is an island off the coast. Do you know it?'

"'Yes, I know it.'

"'My husband's name is Alexander MacDonald. Were you a MacDonald?'

"'Yes, I was.'

"'He is going to meet me in Halifax and I will introduce you to him,' she said. 'Perhaps you two are related.'

"'Perhaps we are,' I said. 'I am part of *clann Chalum Ruaidh*.'

"'So is he,' she said.

"Just then the attendant announced that all passengers with seats at the rear of the aircraft should proceed through the gate, so the woman gathered up all her packages. 'See you at the luggage carousel,' she said. 'Don't forget. My husband has red hair.' And then she was gone. I wanted to wave to her or try to explain, but there was no time and she vanished beyond the attendant taking the boarding passes.

"After she had gone, I stood at the gate for a long time. I watched them shut the plane's doors and watched the plane itself as it taxied towards the runway and then lifted into the sky. And still I stood there. I didn't realize how conspicuously solitary I was until an attendant came up to me.

"'Is there anything we can do for you, ma'am?' he asked. 'There is not another flight from this gate for more than an hour.'

"'No,' I said. 'Sorry. No, there is nothing you can do for me.'

"Did you know," she said, changing the subject, "that James Wolfe had red hair?"

"No, I didn't," I said.

"Well," she said, "he did."

29 Now my car moves south and west towards the descending sun. Farther south the pickers view the day's decline from differing perspectives. The urban families are glad the day is done and look forward to their evening meals and the comfort of rental videos and long conversations with their friends. The children will have school on Monday.

The families of the Mexican Mennonites and the Jamaicans will pick until the sun goes down, as will the families of the French Canadians from New Brunswick and Quebec. For many of them school is, perhaps, a luxury and they see themselves within a foreign land where the authorities pay little attention to their existence. In New Brunswick, the academic year is altered to accommodate the needs of varied harvesters, and there is leniency in Quebec.

Later in the season, when they are no longer needed, the pickers will leave their tiny cabins and begin their long return journeys. Sometimes the Mexican Mennonites will have trouble at the various borders because of the complications of their lives. Vehicles may have been purchased or, perhaps, children born since the time of their last border crossing. Sometimes when they attempt to enter the United States they will be pulled aside by the immigration authorities and the same may happen to them thousands of dusty miles later as they try to leave the state of Texas.

They may be herded into small overcrowded rooms, clutching their vehicle permits, their creased and tattered birth certificates, their yellowed work visas, and their passports containing the uncertain photographs. The children will clasp their parents' browned hands. They will be asked to take a number and later to answer the complicated question of exactly who they are.

On their homeward journeys, the French Canadians may stop to visit their relatives in St. Catharines or in Welland before the final push. Reacting to economics, some will fill up their gas tanks on the Ontario side of the border because Ontario gasoline has traditionally been cheaper. Others motivated by patriotism will coast their near-empty cars across the border, filling their tanks with more expensive gas in Rivière-Beaudette or St. Zotique. All of them will point out to their children the superiority of Quebec's highway rest areas compared to those of Ontario, indicating the plentitude of free hot water and the lack of the commercial pressures. They will rest easily within the boundaries of their region.

In the period prior to their long homeward journeys, many of the men will work upon their cars. Nearly all of them are, by necessity, mechanically knowledgeable and they go to garages as rarely as they visit the dentist. In the sundowns of the late autumn evenings they will bend beneath the raised hoods. They will replace their water pumps and fuel pumps and seal their hissing hoses with strands of electrical tape. They will check their carburetors and clean their spark plugs and tighten their fan belts and listen with fearful practiced ears to the ticking of their engines. Later they will rotate their worn tires and check the lamps of their headlights for their journeys through the night. But that will be in the future. This late afternoon and evening there is still work to be done before the sun's final descent and the achievement of Saturday night. Then, perhaps, there will be beer and the flickering television shows which come to many of them in a foreign language. They will lean forward and concentrate intently, taking their cues at times from the insistence of the canned-laugh tracks. Some will play cards and others dominoes.

Tomorrow, which is Sunday, will see some of the single young men change their clothes and venture, perhaps, to the pebbly beaches. There they will often laugh too loudly and call out to the young women in their fractured versions of English, in French, in Spanish, or in Jamaican patois. They will receive basically unintelligible responses and console themselves by punching one another on their upper arms or heavily muscled shoulders.

30 During those months on the Canadian Shield, when the life of Marcel Gingras touched mine, it seemed as if we were like gently nudging planets or perhaps helium-filled balloons. We came in contact with one another but did not collide and although our outer perimeters brushed we were still deep within the private areas of our own circumferences. Sometimes when the shifts were changing we

would nod to one another. And once or twice the management of Renco Development asked me if I would help him to interpret the signals of the hoist or to read the directions on the dynamite cases. On two nights when there were breakdowns, Renco Development paid each of us to sit high on the headframe's deck and explore the basics of the French and English languages.

We would begin with the obvious parts of our bodies, pointing by turns to our heads, our eyes, our mouths and shouting, "*la tête*," "*les yeux*," "*la bouche*" to ourselves and the twinkling stars. Later we would move to the contents of our lunch cans, shouting, "apple" and "*la pomme*" and "cake" and "*le gâteau*" and "bread" and "*le pain*" as we held up each item for the other's scrutiny. He would punch the air with enthusiasm when the answers were correct and we would move from the designations of food to whatever objects of work lay before us on the deck-room floor, pointing to *une chaîne, la dynamite, la poudre, la poudre de mine*, being impressed and surprised by how similar many of our words were although our accents were different. It seemed, at times, as if Marcel Gingras and I had been inhabitants of different rooms in the same large house for a long, long time. There was a rumour that Renco Development planned to train both of us as hoistmen in some near or distant time.

During that period Renco Development was eager to meet its own objectives and deadlines, as were we. All of us joined in the relentless rush towards the black and radiating uranium which lay beyond the walls of rock.

In the dark and dripping coldness of the underground and the stifling heat of the surface bunkhouses, time seemed to compress and expand almost simultaneously. When we were underground it was impossible to distinguish night from day. If we went to work at seven in the evening we would emerge at seven in the morning at first unaware that we had gone to work on one day and emerged on another. We would blink our eyes to the unfamiliar sun. At times we seemed like jet-lagged travellers, passing through time zones where everything appeared to be the same but was also somehow different. In the cloying daytime heat of the bunkhouses it was often difficult to sleep, the sheets clinging damply to our bodies and the perspiration beading upon our brows. On awakening, it was at times a challenge to focus upon the time of the day or the day of the week or even the week within the month. It was easy to become annoyed at the radio playing in the next room, or to become irritated by interruptions to the boring familiar rituals we had ourselves grown tired of following.

One hot sticky day I heard a voice saying, "Hey, hey," as I became aware of someone pushing on my shoulder. I had been sleeping in a sweaty troubled way, and at first the voice and the nudging seemed to come from a muffled distance. As the voice and the nudging grew more intense I opened my eyes to a worried-looking security guard. He would advance, nudge, and say, "Hey, hey," and then jump back a short distance, as if he feared he were touching a dangerous trap which might uncoil and do him harm.

"What? What?" I said, trying to swim up from the uncertain regions of bleary sleep.

"Are you Alexander MacDonald?" he asked, still standing at what he assumed to be a safe distance from his newly awakened objective.

"Yes," I said, "I am."

"Well, you're wanted on the phone. Come to the front gate. You know I'm not supposed to take or to deliver phone calls or leave the gate, but this is long distance, so hurry up."

He turned and walked quickly through the door in a state of what seemed like relieved agitation.

I looked at my watch and glanced rapidly around at my surroundings. It was eleven a.m. and no one else was in the room. I pulled on my trousers and my open shoes and followed the route the security guard had taken. By the time I got to the door his diminishing form was already entering the plywood hut.

The telephone swung at the end of its coiling cord.

"Hello," I said.

"*Ciamar a tha sibh?*" said Grandpa from far away. "How are you?" he repeated in English.

"Okay," I said. "How are you?"

"Not bad for an old man. I wanted to tell you he's coming tomorrow."

"Who's coming?" I said, trying to dislodge the sleep from my head. "Coming where?"

"Your cousin," he said, "*cousin agam fhein*, from San Francisco. Remember the letter Grandma read you on the day of your graduation? The one from my brother and her sister? Well, he's coming to Sudbury tomorrow. At three in the afternoon. They wrote from San Francisco. It's all arranged on their part. Now we have to do ours."

"What?" I said, still groggy.

"Are you awake?" said Grandpa, his voice verging on annoyance. "What time is it there? It's a little after noon here."

"Yes," I said somewhat unconvincingly, "I'm awake."

"Did you have your breakfast?" he said. "Did you have porridge or that other stuff?"

"What other stuff?"

"I forget what you call it," he said. "It looks like little bales of hay."

"Oh, shredded wheat. No, I didn't."

"Good for you. Stick with the porridge. Now at least you sound more awake. You sounded as if you had been out all night with a girlfriend or something."

"No," I said, "there are no girlfriends here."

"Oh well," he said. "Too bad. Maybe someday. Now although you've never seen this young man, it's like that poem your grandfather is always quoting: 'Mountains divide us and the waste of seas – Yet still the blood is strong, the heart is Highland.' I hope you remember that."

"Yes, I remember."

"Good. Have a drink for me in Sudbury. Are there lots of taverns in Sudbury?"

"Yes," I said. "Lots of taverns in Sudbury."

"Good," he said. "My hope is constant in thee, Clan Donald. Here's Grandma."

"Hello, *'ille bhig ruaidh*," she said. "As Grandpa said, he is arriving in Sudbury tomorrow at three. Is Sudbury far from where you are?"

"About one hundred and sixty miles," I replied.

"Oh, that's not too bad. Ask Calum to go with you. I suppose I should talk to him as he is the oldest and our grandson too, but you are our own *gille beag ruadh* and we have given you the best we could for all these years. Blood is thicker than water, as you've often heard us say. If our brother and sister had not gone to San Francisco we would have all been together these years, and this war would not affect us in this way, but now all we can do is our best. We always have to do our best with what we're given. Are you still there?"

"Yes," I said, "I'm still here."

"Good," she said. "Well, you will have to get up early in the morning. Grandpa says to tell Calum he was down to the old shore yesterday and brought Christy some apples. He tries to whistle like Calum used to do, but he says that Christy knows the difference. She comes to him, but she is always looking over his shoulder for someone else. He says it is because they were never young together, through the good times and the bad. But she is fine. Tell him that."

"Yes, I'll tell him."

"Goodbye for now," she said. "God bless. *Beannachd leibh.* Love to all."

"Okay, goodbye. *Beannachd leibh.*"

I hung up the phone, thanked the security guard, and pre-pared to look for Calum. Although we had come off our shifts at seven, I knew he sometimes found it hard to sleep because of the heat and he sometimes wished to be alone with his own thoughts. As I stood uncertainly outside the security guard's door I saw Calum approaching from the area beyond the gates. I waited for him and we walked together towards our bunkhouse.

At first I did not know how to approach the subject, as I had forgotten to tell him of the letter from San Francisco in the confused time which followed its arrival. It seemed a long time ago, although the death of Alexander MacDonald did not and remained constantly with us. For a moment I felt as I had on that long ago day when I had forgotten to bring the can of oats for Christy.

I began to explain the situation.

"Who is coming?" he said. "Coming from where? Why? Slow down."

I repeated the information, stressing the call from Grandma and Grandpa.

He was thoughtful for a while, turning over the pebbles on the path with the sole of his boot. Finally, he asked, "Is this important to you, *'ille bhig ruaidh?*"

"Yes, it is. It's just that Grandma and Grandpa . . ."

"Okay, it's important to me too. Grandma used to say, 'Always look after your own blood,' and she used to say to you and your sister, 'If I did not believe that, where would you two be?'"

"Yes," I said "she did."

"Well," he said, "we have to respect that. After our parents died we could not have looked after our sister and you. We could hardly look after ourselves, and when we went back to the old house we could not have survived without the help of all those people who brought us chains and saws and a boat and horses."

He was silent for a moment. "And I know," he continued, "that you don't have to be here with us either. You could be in your white lab coat in Halifax. It's just that when Alexander was killed we needed another man." He paused momentarily. "Ah, *'ille bhig ruaidh*," he said, "I appreciate that you're here. We'll go to Sudbury. But first we'll have to find a car."

"I can get a car," I said. "At least I think I can. And, oh, by the way, Grandpa said he saw Christy yesterday and brought her some apples. He said she was looking over his shoulder for you."

"Ah yes," he said. "Poor Christy. She always kept her part of the bargain."

We had stopped walking and were standing in the middle of the path when we saw Fern Picard approaching. The path was narrow and we stood two abreast. His pace seemed to quicken when he saw us, and his increased speed seemed to emphasize how big he was. There was no space for him to pass without his leaving the path, and it seemed certain he was not going to do that.

"Well, I have to go," I said at the last moment, vacating my place on the path. Fern Picard's shoulder brushed my brother's as he passed and we heard him say, "*Mange la merde*" under his breath. "*Mac an diabhoil*," I heard my brother say, and each of them spat, as if on cue, into the centre of the path. The gobs of silica-coated phlegm lay glistening in the sun.

Overhead in the trees the crows and ravens screamed. Once, my brother told me, they were working in the Bridge River Valley of British Columbia. There was a man who used to wrap pieces of bread around live blasting caps and toss them to the ravens. The ravens would swoop down for the bread and seconds later when they were airborne the caps would explode, as would the birds, their black and shining feathers still clinging to flesh wafting down over a wide area from the sky. One night the man was beaten badly by someone with a wrench, and he left without collecting his pay and was never seen again.

I went in search of Marcel Gingras. Because of the encounter with Fern Picard I did not want to go too near the bunkhouses of the French Canadians, but I found Marcel sitting in the dining hall. He was seated on a stool drinking a cup of coffee and seemed lost in his own dreams. When I sat down suddenly beside him he started. "*Tasse à café*," I said, pointing to the object in his hand. "Coffee cup," he said with a laugh.

I thought I had understood him to possess some kind of car, but to make sure I drew a primitive automobile on a napkin and then pointed to him and to myself. "*À Sudbury?*" I asked. "*Oui*," he said and nodded. In our monosyllabic way, accompanied by many gestures, we agreed to meet outside the camp gates. He did not wish to be seen in my company more than was necessary, he indicated, because he was afraid of Fern Picard and the potential threat of losing his job.

When I joined him in the parking lot outside the camp gates, he was standing beside a rusting black Chevrolet sedan. The tires were balding and the windshield was pockmarked from the onslaught of a series of flying stones. There was also a giant wavering crack which coursed like an uncertain river across the total expanse of the glass.

Marcel pulled open the unlocked door. On the front seat there was a woman's makeup bag with the long handle of a pink comb protruding. On the floor there was a pair of white high-heeled shoes which were badly smudged. He shrugged his shoulders and extended his hands with their palms upward in a gesture of non-comprehension. Perhaps someone had been sleeping in his car?

Hanging from the rear-view mirror there was a pair of large

Styrofoam dice and a woman's frilly garter – the kind which is often thrown at weddings. The ledge before the rear window bore the figure of a brown dog made from hard plastic. The dog's head was attached to a spring which would cause it to bob up and down when the car was in motion.

Marcel handed me the keys. They were attached to a small metal disc which read, "*Je me souviens.*"

We returned to the camp separately to avoid detection.

That night our work did not go well. The air hoses seemed to rupture constantly and the dynamite seemed damp to our touch. The jackleg drills seized or malfunctioned, spraying our faces with foul and overused oil. We lost more than we gained and were embarrassed to confess our non-progress to the oncoming shift left to confront our mess.

After we showered and had a cup of coffee, Calum and I decided to dispense with sleep and leave for Sudbury immediately. When we reached the parking lot he looked at the car with disapproval.

"Is this your car?" he asked, trying unsuccessfully to veil his annoyance.

"Yes," I said. "This is it."

I opened the door and slid into the driver's seat. The makeup bag and the smudged shoes were gone.

During the first few miles we said little. We had not slept the day before, nor the previous night, and our accumulated exhaustion seemed to manifest itself as soon as we settled into the passivity of our sitting positions. I noticed that the gas gauge did not work and the needle rested permanently on empty. We pulled to the side of the road and broke a willow branch from one of the trees growing at the edge of a murky swamp. We inserted the branch in the gas tank. Our willow gas gauge indicated that the tank was more than three-quarters full.

We talked in a desultory manner about the man we were driving to meet. Because I had been raised by my grandparents I knew slightly more about him than did my brother. I tried to recall in more detail the conversations of my grandparents concerning their siblings who had moved to San Francisco. "Do you think," asked Calum, "that if Grandpa did not get that job at the hospital they might all have gone to San Francisco?"

"I don't know," I said.

"If they had," he said thoughtfully, "things would be much different for us."

"Yes, they would."

"From what I understand of this war," he continued, "those people are only fighting for their own country and their own way of being. It's hard to say they should be killed for that."

"I know," I said. "Wars touch all of us in different ways. I suppose we have been influenced by lots of wars ourselves. We are probably what we are because of the 1745 rebellion in Scotland. We are, ourselves, directly or indirectly the children of Culloden Moor, and what happened in its aftermath."

"Yes," he said with a smile, "the old men at home, the *seanaichies*, always used to say, 'If only the ships had come from France . . .'"

"Maybe" I said. "We'll never know. Perhaps it was all questionable from the start. Talking about history is not like living it, I guess. Some people have more choice than others."

"Yes," he smiled again. "Grandpa used to say, 'I don't want to be like the bull's cock and just go wherever I'm shoved.'"

"My hope is constant in thee, Clan Donald," I said. "He said that too. He said it to me yesterday on the phone."

We were silent for a while. "Oh well," Calum sighed, looking out the window at the jagged rocks and mangled trees, "too many bodies and too many wars. I often think it ironic that our father came through the war unscathed only to die beneath the ice at the end of a sunny March day."

"Yes," I said, "If you had been with them you would have gone down too."

"I look at it differently," he said, "If I had been with them I might have saved them."

31 The heat began to intensify as the sun rose higher. It shone through the cracked windshield until it seemed as if we were behind the glass of a green-house. We rolled down the windows and rested our arms on the car's window frames to feel the rush of the passing air. Our arms were white from the long hours underground and seemed almost to recoil from the blazing power of the sun.

"When we used to cross from the island in the summer," said Calum, "Father sometimes used to look at the sun. If it was at a certain angle and if the waves were rolling in a certain way, he used to gun the engine of the boat. It was a big boat supplied by the government and if he gunned the engine in a certain manner and steered at a certain angle to the sun the spray would fly up and the water droplets would be caught in the sun's slanting rays. It had the effect of a rainbow which seemed to be following us. It must have been before you and your sister were born because Colin was just a little boy. He always used to say, 'Dad, Dad, make the rainbow.' One day he said to our mother, 'Mom, isn't there supposed to be a pot of gold at the end of the rainbow?'

" 'I don't know dear,' she said, 'some people say that it's so.'

" 'Well,' he said, 'I think that for us, our pot of gold must be at the bottom of the ocean.' "

Calum was silent for a while. "When I went back to the old shore," he continued, "I used to take our boat out by myself and angle it in different directions off *Calum Ruadh*'s Point to try to recapture the effect, but I never could. People would ask me what I was doing out in my boat those afternoons. I was always too embarrassed to say I was looking for a rainbow, so I would say I was just fooling around. They would generally say, 'It looked to us like you were just wasting gas,' so after a while I stopped."

"Perhaps it was just the difference in the boat," I offered.

"Perhaps," he replied, "it was the difference in the boat or perhaps it was the difference in the man. There were a lot of things I could have learned from father, but we both ran out of time." He paused.

"Four years ago we were in Timmins," Calum continued, "and we talked all one day and night about the island. In the end we couldn't stand it any longer so we phoned up Grandfather and first we asked him about the weather. 'It is lovely weather here,' he said. We asked him about the island. He hesitated at first and then said, 'The island?'

"'Yes, can you see it clearly today?'

"'Yes, I see it every day of my life. But today there is a slight southeast wind. You know what it is like when there is a southeast wind, the island always seems closer than it really is.'

"'Can you land a boat there?' we asked.

"'Not easily,' he said. 'There's no longer any government wharf, but if it's a calm day you can get fairly close and anchor and then take a skiff or even wade, but the water will be up to your chest.'

"'If we came,' we asked, 'could you get us a boat? It is about seventeen hundred miles and the roads are not that good. It will take us a few days.'

"'If you come seventeen hundred miles,' he said, 'I will get you a boat. I will be waiting for you.'

"'Okay,' we said. 'Tell Grandma and Grandpa we're coming.'

"'I will tell them,' he said. 'Take care. *Beannachd leibh.*'

"We bought an old pickup truck and a generator and a compressor and rented a jackleg and some drilling bits and steel from the company. We were ahead of our schedule and knew the manager and promised we would be back.

"'Okay,' the manager said. 'I suppose if I said "No," you would just go anyway.'

"The three of us squeezed into the cab and took turns driving. Just outside of New Liskeard a car passed us at high speed. As it receded into the distance, someone flung a kitten through the open window and into the ditch. We all looked at one another and thought the same thing. We pulled over and began to search the grass beside the ditch. We found her with blood coming out of her nose and you could see her heart pounding behind her ribs. She was grey and white. We took turns holding her on our laps and later stopped in Temagami to buy her some milk and a can of tuna, but she was too frightened to eat or drink. We called her *Piseag*, 'pussycat,' and sang little Gaelic songs to her. Once, in a parking lot outside of Ottawa we thought we had lost her and went around calling, '*Piseag, Piseag*,' as if she could understand Gaelic," Calum said with a laugh. "Sometimes we even tried 'Meow, meow.' A half-hour later we found her sleeping on the floor of the truck beside the gas pedal. She remained there for most of the trip and whoever was driving had to hold his foot at a certain angle so she would not be disturbed.

"When we got home, Grandpa was so glad to see us he almost buried us in beer and Grandma hugged and kissed us. Grandfather said he had made arrangements for the boat. Grandpa looked inside the cab of the truck. 'What's this?' he asked.

"'That's *Piseag*,' we said. 'She was born in Northern Ontario but she's going to live here now.'

"'Oh,' he said, 'welcome *Piseag, ciamar a tha sibh*? Would you like some milk?'

"The next morning we left early. Grandfather had borrowed a boat and had a small skiff tied behind it. We loaded our bits and steels and our generator and compressor and Grandpa brought two cases of beer. 'God,' Grandfather said to him, 'can't you go anywhere without that stuff? You'll fall overboard and the seals will think you're trying to steal their mates.'

"Grandma had packed us a lunch and Grandfather had brought some lumber for a staging and some grappling hooks. The sea was as smooth as glass. When we approached the island we could see its reflection in the water and we seemed to be gliding over its surface.

"We hung from the grappling hooks, and using the lumber for the jackleg's support we drilled our parents' initials into the face of the rock. We drilled their initials and their dates and Colin's, too. He was born on the island because it was too stormy for mother to cross. He was never circumcised and when he used to pee we would laugh at him because he didn't look like the rest of us. Grandpa tied a bunch of beer bottles together and put them in the ocean to keep them cool. The seals swam nearby.

"We walked up to the old house. It had been abandoned since they installed the automatic light which had replaced the duties of the man from Pictou – the one who shot our dog. Someone had stolen the door frames and the window cases, but the rooms were much as we remembered them. There were rabbits hopping in and out of the rooms.

"Mother used to have a patch of rhubarb beside the garden and it had all gone wild," Calum recalled. "The stalks were like those of the tropical plants you see in Peru. The tops came up to our shoulders, trembling under the weight of their white, clumped seeds. You would need a machete to get through the rhubarb patch. Some of the flowers had taken seed as well and were growing wild. They were pink and yellow and blue, struggling hard, it seemed, amongst the weeds and the grass. We pulled some of the weeds away from them to give them a better chance. When we were children, we used to complain when mother asked for our help in planting her flowers.

"We went down to look at the well. It was still there, although we had to clear some of the foliage and dead leaves in order to find it. We all lay on our stomachs and drank from it. The water was as sweet as we remembered it, pouring up out of the rock into the brambles and vines and decayed vegetation that threatened to overwhelm it. Grandpa went and pulled on his string of beer bottles. They emerged from the water like a catch of glistening fish. He pried off the caps of five bottles and spilled the beer on the ground and then he knelt by the well and filled the beer bottles with the clear, fresh water.

" 'For old time's sake,' he said.

"Grandfather took out his pocket knife and cut a branch from one of the overhanging willows. He fashioned five willow plugs and inserted them into the necks of the bottles so the water would not spill. He stood for a while looking at the overflowing water. 'It seems sad,' he said, still looking at the bubbling well. 'It seems to be pouring out its heart and nobody knows the difference.'

"We were quiet on the return journey.

" 'I guess they're still under there somewhere,' said Grandfather, looking over the boat's side into the glassy sea.

"We were all silent for a while, straining our eyes while looking over the side of the boat and then concentrating on the white water that foamed in the boat's wake as the island receded behind us.

"'Well,' said Grandpa, 'there is lots of beer here. Why don't you drink some of it? It will help you to forget.'

"'They didn't come all this way,' said Grandfather quietly, 'because they wanted to forget.'

"Grandpa was silent for a while. 'No,' he said. 'I guess they didn't.'"

Calum stared out the window.

32 We were now on the paved roadway of Highway 17. Once in a while to our right, and through the trees, we could glimpse the small uninhabited freshwater islands of the North Channel and Georgian Bay.

"You must be tired," said Calum. "I'll drive for a while."

I pulled the car to the side of the road and we got out and exchanged places. Blotches of damp perspiration darkened the backs of our shirts, and our pale arms, which had been exposed to the sun, were beginning to redden.

"You burn faster than I do," he said, "because of your reddish complexion. You'll burn over and over again and it will never stop. You'll have to be careful."

As he eased the car back onto the road, he said, "I was thinking of all those flowers that mother planted on the island. She was very fond of flowers, even wild ones, and she always had vases of them in the house.

"Sometimes, in the summer," he recalled, "she and father would lie in the grass and make chains of dandelions and daisies. It seems a funny thing to remember. You seem always to think of your parents as old and it seems unnatural to be gaining on them and passing them eventually. Perhaps when they were lying in the grass, they were becoming sexually aroused, but we never thought of such a thing. They were old to our eyes, but probably young to their own. I am perhaps remembering them from a time before you and your sister were conceived. If it had happened earlier you might never have been born. I guess," he paused, "the same can be said of all of us."

He drummed his fingers on the steering wheel as if he were embarrassed.

"Once," I said, remembering a distant scene, "when I was perhaps five or six I had a nightmare. I remember shouting and crying and Grandpa came to my room. 'Would you like to sleep with us?' he asked. 'We will look after you and you won't be afraid.'

"'Yes,' I said.

"I went to sleep between them. Grandma must have risen early to do her work and then someone came to the door of the house looking for Grandpa. Grandma came and knocked on the bedroom door and we both awoke with a start. He started to roll and rise from the bed before he was fully awake and bumped against me. He had an erection which had come to him during sleep and for a second he was unaware of his condition. When he noticed himself, he took a huge step across the room and began hurriedly putting on his trousers which he had flung on the chair. He dressed with his back to me. 'Don't worry,' he said over his shoulder, 'it's only nature.' Then, regaining his composure and good humour, he added, 'But if I weren't capable of that, where would you all be?'

"I drifted back to sleep and when I awoke the sun was streaming through the window. I did not know what he meant at that time, so his remarks and his condition seemed of little significance to me. I did not remember them for a long, long while because they had very little to do with my life as I thought I understood it at the time."

33 Suddenly we were aware of a repetitive thumping and Marcel Gingras' car began to vibrate. "Shit," said Calum. "Does this car have a spare?"

"I don't know," I said. "I never looked."

Over a rise and through the waves of shimmering heat we saw what we thought was a service station.

"We'll try to make it there," he said.

We wobbled into the station's lot amidst the odour of burning rubber.

"You have trouble," said the man at the station with a helpful smile. "You're lucky you didn't ruin the rim."

We inquired about a tire.

"If you put a new tire on that car," he said, "it will handle poorly because the treads are so worn on the other three. I'll sell you a used tire for ten dollars. It will be no worse than the other three and it will get you to wherever you're going. Perhaps you picked up a nail in this one, but all of your tires are bad, and this one here is ruined."

"Something has been troubling me," said Calum as we pulled back onto the road. "The day that Alexander was killed most of us had come out of the underground early. We had had a bad night. We had blowouts at the face and made no progress. Something like last night, only worse. I went for a walk outside the camp gates by myself. It was about five-thirty or six in the morning and I met Fern Picard. He was probably scheduled to start at seven. I think he had heard of our bad luck and he laughed and grabbed his crotch. I hit him with my fist as hard as I could in the mouth. His right hand was still down at his crotch when I hit him, so he was taken by surprise. He fell into the bush and before he could move, I went and stood over him. He was at a disadvantage and looked at my boots as if I might kick him in the head. He was afraid to move and I was afraid to turn my back on him. He lay there and I stood and our eyes locked. Five years ago in Rouyn we were in a tavern brawl with them. There were about twelve of us with nothing but bottles and chairs in our hands, and our backs to the wall. There was a sea of them because we were on the Quebec side of the border. I remember thinking in Gaelic, '*Sin agad e*,' that's it, and I looked directly into Fern Picard's eyes. He knew he had me, but then the police came. He took three or four steps backwards and spat on the floor while still keeping his eyes fixed upon me. We were charged with creating a disturbance and all of us lost our jobs.

"I looked at Fern Pickard lying at my feet and took three or four careful steps backwards. He got up carefully and took three or four steps backwards as well. Both of us were afraid to turn our backs on the other. We spat on the ground and continued to move away. When we were a dozen steps from each other, he turned and walked towards the camp gates where the security guard apparently had been watching us. 'This isn't over,' he said as he turned, speaking in clearer English than I thought he had.

"That afternoon someone came and said they needed a man to clean the sump. Alexander was well rested and he needed the money from the extra shift. When the ore bucket came down and decapitated him, the hoistman said he had been given the wrong signal or had misunderstood the signal. He was a young hoistman and had difficulty expressing himself in English. When we came back after the funeral, I went to look for him, but he had quit and returned to Quebec.

"I never told anyone about hitting Fern Picard in the mouth that day. Later we realized that all of our crew were on the surface and probably sleeping when whoever it was came for Alexander. The only people working were Fern Picard and his crew. If Alexander had asked me, I would have told him not to go, but he probably didn't want to wake me. I would have told him that under the circumstances, and on that day, it was best for him 'to stick with his own blood,' as Grandma used to say."

My brother turned towards me. His palms were slipping from perspiring on the steering wheel and he took a soiled handkerchief from his pocket and tried to wipe them dry.

"A lot was happening," he said, "on your graduation day."

"Poor Grandma," he continued, "she always used to say, 'You'll get used to almost anything except a nail in your shoe.' Perhaps she was wrong. Anyway, I'm having a hard time getting used to this. Or else this is the nail in my shoe."

He looked in the rear-view mirror above the swinging dice. "Now what?" he said.

I looked over my shoulder. Beyond the bobbing head of the plastic brown dog, the police cruiser's headlights rose and fell in concert with the undulations of the road. The rooflights flashed in rhythm on the shimmering metallic roof, which seemed to send its heat waves back in the direction of the sun.

We pulled over to the shoulder of the road. The police officer approached the driver's side of our car. "Can I see your driver's licence and your registration and proof of insurance?" he asked.

He looked at the car with disapproval. "The licence plates on this car are expired," he said. "We're tired of you guys from Quebec driving these old cars on Ontario's highways."

We looked in the glove compartment, but there was no registration. The makeup bag with the pink-handled comb was stuffed at the back of the compartment, but there was nothing more.

The officer looked at my brother's licence. "What are you doing driving a Quebec car with a Nova Scotia driver's licence?" he asked. "Where is the car's registration? Perhaps you stole this car?"

"If I was going to steal a car," said Calum, "I'd steal a better one than this."

"Will you step outside of your car, please," said the officer. "Will you open the trunk?"

We both got out of the car. I noticed the officer's name tag read Paul Belanger.

The trunk of the car contained two tire irons but no tire. There were two or three empty oil cans and an old ripped checkered shirt which I remembered seeing Marcel wear. There was also a pair of worn gloves and a length of chains. In one corner there was a soiled and crumpled bill from a garage near Temiskaming which bore Marcel's name and address. The bill was for a second-hand replacement radiator.

"Is this the owner of the car's address?" asked Paul Belanger, looking first at the bill and then at my brother.

"Yes, it is," I said.

"I'm not talking to you, sir," he said. "I'm talking to the driver of the vehicle."

He took the bill and my brother's licence and walked back to the cruiser with its flashing lights.

"You can wait in your car," he said over his shoulder. "This may take a little while."

When he came back he walked around the car, noting its worn tires and scrutinizing the meandering crack across its windshield. He returned to his cruiser once more. When he came back the second time he handed my brother what seemed like a sheaf of summonses or tickets. He told Calum to read them carefully.

When we resumed our journey he followed us for what seemed like a very long time. We drove very slowly and noticed, for the first time, that the speedometer was also broken. When the cruiser roared past us my brother took the sheaf of papers, crumpled them into a ball, and threw them out the window.

When we arrived at the Sudbury airport we realized how tired we were. We had slept very little in the past two days, and our heads kept dropping forward. We tried to fortify ourselves with coffee, but it turned brackish within our mouths. We went to the washroom and splashed water on our faces. When we looked in the mirror we remembered that we had not shaved. Our eyes were bloodshot and our arms burned from the sun. We splashed water on the backs of our necks and ran our dripping fingers through the black and redness of our hair.

When the passengers came off the plane we watched them carefully. Although we had never seen this Alexander MacDonald before, there was no doubt in our minds concerning recognition. "There he is," we said simultaneously. He had shoulder-length red hair and wore a buckskin jacket. He looked like a young Willie Nelson and he extended his hand when he saw us approaching.

He seemed as tired as we were, as we went to retrieve his luggage at the baggage carousel. He had two duffel bags and a metal footlocker guarded by an iron hasp and a combination lock. We carried the luggage to the car. "Not much of a car," he said, although his tone was non-committal. "Beggars can't be choosers," said Calum, also non-committal. He sounded, for a moment, like Grandma, falling back into the familiarity of cliché.

"Here, you drive for the first part," said my brother, tossing the keys in my direction. "We have to hurry up. We have to go on shift in a few hours."

He eased himself into the back seat while our new companion took the front.

Outside of Sudbury the rocky landscape stretched on either

side as we journeyed to the west and towards the descending sun.

"Pretty barren around here," said our cousin. "It looks like photographs of the moon."

"Any port in a storm," said Calum. He paused for a second. "'When you have to go there, they have to take you in,'" he added. "Isn't that from a poem of some kind?" he asked, directing his eyes towards me via the rear-view mirror.

"It's from a poem by Robert Frost," said our cousin. "It's called 'The Death of the Hired Man.'"

I drove back as rapidly as I dared. Without the speedometer to guide me, I glanced frequently above the swinging dice and beyond the bobbing dog, hoping that I would not see the flashing lights of Paul Belanger or one of his fellow patrollers of the road. My companions' heads tilted gradually towards their chests and soon they were both snoring softly.

When we left Highway 17, my brother woke with a start. "Sorry I slept so long," he said. "Here, I'll drive the rest of the way." We exchanged places. Our companion slept on. His red hair fell forward from his shoulder and his left hand lay limply on the soiled upholstery of the car's seat. We noticed that he wore a Celtic ring upon his finger. The never-ending circle.

When we arrived back at the camp we left the car in the parking lot and my brother handed me the keys. Each of us carried a piece of luggage past the security guard's post. He was reading a paperback novel when we approached, and his shift was nearing its end.

"Been to Sudbury," said Calum. "This is our new man. He'll have his identification in the morning. *Cousin agam fhein*," he added with a smile. The security guard waved us in.

On the path to our bunkhouse we met Marcel Gingras. "*Bonjour,*" he said, "*comment ça va?*"

"Why don't you speak English?" said our cousin. "This is North America."

Both Marcel and I raised our eyebrows. "*Merci,*" I said, tossing him his keys.

Calum had gone on ahead and we followed him to the bunkhouse. Our crew was ready to work their shift and were waiting impatiently. They had ordered our lunch cans for us and after brief introductions we were on our way. I told the new Alexander MacDonald he could sleep in my bed for the night and we would make other arrangements in the morning. He seemed grateful. He stuffed his footlocker and his duffel bags under the bunk and lay down, still clothed, upon the blankets.

The night seemed long because both Calum and I had slept little during the past two days, and sometimes our heavy steel-toed boots stumbled against the rocks and the yellow-hissing hoses which snaked behind us. The incessant hammering of steel on stone seemed to vibrate within our throbbing heads and sometimes I would rest my hand against the walls of rock to forestall the bouts of dizziness. The rest of the crew, however, were well rested and shouldered more than their burden. We waved to each other above the clamour. When we raised our hands to wave, the water within our gloves ran down to the bends of our elbows.

The next morning we were bleary, but Alexander MacDonald was rested. We found among our luggage and assorted papers the pinkish-brown employment card that had belonged to the red-haired Alexander MacDonald. It was more fragile than the current plastic S.I.N. cards, but the numbers were still intact. Calum took the card to the timekeeper. "This man will be working with us tomorrow," he said.

Whether Renco Development knew the difference or cared did not seem terribly important. "Sometimes, to them," said Calum, "we all look the same, and I guess we do. As long as the work goes forward."

We also found the security pass of the red-haired Alexander MacDonald, which allowed our new man to pass freely in and out of the gates.

It was somehow as if the red-haired Alexander MacDonald had merely gone on a short vacation and had now returned to resume his appointed tasks. Perhaps that was how it would appear on a company payroll. Someone might ask, "Wasn't this man here a few months ago? Maybe something happened to him, but now he has returned?"

More than fifteen hundred miles away the body of the red-haired Alexander MacDonald lay silently beneath the gentle earth. On the last day of his life he had been deeper in the earth than he now reposed in death. In the darkness of his oak casket, perhaps, his severed head lay quietly beside him. By now the hopeful spring vegetation had given way to that of summer and his parents had, no doubt, planted flowers on the brown mud beneath his cross.

His ongoing documentation took on a life beyond his actual existence. It seemed as if a part of his life continued to go forth, as the hair and the fingernails of the dead continue to grow, beyond the cessation of their host. It was almost as if the new Alexander MacDonald was the beneficiary of a certain kind of gift. A gift from a dead donor who shared the same blood group and was colour-compatible, although the two had never met. A gift which might allow an extended life for each of them. An extended life, though false, allowing each of them to go forward. Not for a long journey. Just for a while.

34 "The people of Glencoe," said my sister once in her modernistic house in Calgary, "believed that when the herring came they were led by a king. When they were scooping up the silver bounty they were always on the lookout for the king of the herring because they did not want to harm him. They thought of him as a friend who was bringing them food and perhaps saving them from starvation. They believed that if they kept their trust in him, he would return each year and continue to be their benefactor. It seemed to work for a long, long time."

She paused and looked through her magnificent picture window at the city spread out before her, it seemed, like a painting in the sun.

"Grandfather told me that story once," she continued. "And then he asked, 'What do you think of that?'

"'I don't know,' I said, 'I like the part about believing in the king – even if he was just a herring.' I was perhaps in Grade 7 or 8. Grandma had sent me over to his house with some cookies.

Grandfather smiled and even laughed a little and poured me a glass of milk.

"'Think of it from the point of view of the other herring,' he said. 'They were really being betrayed by him. He was leading them to their deaths and they probably didn't realize it until it was too late.'

"I didn't like the picture nearly as much once he told me that. It was as if I had to think too much."

"Perhaps the herring should have thought more," I said.

"The herring," said my sister, "were following patterns as old as time. To me they flow above and beyond whatever we think of as thought. To me they are governed by the moon. And they are faithful in their force. There was an old Gaelic song that Grandma used to sing that was composed when the people were leaving Scotland. There was a line in it which said, 'The birds will be back but we will not be back,' or something like that. Do you remember it?"

"Yes," I said, "'*Fuadach nan Gaidheal*,' the 'Dispersion of the Highlanders.'" We began to hum the song and then the Gaelic words came to us, hesitatingly at first, it seemed, and then gaining force, welling up from wherever it was that song was stored. We sang all that we knew in Gaelic, three verses and the chorus, looking to each other for clues at the beginning of lines when we seemed uncertain. When we finished we stood and looked at one another, almost embarrassed in our expensive clothes amidst the opulence of my sister's majestic house.

"Well," she said, "I think of the herring like the returning birds. That they came back regardless of what had happened to the people. That they came back whether or not there were people on the shore waiting for them, whether or not there were people there who believed they had a king."

"Grandfather once said," she continued, "that on Culloden Moor the Highlanders sang. Standing there with the sleet and rain in their faces, some of them sang. To cause fear or to bolster confidence or to offer consolation. None of the Highlanders ever went into battle without music.

"Do you remember," she asked after a pause, "how Grandpa and Grandma and all their friends used to sing? Grandma said that when she was newly married, all of the women used to take their washing down to the brook. They would make a fire and heat water in those black pots they used to have and they would sing all day, slapping the clothes on the rocks in perfect rhythm. And they would do the same thing when they were making blankets, fulling the cloth, all of them sitting at that long table. They believed the music made the work go faster. And the men all sang when they were pulling their ropes and their chains."

"Yes," I said. "Remember when they were older? The house would be full of people and late in the evening they would sing those long, long songs with thirteen or fourteen verses. Grandpa would be addled because he was so full of beer and he would say to us, 'Run over and get your grandfather. He knows all the verses.' Grandfather would be sitting in his freshly scrubbed kitchen all by himself, reading his history book, but he would always come. When he would enter the kitchen, at first everyone would pause as if he were a foreign element entering their merriment. 'It's because he's so damn smart and so damn sober and so damn clean,' Grandpa would always say later; but then Grandfather would begin to sing and everyone would go along with him. 'When he comes in,' Grandpa used to say, 'it's like a stone dropped into a pool. It causes a ripple at first but then everything is fine.'

"Remember," I said, "how in the enthusiasm of the moment, they would sometimes veer into the opening lines of those mildly off-colour songs and then they would remember he was among them and raise their eyebrows or gesture towards him with their heads and try to change the song in mid-line? Otherwise he would put on his hat and walk out. He was like a precise clergyman who didn't wish to be at a stag party."

"Yes," said my sister. "He was always troubled by the sexual circumstances of his own birth. And perhaps also by the circumstances of our mother's birth. Grandma used to say he felt guilty about his wife's death — that if he had not impregnated her she would not have died in childbirth. They only had one year of married life."

We were silent for a moment.

"Grandma once told me," continued my sister, "that before our mother had her first period he came over to Grandma's and asked her to explain 'the facts' to our mother, who was then just a little girl advancing towards puberty.

"'The poor dear man,' Grandma said. 'He came and sat on a chair with his hat on his knee and hummed and hawed and was all red in the face. I didn't know what he wanted as he was usually so direct. When I finally found out I said, "Of course I'll do it. There's not much about menstruation that I don't know."'

"It was, I guess," said my sister, "peculiar to his personality. He could iron our mother's clothes and braid her hair. He could frame a house all by himself in two or three days and do quadratic equations without ever having gone to high school, but he couldn't handle menstruation. He was raised in a house without a father, only a mother, and years later he was with a daughter who had no mother, only a father. He was always in the midst of loss. They say," said my sister quietly, "that his mother used to beat him – just because he was born."

"Yes," I said. "She was our great-grandmother. Her blood also runs through our veins."

"Yes, it does," she said. "I often think of that."

"Once after a night of singing," I said, "I walked home with him." 'Music,' he said, 'is the lubricant of the poor. All over the world. In all the different languages.'"

"Yes, I think of that even when I watch the news."

"The Zulus," I said, recalling earlier conversations, "always sing in the miners' compounds. Our brothers said that after a while they could almost sing the songs, although they didn't know their meaning. It was as if it were one musical people reaching out to join another."

"I don't suppose," she said after a moment of reflection, "that you sing at your work?"

"No, I don't."

"Do you subscribe to a concert series?"

"Yes," I said.

"So do I," she replied. "The performers are quite wonderful."

"Yes, they are."

"Sometimes when we attend concerts here or when we go to performances in Banff I look at the performers and then around me at the members of the audience. Sometimes the women, including myself, have exclusive dresses and the men are in tuxedos. I suppose it is the same where you are. 'Most of those people,' I say to myself, 'go to the orthodontist.' Am I right?"

"Yes. Most of them go to the orthodontist."

"I don't suppose," she said, "that many of the Zulus go to the orthodontist?"

"No, I wouldn't think so."

"I don't know why I think this way," she said, "but I am always moved by those African documentaries. The Zulus thought their world would never end. They seemed to be such a tall athletic people. Swaggering and arrogant. They believed in their battle formations and in their songs and in their totems. They believed in their landscape and in their armies of the thousands. When they moved across the veldt, singing, people say the ground trembled under the impact of their bare feet. They believed they were invincible and I suppose, in human terms, they were. They just weren't ready for machine guns, and the documentation that followed.

"A few years ago," she continued, "Mike and I went on one of those African safari tours. To see the animals on the plain at the base of Mount Kilimanjaro, in the south of Kenya near the border of Tanzania. The animals will take your breath away. All the different species grazing together and followed by their natural predators. Almost intermixed with the animals are the Masai following the grass cycle with their cattle herds, living off the milk and blood of their cows. We would go early in the morning from a base camp in Land Rovers and all-terrain vehicles, armed with cameras and binoculars. The tour operators apologized for the presence of the Masai. They realized that we had paid a lot of money to see wildlife, not families of people following their cows. There were borders and boundaries to the game preserves and the national parks, explained the tour operators, but the Masai refused to recognize them. They just followed the water and grass. They had always been 'troublesome,' according to the tour operator, and when colonization first came to Kenya they had attacked rather than co-operated. 'What will be done with them,' asked a member of our tour group, 'to get them out of this beautiful place?' 'I don't know,' said the tour operator. 'Something. Soon, I hope.'

"Sometimes," said my sister, "when our vehicles passed the Masai on the plain, I would try to look into their eyes. Perhaps what I saw there, or imagined I saw, was a combination of fear mixed with disdain. We were high above on the roofs of rubber-tired vehicles and they were in bare feet on the ground.

"But, this is a long digression," she sighed. "What do I know of Africa, anyway? I've never been there in my bare feet."

We both got up, as if on cue, and looked out the window. The Bow River sparkled below us. It snaked and glimmered through the newness of the city built upon its banks.

"Did you know," she said, "that Calgary gets its name from a place located on the Isle of Mull?"

"No," I said. "Well, I'm not sure. I guess I haven't thought about it very much."

"Well, there are none of the native people there any more, either," she said.

"Everyone used to say that when our parents came in from the island, our mother would often go to visit her father, just by herself. Sometimes she would ask Grandpa and Grandma if it were okay if she could leave her small children with them for a while and then she would go to see him. They would sit there in his bright, clean kitchen drinking tea. I often think of the two of them sitting there together. I wonder what they talked about? They had been together longer than she was with her husband or he was with his wife. He had always been there for her and as Grandpa used to say, 'That man is as solid as a rock.' He had been with her through a lot of changes in her life, though, of course, not the last one, and no one could have foreseen that. Grandma said that when our mother was a little girl she was always dressed so meticulously and her hair always braided to perfection. Grandma said that he was trying hard to give her the care her mother might have given. Perhaps he was also trying to relive and improve upon his own situation as a child. Grandma said he told her that when he was a little boy he used to sit on the doorstep in his short pants and look down the road for the coming of his father. He used to wish and wish that his father would come and make his life better." She paused. "It is hard to imagine Grandfather in short pants."

"I am sure they were clean," I smiled.

"Maybe they weren't," she said. "Maybe his cleanliness was a trait he later developed within himself. Anyway, his father never came. He never had even a picture of him. His mother would become enraged if he ever mentioned the circumstances of his own conception. Perhaps in addition to being bitter she was also embarrassed.

"I think he was always haunted by the fact that the night he was conceived, if it even was at night, his father may just have been having a good time. A young man going off to the woods of Maine, like all those young soldiers you read about, going off to the wars. Perhaps that's why he was always so ill at ease when Grandpa would start those little jokes about the man taking the girl behind the bushes. I think now I understand him more," she said.

"Perhaps that's why he became so interested in history," she went on. "He felt that if you read everything and put the pieces all together the real truth would emerge. It would be, somehow, like carpentry. Everything would fit together just so, and you would see in the end something like 'a perfect building called the past.' Perhaps he felt that if he couldn't understand his immediate past, he would try to understand his distant past."

"Not so easy," I said.

"I know not so easy," she answered. "And he knew it too. But he tried, and he was interested, and he tried to pass it on to us. Living out here where everything is so new, I miss all of those people," she continued. "I miss them as a group and then sometimes I try to separate our parents from the group. Sometimes perhaps you and I idealize our parents too much because we scarcely remember them. They are the 'idea' of parents rather than real people. Perhaps we are doing the same thing that Grandfather was doing with that young man who was his father."

"Perhaps it's genetic," I said. "And I'm not mocking."

"Oh yes, genetic," she said. "Sometimes I think of *clann Chalum Ruaidh*. All of those people with their black and red hair. Like you and me. All of them intertwined and intermarried for two hundred years here in Canada and who knows for how many years before. In Moidart and Keppoch, in Glencoe and Glenfinnan and Glengarry."

"Don't forget the prince," I said. "He had red hair."

"I'm not forgetting the prince," she said. "Still, you can't have generic parents. You only have two individuals. Sometimes I have thoughts and feelings and I say to myself, 'I wonder if my mother ever thought or felt like this?' It would be nice to ask her. Perhaps that's the type of thing she used to discuss with her father when they were drinking their tea. I suppose this is the way adopted children feel when they wish to seek out their bio- logical parents. They are perhaps looking for foreshadowings of themselves. Forerunners. Signs of the way that they themselves might later develop. In our case, though," she said with a smile, "I guess we were hardly adopted. We were left with more than Grandfather, who never even had a picture of his father."

"On the day of my graduation," I said, "he told us that his father came to him twice: in a vision and in a dream. He saw him in the vision as a younger man than he was himself — probably, I suppose, because he had been stopped by death and time. He remembered what he looked like, although, of course, he had never seen him in a physical way. In the vision he unnerved him, but in the dream he consoled him and, I guess, gave him advice as to how he might live his daughter's life and his, for a while.

"The day before," I continued, "he had confirmed his suspi- cions about Wolfe. Authenticated that passage where Wolfe refers to the Highlanders as 'a secret enemy.' It sort of changes the conventional picture of Wolfe with his 'brave Highlanders.' "

"I suppose," she said, "you can be brave and also misunderstood. Brave and betrayed. After Culloden many of those Gaelic-speaking soldiers went to France. After they were pardoned and came back to fight under Wolfe they could speak French as well as Gaelic. *Two* languages that probably didn't make Wolfe feel particularly comfortable with his circumstances."

"If MacDonald had not been able to speak French, to fool the sentries, the history of Canada might be different," I added.

"Who knows?" she said. "If the MacDonalds had been placed on the right of the line instead of the left, Culloden might have been different. They believed it was their traditional spot since Bannockburn, but their commanders were largely of a different culture. They didn't know what they were talking about, and probably thought of them as being sulky or petulant, which they probably were. Muttering to themselves in the strangeness of their Gaelic language."

"Troublesome," I said.

"Yes," she said. "MacDonald of Glencoe in the previous century was considered troublesome as well. That's why they shot him in the back of the head when he turned to offer them whisky. Talk about betrayal. He thought a piece of paper would protect him."

"Oh well," I said, "as Grandpa used to say, 'No more sad stories.'"

"I guess you're right," she said. "But when I read about Montcalm he seemed to face almost the same problem. A lot of his troops were French Canadians. They had been 'in the country of winter,' as they say, for generations. They had evolved differently and knew their land, and he was a *français de France*.

And he didn't know what to do with his allies, the Indians. He didn't understand them or their language or their customs or their methods of attack. He felt their independence was indicative of untrustworthiness. Did you know," she added, "that the Indians believed that if they saw a dog in their dreams it would mean they'd win the battle?"

"No, I didn't know that."

"Well, anyway," she said, "Montcalm probably felt he was in command of a lot of undisciplined primitives, and they probably thought of him as effete, with his ruffed clothes and strange European battle formations. No wonder he kept looking yearningly out to sea for the ships from France."

"Yes," I said, "if only the ships had come from France."

"Before the Plains of Abraham," she said, "Wolfe launched an attack, a landing at Beauport. They were badly beaten back and he was furious at the Highlanders because they wouldn't retreat until they had carried their own wounded from the field. They waded back in the face of fire to get their own people, although they had been ordered to leave them there. It wasn't a very sound military tactic, I suppose, but by that time they were probably fighting with their hearts rather than their heads. The French in front of them and Wolfe and the boats behind them, and their wounded on the Beauport shore. They didn't know about his earlier letter describing them. I still remember some of the phrasing: 'They are hardy, intrepid, accustomed to a rough country, and no great mischief if they fall.'

"I suppose I seem to be trivializing it," she said, "but they seem at times like a great sports team which may have lost faith in its management or its coach, but are out there anyway in the bloodied mud and the smoke, giving their hearts and their sinew not for 'management' but for the shared history of one another.

"In my modernistic mind," she added, "I sometimes imagine Wolfe standing there with his calculator. I know it is untrue and unfair to him. He was supposed to be a great general and he did have red hair. I'm not a very good military historian," she admitted. "If I had been there myself, I probably would have wept. More so if I had read the letter.

"Perhaps I think about all this too much," she said. "Both Grandpa and Grandma used to say, 'If you spend too much time thinking you'll never get your work done.'"

"Yes," I said, "and they worked very hard, especially Grandma."

"I know," she said. "When we had to do our work, cleaning our rooms or doing the dishes or scrubbing the floor, I used to say sometimes, 'But I'm tired.' She used to say, 'Everybody's tired, dear. I'm tired. The world doesn't stop because we're tired. So hurry up and it will be all done in a minute.' And sometimes if her own tiredness were showing she would say, 'I bet if your brother Colin were alive he wouldn't be whining about cleaning his room. You've already passed him in age, and he will never grow older. Poor little soul. He was so happy the last time I saw him in his new coat. We should all be grateful that we're alive and have each other, so hurry up and make your bed. Your older brothers in the country would probably like to have clean rooms.'

"'But they never make their beds,' I said. 'They never have to clean the bathroom. They don't even have a bathroom.'

"'I know,' she said. 'You should consider their lives.'"

My sister was silent for a moment.

"Calum once told me," I said, "that when they went back to the country, they went one day to cut a timber for the skidway they were making for their boat. They went into a tightly packed grove of spruce down by the shore. In the middle of the grove, they saw what they thought was the perfect tree. It was tall and straight and over thirty feet high. They notched it as they had been taught and then they sawed it with a bucksaw. When they had sawed it completely through, nothing happened. The tree's upper branches were so densely intertwined with those of the trees around it that it just remained standing. There was no way it could be removed or fall unless the whole grove was cut down. It remained like that for years. Perhaps it is still there. When the wind blew, the whole grove would move and sigh. Because all of the trees were evergreen they never lost their foliage, and the supporting trees extended their branches every year. If you walked by the grove, Calum said, you would never realize that in its midst there was a tall straight tree that was severed at its stump."

"I guess things are not always as they appear," she said. "In any of our lives. When I first wanted to be an actress both Grandpa and Grandma thought it was strange. 'Why would you want to be an actress?' they asked. 'Why would you want to spend your life trying to pretend you're somebody else? Wouldn't it be easier just to be yourself?'" She touched her fingers to her hair. "Let's look at the photo album."

We took out the photo album and looked at the pictures of our vanished parents. All of the pictures were taken out of doors.

There are no pictures of our parents by themselves. They are always in large groups of *clann Chalum Ruaidh*. Sometimes they are holding children and sometimes they have their arms draped over the shoulders of whoever is standing next to them. Because there are so many people in the pictures, the amateur photographer had to stand far back to incorporate them all within the lens. In one, our father is down one knee in the front row, and our mother is behind him with her left hand on his shoulder. She is holding Colin in the crook of her right arm and he has his thumb in his mouth. Our father has his hands clasped around the brown dog, who is sitting on the ground in front of him. His fingers are interlaced across her chest and her head is tilted back and upwards towards his face. She is trying hard to lick his chin.

We touched the faces of our vanished parents and our older brother who, unnaturally, became our younger brother, stopped like his great-grandfather by death and time. We looked at the dog in her devoted happiness.

"Poor *cù*," said my sister. "She went through the ice with them and then swam back and came to get help. Later she died, I guess, for a lost cause but she didn't know that. Gave every fibre of her small being. Never wavered. As Grandpa used to say, 'You can't ask more.' Cared too much. Tried too hard."

We continued to look at the pictures. "I thought, with modern technology," said my sister, "I could separate our parents from these large groups. I took these pictures to a photo studio and asked if it were possible to isolate our parents and then have their individual photographs enlarged. Blown up. I would like to have their pictures on the wall. The photo studio tried, but it would not work. As the photographs became larger the individual features of their faces became more blurred. It was as if in coming closer they became more indistinct. After a while I stopped. I left them with their group. It seemed the only thing to do.

"If you stay another day," she suggested, "we can go to Banff tomorrow. In Banff you can 'see the weather' on the mountains. You can see patches of rain and areas of sunlight and cloud formations that shift and change. And patterns of mist that rise and descend, that cover and reveal. It is very beautiful.

"Remember as children when we used to look across at the weather on the island? Sometimes it would be raining where we were, but the sun would be shining there. And sometimes it would be the reverse. Sometimes in the snow or the fog we could not see it at all, but then 'the weather would lift,' as Grandpa used to say, and there it would be. Constant in its way."

"I remember," I said. "Yes, I can stay another day."

She smiled. "Do you know where Wolfe was when he wrote his 'no great mischief if they fall' letter to Captain Rickson?"

"No, I don't."

"It was written from Banff," she said. "Banff, Scotland. Wolfe was not very happy there. Banff was dreary and cold and he didn't like the people. He was probably happy to get to Quebec, although he didn't know what was ahead of him."

She was silent for a while. "Maybe we can go farther than Banff," she said. "Maybe we can go as far as the Great Divide."

35 *T*he new Alexander MacDonald seemed, to casual eyes, just another one of us. To Renco Development and the French Canadians and the construction crews and the dining hall staff he seemed to be a part of the fabric we presented to the outside world.

Because it was thought he might have more in common with me, he moved into my bunkhouse, and one of our cousins moved to an adjoining building.

He had been an outstanding high-school quarterback and as he talked I remembered some of the clippings his grandparents had sent to Grandma and Grandpa. He had some of his clippings from the San Francisco area newspapers with him, folded neatly in a manila envelope, carefully preserved at the bottom of his footlocker. They told of his strong arm, his ability to read his opponent's defences, his ingenuity and his quickness in making last-minute decisions. Many of them stressed the fact that he was absolutely fearless. He would stay in the pocket until the last possible split-second, undeterred by the large hulking linemen thundering down upon him. "MacDonald Leads Team to Victory in Dying Seconds," read one. "Red MacDonald Brings Home Yet Another Championship," "MacDonald Engineers Come-From-Behind Triumph," "MacDonald Voted to All-Star Team," read others.

Once, he told me his grandfather said to him, "You're not afraid of anything. You would be great for war. If I were at Culloden I'd want you by my side."

We were lying on our bunks looking at his clippings. "Culloden was where they lost," he said, "right?"

"Yes," I said.

"But they won some of the time?"

"Yes," I said, "they won some of the time."

"My grandfather gave me this ring," he said, holding up his left hand. "It's a Celtic design. The never-ending circle."

"I noticed it," I said, "the first day that you came."

36 Our cousin had been highly recruited by various universities, but nearing the conclusion of his final season he had been badly injured in a game. He had remained in the pocket a portion of a second too long and, perhaps, his bravery had betrayed him in the end. His left leg had been firmly planted just before he released the ball, and it had supported most of his weight. When he was blindsided, the leg crumpled beneath him. The ligaments of his left knee were torn, and although he underwent reconstructive surgery he was never to regain his former quickness and lateral movement. The recruiting universities lost interest, fearing that he might be

damaged goods, but apparently he recovered enough agility to be deemed fit for military service.

And he was tremendously athletic; quick in his movements and poised and balanced upon his feet, and muscled and strong from his years of disciplined training. Those of us who saw him for the first time that summer could not imagine that he might ever have been better, physically, at an earlier time; although when he stood next to us in the showers, the scars from his surgery were jaggedly visible on the raised pink flesh that surrounded his knee.

He was also, or so it seemed, in the words of his grandfather, "not afraid of anything."

"He catches on to things really quickly," said Calum. "I was worried he would be bothered by the underground, by the dynamite and the darkness and the heaviness of the work, but he never complains. He always pulls his weight and you only have to show him how to do something once."

He was also very adaptable socially. He would talk willingly on most subjects and was quick to pick up the prevailing attitudes of those around him. He mingled easily with people from other groups but was careful never to reveal his true identity. And when he played poker, which few of us did, he was unusually successful because neither his facial expression nor his body movements gave any indication of what cards he was concealing in his hand.

"All good quarterbacks are like that," he said with a laugh. "You never let your eyes betray what your mind is thinking."

That summer we talked about different things. We were aware that there were events taking place in the outside world.

Newspapers arrived, although they were sometimes two days old, and items of information somehow seemed to be parachuted in through the static of the tiny radios. Some of the reported events were more relevant to some of us than to others. Some of them, directly or indirectly, affected us all.

That summer it was reported that a bone fragment of early man was located in Kenya. It was said to be two and one-half million years old. Pierre Trudeau replaced Lester Pearson as prime minister of Canada. Lester Pearson had long represented the riding of Algoma East, where we worked, but few of us ever voted because we did not meet the residency requirements. Pierre Trudeau, like Lester Pearson before him, suggested that there be a cessation in the bombing of North Vietnam. Lyndon Johnson was not impressed by such suggestions. Charles De Gaulle, after his return to France, continued to offer advice concerning an independent Quebec. Pierre Trudeau, like Lester Pearson before him, was not impressed by such suggestions. James Hoffa was in jail. Ronald Reagan remained as governor of California. Robert Stanfield left his post in Nova Scotia and replaced John Diefenbaker as leader of the Progressive Conservative party. The civil-rights movement intensified. There were marches and there were shootings and there were fires and there were riots. Stokely Carmichael and Rap Brown advocated their own form of change. Martin Luther King, Jr., who had led his own host of thousands, had been assassinated in April. James Earl Ray, the man who killed him, was arrested at Heathrow Airport carrying a fraudulent Canadian passport. His arrest occurred three days after Robert Kennedy was shot in the head after making a speech in California.

There were reports of new uranium findings in the area where we worked. Perhaps Renco Development would begin sinking new shafts farther to the north? Canada led the world in the production of nickel and zinc. There were new mineral findings in Nevada, New Mexico, Utah, and Montana. Reportedly, experienced shaft and development miners were in demand, but a knowledge of English was required. My brothers said that when climbing to the high altitudes of Utah and Montana, it was sometimes necessary to adjust the carburetors of their cars because the air was so thin. The air, they said, was almost as rarefied as that of Peru.

California led the United States in its number of draft evaders. It was reported that many such young men were working in Canada under assumed names. We read that 26,907 American soldiers had died since the beginning of the conflict. Cassius Clay expressed the opinion that he had no wish to join them. He had nothing against the Viet Cong, he said. Willie Mays continued his spectacular play for the San Francisco Giants. Dr. Benjamin Spock was given a two-year jail term in Boston because he was opposed to the draft. J. Edgar Hoover was still in control of the FBI and, perhaps, like a good quarterback, he did not let his external signs betray what his mind was really thinking. The knitting manufacturers of Toronto earned lucrative contracts for the production of green berets, as did the leading shoe manufacturer for the production of military footwear. Its spokesperson was later to say, "We made millions from that war and didn't lose a man."

"I'm not here because I'm afraid," said Alexander MacDonald. "I'm here because I'm not stupid."

The music of Bob Dylan wafted in on the tiny radios.

Sometimes we talked about the Oakland Raiders and the San Francisco 49ers. The Montreal Canadiens possessed the Stanley Cup, which gave Marcel Gingras and his friends a certain sense of satisfaction. Some of them had the logo of the Canadiens on the windshields and the bumpers of their cars.

In the country of Marcel Gingras, the Rouyn car dealer Réal Caouette had captured his people's imagination. As leader of the Créditistes he had garnered fourteen seats in the recent election. Many people were surprised. Réal Caouette expressed no wish to secede from Canada. Rather he advocated the creation of an eleventh province. It would straddle the border of eastern Ontario and western Quebec. It would include places like Rouyn-Noranda, Cobalt, Temagami, Kirkland Lake, Larder Lake, Temiskaming, and Abitibi. His reasoning was that the people of that region had more in common with one another than they had with those whom they felt controlled their destinies from the distant cities of Toronto and Quebec City, people who shared neither their weather, their landscape, their daily concerns, nor their sensitivities. Quebec City and Toronto were cities which were remote in many different ways and, to a proportion of the people from the proposed new province, they were distant places that they had heard about but never seen. The proposed new province would be something like the Republic of Madawaska, that region of the country where the boundaries of New Brunswick, Quebec, and Maine are so close to one another that in the end they vanish within the consciousness of the region's inhabitants. Once again, Quebec City is far away, as is Fredericton, while Augusta, the capital of Maine, is more distant still. The citizens of Madawaska sing their own songs, and they sing them mostly for and to themselves.

The citizens of Réal Caouette's proposed new province possessed a body of song as well. Sometimes Marcel Gingras would sing one or two songs to us, although they often surpassed our understanding. They affected him, though, quite deeply and sometimes his eyes would fill with embarrassed mist as he ran his hand over the tattered map, outlining the lines that did not visually exist. They existed, however, for him, and in the old dream: *le pays des Laurentides.*

That summer Marcel Gingras greatly increased his English vocabulary. He was highly motivated and would pore over the discarded newspapers, wrinkling his brow in an attempt to make sense of what seemed like an unruly language. Sometimes, if there were few people around, he would bring the newspaper to me and point to individual words. I would scramble around for the French equivalent, relying on the not very well stocked warehouse of French I had acquired in high school and university. We could make progress with the nouns and verbs, but many of the abstractions were more complicated. It seemed almost possible, however, to live a life based on "person, place, and thing" plus action. Sometimes Marcel Gingras would point to a certain word and look inquiringly at Alexander MacDonald. Because we were of roughly the same age, he assumed we had the same smattering of French. He had no way of knowing we had come from different educational experiences, for to him we both looked pretty much the same.

At first, perhaps, Alexander MacDonald viewed Marcel Gingras and his comrades as "quaint." Later, perhaps, he viewed them as he might have viewed the large Hispanic or Mexican population of his native California. People who did not always speak the mainstream language, yet were very much there. Alexander MacDonald's warehouse of Spanish words and phrases was likely equivalent to my ill-stacked one of French. I say all of this now as conjecture, because he was careful in what he chose not to reveal.

Yet, as I said, he was sociable and affable. He would nod and smile when he met Fern Picard on the pathways and bore him none of the grudges which most of us carried. It was rumoured that sometimes, at night, he even ventured into the French-Canadian bunkhouses to play poker. It was said that at first they regarded him as a spy sent to seek out information across enemy lines. But then they saw that if he were a spy, he was a very naïve one. Maybe he was a bit unbalanced mentally? Maybe he needed protection from the realities of life?

On the rare occasions when Marcel Gingras visited our bunkhouse he was regarded in much the same way. He was not appreciated historically, but as an individual struggling with a language not his own he was difficult to dislike. No one wished to hit him with a wrench. .

Possibly Marcel Gingras, Alexander MacDonald, and myself were protected for a while because we did not share the same history as the others. We shared some of it, but not all. None of us had been present at the brawls in Rouyn-Noranda, and no one had spent much time calling us "frogs" or "porridge eaters" or visiting real or imagined sabotage on us. We had not seen other people wearing our clothes. In many ways we did not bear the scars, and none of us had been present at the death of the

red-haired Alexander MacDonald. I myself had been half a con-
tinent away. I was probably having my picture taken when the
bucket came down upon him. There was probably a mortar
board on my head in the instant when he had no head at all.

So for us, the nail did not protrude in the same way. It was not
as deeply embedded in the bottoms of our shoes.

The new Alexander MacDonald appeared the most
unaffected of all. Probably, as I have said, it was because he was
the one who was the most removed from our immediate history.
Concerning our relatively recent past he had nothing to forgive
or to forget. Of all the members of our branch of *clann Chalum
Ruaidh*, he was the only one amongst us who had never seen or
known the dead man whose identification papers he carried
upon his body.

He continued, though, to work hard.

One day Calum asked me, "Do you think he will stay with us
for a long time?"

"I don't know," I said. "He never mentions anything like
that."

"If he were to stay with us for a while," said Calum, "perhaps
you could go back? I suppose it's too late for your lab and your
white coat. Is it?"

"Yes," I said, "it's too late for this year."

"Perhaps you would just like to go home for a rest?" he asked.
"He is a good worker and perhaps now we could get along
without you.

"But perhaps," he added, "if you were to leave he would not
be as comfortable among the rest of us. I suppose it's because of

your agreement with Grandpa and Grandma that he's here in the first place."

I considered it for a while. "I think I should stay," I said.

"Okay," he said. "We'll go forward."

"Most people," Grandpa used to say, "try to do the right thing. If your parents knew they were going to drown, do you think they would have started across?"

The work went forward.

37 Alexander MacDonald worked hard, as did the rest of us. When he was not at work, he slept, it seemed, for only brief periods. Sometimes, late at night, I would awaken to see or to hear him moving in the darkness. Sometimes he would open his footlocker, where the clippings from his days of glory quietly reposed. At times when we were together, we would talk about sports teams or books or music or movies from the previous months. *A Man for All Seasons*, starring Paul Scofield, had won the major award the previous year. We both had seen it.

On a Saturday in early August the hoist broke down. It was about three in the afternoon. We could move neither men nor material, so everything came to a halt. In terms of the contemporary world it would be as if the only elevator in a twenty-storey building ceased to function. Except, in our case, we were beneath the ground instead of above it. When we realized what had happened we began to climb our way to the surface. Beside the shaft there was a series of wooden ladders constructed in case of just such an emergency. So that we would not be trapped at the bottom.

We began to climb upward in single file. The lights on our helmets shone upon the glistening rock and the water dripped from our helmets' brims to beneath our collars, and then trickled in small, cold rivulets down our backs. Each man could only move as fast as the man before him. If you were too eager, your fingers would be stepped on by the steel-toed boots of the man above. Small rocks and bits of dislodged mud fell from our passage and from the bottoms of our boots. Those farther down the line were constantly bombarded by small showers of debris rattling upon their helmets. They had to keep their heads down while also attempting to look upward in order to grasp the next rung upon the ladder.

If someone's legs began to tremble or if breathing became hard, the individual might stop for a moment to catch his breath and to lean against the walls of stone. But if he did so, he would halt the progress of the climbers beneath him. Impatient voices would echo upward from the darkness. "What's going on up there?" "Who's holding up the line?" "Who's sending these rocks down on top of me?" "We've got to get out of here. *Greas ort!* Hurry up!"

We emerged wet and trembling to stand blinking under the rays of the blazing sun.

At first the usual rumours circulated. The hoist was being repaired. It could not be repaired. A new one was being trucked in. The installation would take two hours. Perhaps it would take half a day. Perhaps a whole day. Because it was late Saturday afternoon, the suppliers were not answering their phones. In the end it seemed that nothing could be done until the conclusion of the weekend. We would not be able to descend again until, probably, Monday morning.

Almost immediately, the taxis began to appear outside of the camp's main gates. In retrospect it is hard to imagine how they got there so fast. Maybe they were forewarned. Sometimes I think of them as being akin to circling birds in the lower regions of the sky. Drawn by instinct or intuition. Aware that something is going to happen in the near landscape that will be beneficial to them all. These taxis, however, did not circle. They either waited near the entrance of the gates or drove directly into the adjacent parking lot. Those waiting for passengers were the former. Those with something to sell were the latter.

As the sun continued its decline, we were beset by a certain restlessness. Generally when some of us were above ground, either resting or sleeping, the others were at work. But now we were all on the surface together. For a while some of us wrote letters or lay on our bunks and tried to listen to the radio. Some people played cards. Someone tried to play the violin, briefly, but then put it aside. We walked to the coffee shop and then returned. We waited for supper. In the dining hall there were more men than usual because no one was underground. People jostled one another. The cooks ran out of food. We returned to our bunkhouses. No one was particularly tired and it was too hot to sleep casually. We walked outside the camp gates. We walked to the parking lot. We sat on the rocks which were still warm from the earlier heat of the sun, or sat on the bumpers of some of the old cars. A man approached us and asked if we would like to have a good time. Calum said he didn't think it was possible. The sun continued its decline and then it was dusk. We continued to sit on our rocks and our bumpers. Sometimes individuals would separate from the group and stand and urinate at the parking lot's edge. We could hear the hiss and see the steam rising from the hot rocks.

"What the hell!" said Alexander MacDonald. "I'm going to buy you guys a beer." He approached one of the taxi drivers and soon two large cases of beer were deposited at our feet. There was also a bottle of cheap rye whisky. It must have cost a lot of money.

Across the parking lot Fern Picard was sitting with his men. When he saw Alexander MacDonald make his purchase, he sent one of his men to do the same thing. It was almost as if he did not wish to be outdone.

As the man passed our group, someone said, "Monkey see. Monkey do."

"Fuck off," said Fern Picard's man.

We sat in the dusk and sipped on the warm beer. Some people passed the whisky bottle around. We thanked Alexander MacDonald.

As it became darker, someone turned on a car radio. Alexander MacDonald got up and went back towards the bunkhouses. Later he returned and sat with us. There was movement among the

French Canadians as well. Shadowy figures departed and returned. The stars began to appear and then the moon. It was our only light.

Out of the semi-darkness Fern Picard appeared. "*Maudits enfants de chienne*," he said and spat on the ground.

He was standing over Calum, who was sitting on a rock. Calum perceived his disadvantage and bent forward slightly from the waist. "Fuck off," he said. "Mind your own business."

Now we were aware of Fern Picard's men moving out of the shadows to stand behind him. Those of us who were sitting rose to standing positions.

"*Vous êtes des voleurs et des menteurs*," said Fern Picard. "*Vous êtes des trous de cul. Ta soeur!*"

Calum sprang forward from the rock, tackling Fern Picard below the knees and attempting to knock him backwards. Instead, because of Picard's size and the way his feet were planted, he fell forward so that he was almost extended across Calum's back. They rolled together across the rocky ground of the parking lot. And then they were all upon us, as we were upon them.

Members of the various construction crews who happened to be in the parking lot moved away quickly, although some stayed to watch from the shadowy edges near the trees.

"I didn't come here to die in the boondocks," I heard Alexander MacDonald say, as he vanished into the trees behind us.

In the darkness there was only the muffled thuds of fists on flesh and the uneven gasps and grunts of great exertion. I rolled across the parking lot with my hands around the neck of a young man even as his hands pressed tightly against my throat. Each of us was trying to do the same thing to the other. Each of us was trying not to be on the bottom when our revolutions ended. If it seemed that he had me pinned upon my back and might complete his throttling, I would heave myself against his leg and roll to the right until our positions were reversed. He would do the same. Sometimes we would have to relinquish our grips on one another's throats to regain our leverage. When we did so, we would each attempt to hit the other in the face with whatever hand was free. I did not even know his name.

Someone kicked over one of the beer cases, and when the bottles were broken, their agitated contents foamed upward and outward beyond their circles of confinement. We could smell the yeasty odour in the air.

I heard car doors or trunk lids slam, and then the sound of steel on stone. Someone had introduced car jacks or tire irons or wrenches or chains to the complications of the conflict.

There are many things that people will do in the dark that they will not do in light. The man with his teeth fastened in his opponent's ear, or the man trying to insert the blade of his pocket knife between his opponent's ribs, will be embarrassed by the smallness of their actions if they are exposed to light. Suddenly someone turned on the headlights of some of the surrounding cars, and then the tenor of the conflict probably altered in some ways. Altered, but did not diminish.

In the now well-lit arena my opponent and I rolled across the rocky surface. The backs of our shirts were bloodied because of the sharp stones that had penetrated the fabric. We could smell and taste the salty odour of our mingled blood.

The car radio continued to play. Charley Pride was singing "Crystal Chandeliers."

Someone threw a huge heavy-duty pipe wrench either to us or at us. I was beneath my opponent when it landed with a clunk at our side. Our positions had altered so that now he was astride me, but I had a grip on each of his wrists so that he was unable to move his hands. He looked yearningly towards the wrench. Blood and spittle trickled down upon me from his chin.

Calum fell beside me with a thud. He landed on his back but was able, partially, to block the fall with his shoulders so that his head did not land upon the stone. His face was covered with blood, and almost as he landed Fern Picard was on top of him, hitting him with his right fist and then his left. He forced his thumb against Calum's windpipe. Calum's eyes rolled upward in their sockets and his breath began to rattle.

My opponent, noticing that I was distracted, suddenly jerked his right hand free and lunged sideways towards the wrench. I tried to recapture his escaped wrist and, as we rolled, our tangled bodies nudged the wrench not to us but in the opposite direction. The wrench came to neither of us. Instead it came to Calum. His hand closed around its handle, as it might around a final gift. He heaved himself upward, dislodging Fern Picard, and swung the wrench. The heavy heel of the wrench crunched into the skull of Fern Picard, and he fell with a gurgling sound. He lay on his back and his eyes rolled upward in their sockets. His huge hands twitched, and a dark stain appeared on the front of his trousers. Fern Picard was dead.

Calum hurled the bloodied wrench into the bush. He knelt at the edge of the parking lot and his vomit came forth in waves. My opponent and I had released each other and now stood side by side like spectators at a greater event. Someone turned off the radio and the headlights of the cars. Darkness descended upon us all.

38 After the security guards and the first-aid staff placed the blanket over Fern Picard, everyone waited. They say that roadblocks were set up on the big highways, but no one was apprehended. The police arrived, after what seemed like a very long time. Their sirens screamed and their lights flashed and there was great excitement among their vehicles. I noticed that Paul Belanger was among the police officers. But all of the rest of us were quiet.

We were living in a location where death was not uncommon, but this was different. It was pointed out, by an official, that this was the first death since May, and that had been the death of the red-haired Alexander MacDonald. An industrial accident.

Some of us were questioned on the spot, and some of us were taken to Sudbury. We were asked to tell what we saw. Many had seen the wrench strike Fern Picard. The scene had been illuminated by the headlights of the cars. And yes, it was true that Fern Picard had been unarmed. The security guard came forward to say that earlier in the summer he had seen Calum hit Fern Picard in the mouth and he had been unarmed then as well. We were asked questions about ourselves and where we had lived in the past. I remember thinking that it was a good thing Alexander MacDonald was not there. I had not thought much about him in the past hours. I was asked if I was "sure" I was going to dental school. "We'll check it out," the officer said.

Because it was Saturday night we were held in the Sudbury jail until Monday. On that day Calum was brought before a justice of the peace in the provincial courthouse in Sudbury. He was charged with murder in the second degree. The arraignment lasted about fifteen minutes. The justice of the peace asked the Crown attorney if he wished a detention order. Was there a reason that the prisoner should be detained in custody pending his trial? Was he likely to flee? The Crown attorney responded in the affirmative, pointing out that Calum had a violent past and was a violent man. Behind him there stretched a trail of various offences from various jurisdictions. Some of them dated back to his early youth, while others were more recent, including his assault on the police officer who had tried to stop him on the day he brought home the red-haired Alexander MacDonald in a body bag.

The justice of the peace asked Calum if he were represented by a lawyer. "No," he replied.

"Do you wish to be represented by a lawyer?" asked the justice of the peace.

"I have been looking after myself since I was sixteen years old," said Calum. "I can handle this."

The justice of the peace indicated that it was not a good idea.

Calum was kept in the Sudbury jail pending his trial before the Ontario High Court of Justice. At that time there were judges who travelled the circuit, so it might be five or six months before he came to trial. The rest of us were asked to verify addresses in case we might be subpoenaed, and then we were told we were free to go.

As we were leaving the jail, among those hanging around outside someone said, "Look at how many of them have red hair. They look like people who would be violent."

We went back to the camp, where everything was subdued. The French Canadians began packing their gear. Many of them were going home to Quebec for the funeral of Fern Picard. Some of them threw their belts and their wrenches into the bush, indicating that they would not be back. They had lost their leader. We had lost ours. Fern Picard had negotiated most of their contracts for them, and Calum had done the same for us.

When the Canada geese fly north in spring, there is a leader who points the way, a leader at the apex of the V as the formation moves across the land. Those who follow must believe that the leader is doing the best he can, but there is no guarantee that all journeys will end in salvation for everyone involved. Perhaps in the parlance of the earlier weeks, both Calum and Fern Picard might have been regarded as quarterbacks, but it is unlikely that either of them would have thought of themselves in terms that, to them, were so foreign and so strange.

Marcel Gingras and I met on the path. We raised our eyebrows at one another. It was too dangerous to risk the possibilities of speech.

Clann Chalum Ruaidh went into our bunkhouse. With an iron bar we broke open the footlocker of Alexander MacDonald. In it we found many items we recognized as not being his. At the bottom, above the manila envelopes, we found Fern Picard's wallet. It contained one thousand dollars. It seemed that when Fern Picard called us liars and thieves he knew more than we did.

On one of the manila envelopes we scratched Fern Picard's name and address, which we found on his driver's licence. In the envelope, we placed the thousand dollars. We looked at one another. No one had a stamp.

We resolved that we would take the envelope and the wallet, somehow, across the Quebec border and there we would drop them into separate mailboxes. We would find a stamp and we would send them to *le pays des Laurentides*. It seemed the fitting thing to do.

When management of Renco Development came into our bunkhouse and announced that the hoist was fixed, no one expressed much interest. We said that we would think about it.

We never saw Alexander MacDonald again. I realized later that he had been wearing my MacDonald tartan shirt. The one that the mother of the red-haired Alexander MacDonald had purchased for him on my graduation day, the day that he had been killed. The shirt had been purchased for one Alexander MacDonald who had never worn it. It had been worn by a second and had vanished on the back of a third.

Apparently he never told his grandparents what had hap- pened and, of course, he left before the final events played out to the end. He must have departed in a great hurry, perhaps in one of the taxis which had been so busy in the earlier hours of the evening. His grandparents quoted him as saying when they wrote to Grandpa and Grandma expressing their gratitude for all that we had done for him. It was good, they said, that all of us still believed in sticking with our blood. "Blood is thicker than water," they wrote. "*Beannachd leibh.*"

39 *T*hat winter Calum was convicted of second-degree murder. He was sentenced to life imprisonment at Kingston Penitentiary. The judge, noting what he called the accused's long history of violent transgressions, said that he hoped the sentence would serve as an example for those who chose to break the law.

40 *O*ne of my brothers went back to the Bridge River Valley of British Columbia. He had worked there as a miner as a young man, and now he drives the school bus among the narrow mountain passes.

The other went to Scotland. He was standing on the railway platform at Glasgow's Queen Street Station when a red-haired man approached him. "Hello, MacDonald," said the man. "*Ciamar a tha sibh* – how are you?"

"*Glé mhath*," he replied.

"I'm waiting for the train to the Highlands," said the man. "I suppose you are too. We have time for a dram in the station bar."

"Well," said my brother, "I guess I have time."

"When I first saw you," said the man, "I thought you were from the Highlands, but now that I hear you talk you sound like you're from Canada."

"Yes, I'm from Canada. From Cape Breton."

"Oh," said the man, "the land of trees. That's where a lot of the people went after it all happened. I have probably more relatives there than I have here. Too bad about it all."

"Yes, too bad about it all."

"Well," said the man, brightening, "however long you've been gone, you haven't gone that far to look and talk like you do. What goes around, comes around, I suppose. There is a fish farm near where I live. Come and have a look at it. Maybe you'd like to stay for a while. We can always make room. We can always fit you in. 'Come to the Highlands with me,' as the song says."

"Maybe I will," said my brother. "A few things happened. I was just trying to leave the past for a while."

"Interesting place to come for that," laughed the man. "Perhaps you're coming to the past. Anyway, get yourself a ticket. Then we'll go to the bar. We'll talk about *Bliadhna Thearlaich* – Charlie's Year: 1745-6. If only the ships had come from France!"

41 Grandpa died from jumping up in the air and trying to click his heels together twice. There were a lot of people in his house that evening and he had already attempted to do it on two occasions. Grandma, who was always encouraging, said, "Try it once more. The third time is the charm." He leapt up into the air and then collapsed for the last time on his floor. Neither my sister nor I nor our three brothers were there to see his final fall. Earlier in the evening they had been playing cards. They were playing "Auction" and he had been banging his fist on the table enthusiastically whenever he had the ace of hearts. "I wish I could get as much satisfaction out of having the ace of hearts," Grandfather had often said about him.

When he died, Grandfather said, "What an absolutely foolish way for a man to die." He clasped his hands tightly until his knuckles turned white. Since the death of his daughter no one had ever seen him cry.

Later Grandma said, "Although they were so different they were each other's closest friends. Throughout their lives, they were each a balance to the other."

Grandfather died reading a book called *A History of the Scottish Highlands*. His finger marked the page and the book flipped closed around his finger and his glasses slipped down on his nose. He was reading about the massacre of Glencoe, the old story of betrayal from within and without. He was reading about the "troublesome" man who was killed to serve as an example to those who chose to break the law. The self-reliant man who was overtaken by his own history.

As would be expected, Grandfather left everything in order. He had a list of his pallbearers and the music he wanted performed at his funeral service. As his coffin came down the aisle, the violinist played "Patrick MacCrimmon's Lament for the Children" and on the way to the graveyard the piper played "I Mourn for the Highlands." As we were leaving the church, a woman said, "Who is going to look after us now?"

He had appointed me as the executor of his will. He left his books and his house to my sister, who was his only female descendant, and he divided what money he had among his grandsons.

Neither of my grandfathers died in the hospital which the one had built and the other had maintained. Calum was unable to come to either funeral.

Grandma lived to be one hundred and ten, the same age as her ancestor *Calum Ruadh*. After Grandpa died, she kept all his clothes hanging where he left them. His jackets and his caps hung on their nails in the porch and for a long time you could smell his familiar odour when you entered the house. The specific odour of his tobacco and his spilled beer and his humour and his jolly kindness. The brown dogs lay beneath the hanging clothes for months, their noses resting upon their crossed paws. Caring a lot and trying hard.

Once, he had said to Grandfather, "You should get yourself a girlfriend."

"And you," said Grandfather, "should mind your own business."

Grandma continued to work hard. Her physical strength and endurance, in time, exceeded her other capacities. Towards the end, revellers would see houselights burning brightly at two a.m. Within the house she would have her dinner table set for eleven. Her pots would be boiling merrily on the stove and she would be brushing her hands on her apron. "There now," she would say to the brown dogs, after checking the interior of her oven. "Nearly done. We just need the pickles and then we will be ready. It will only take a minute. A stitch in time saves nine."

After she moved to the nursing home our visits would take on a quality both foreign and familiar. Sometimes I tried to reach her in regard to my own past, but she had more past than I. Always I think of those visits of the past in the present tense.

"It's a nice day today," she says. "It will be good for fishing and for hanging out a wash."

"Yes," I say.

"Are you from around here?" she asks.

"Yes, well, no. Well, yes."

"You have lovely clothes," she says. "You must have a good job. My husband had a good job. He ran the hospital. We always had a regular paycheque. We never wanted for anything. He was a very generous man, my husband."

She pauses.

"One of my sons has a good job too," she continues. "He was in the war, in the navy. Now he is the lightkeeper on the island over there. Look, you can see it through the window. The government supplies him with a big boat and everything. He is married to a lovely girl. The daughter of our friend. They have six children. The youngest two are twins. A boy and a girl. Sometimes they stay at our house for a while. They are never any trouble. Do you have children?"

"Yes," I say.

"Do they make their own beds?"

"Well, sometimes," I reply.

"You should encourage them to make their own beds," she says. "It's good training for life. I have a grandson who lives in southern Ontario. I visited him once. He is a dentist and is a rich man. He and his wife have a lovely big house. They have a cleaning lady. Think of that! When I visited them I used to want to clean the house before the cleaning lady came. I wouldn't want someone else to come in and find a mess, unmade beds and such. I hope you make your own bed. Do you?"

"Well," I say, "perhaps not as often as I used to."

"You should. It only takes a minute."

She pauses again.

"I have a granddaughter," she says. "She acts in plays and things like that. Probably like those plays on television. Do you watch television?"

"No," I say, "not much."

"Sometimes in the afternoon, the people here watch television in the lounge. Oh, those people on television" she flaps her hands sympathetically forward from her lap, "the problems that they have."

After a moment, she begins again. "Most of us are Scottish people here," she tells me. "We are Highlanders. All up and down this coast and inland, too. A lot of us are descended from a man who came here long ago. He was married to a woman in Scotland and they had six children. She died and then he married her sister and they had six more children. She died too while they were making the crossing. He was not a young man when he came here, but not an old one either. He was fifty-five. I think that perhaps he was often lonely, but he was determined and tried his best. He is buried all by himself down by the shore.

"For a long time we never left here," she says. "We were here as a Gaelic-speaking group, and a lot of people never left the island. My husband used to tell a little joke. A man was supposed to have asked another man, 'Were you ever off Cape Breton Island?' And the man was supposed to have said, 'Only one time. Once I climbed a tree.' My husband was like that. He was always full of little jokes. He used to pick them up in the taverns or wherever he went and then he would tell them to me when we were in bed at night."

She looks down at her hands.

"Then the men began to go away. At first to work in the woods during the winter. To mainland Nova Scotia, and then to New Brunswick, to the Miramichi, and then to the state of Maine. Some of them never came back. And then families. My sister and I were married to two brothers. I was her bridesmaid. They went to San Francisco and we never saw them again, although we wrote to one another for years. 'Blood is thicker than water,' we always said.

"Later a lot of people went to the hard-rock mines. All over Canada and the States. To South America and Africa and all those places. They used to send pictures and postcards and some of them brought home those African masks. Once our grandsons brought us a kitten from Northern Ontario."

She is silent for a moment.

"I don't know what happened to some of them out there," she says.

The clack of dogs' nails are heard on the polished floor and two brown dogs enter the room. They go towards her and lick her hand. Suddenly she is back in the present. She leans forward, as if we are conspirators. "Dogs are not allowed in here," she says. "It's a rule, but a lot of the staff here are my relatives so when the dogs come they just look the other way. The dogs come to visit me every day. They are very loyal. Everybody likes them.

"Do you have dogs?" she asks.

"No, I don't."

"You should," she says. "They are man's best friend. Sometimes I think dogs have more sense than half the people." And then she asks, "Do you know any French people?"

"Yes," I smile, "I know some."

"When I used to read I used to think that they were a lot like us. That they were alone with their landscape for a long, long time. That it went into them somehow. Our friend used to say that long ago in Scotland they were our friends, part of the 'auld alliance,' they used to call it. Did you ever hear of that?"

"Yes, I've heard of it."

"Are they nice?"

"Who?"

"The French people."

"Yes, I guess so."

"I suppose they are like the rest of us. Some are nice and some are not so nice."

"I suppose so," I say.

"Are you married?" she asks.

"Yes," I say, "I'm married."

"I was too," she says. "I was married very young. My husband kept pestering me. He said we would be happy and he was right. Neither of us ever wavered. 'All of us are better when we're loved,' he used to say. A lot of people wouldn't think my husband would ever say anything like that.

"Sometimes when he came home from visiting our friend he would tell me all those stories from Scotland. He thought MacDonalds were the best people in the world. Our friend used to say he couldn't see the forest for the trees.

"Sometimes when he would tell me those stories his eyes would fill with tears. People used to say he was sentimental, but it was because he cared. He felt everything deeply. People around here used to call a man like him 'soft.' 'Maybe so,' he used to say, 'but I'm always hard when I have to be, you know that.' He was full of little double meanings like that, my husband."

She pats one of the dogs on the head. It licks her hand. She smiles wistfully. "All of us are better when we're loved," she says.

"Are you a folklorist?" she then asks.

"No," I say, "I'm not a folklorist."

"There are lots of folklorists around now," she says. "They are busy collecting the old songs. We always sang. We always sang when we were working and then we just sang because we liked to. We were used to it. Some of the songs were long, verse after verse. It wasn't until the radio came along that we thought maybe our songs were too long. The ones on the radio only lasted a few minutes.

"My husband and I had a friend," she continues. "He knew a lot of songs. He knew all of the verses in his head and never made a mistake. He could remember everything. We should have copied all those words down while he was still with us. Copied them in a scribbler or something, but we never got around to it. Our friend spent most of his life alone."

She looks at me keenly.

"You remind me, somehow, of our friend," she says. "You even look a little bit like him. Can you sing?"

"No," I say. And then because I no longer wish to say "No," I say, "Yes, yes I can sing."

I begin to sing *"O Siud An Taobh A Ghabhainn."* She joins me instantly. She reaches her hand towards mine and with our hands joined in the old rhythm we are carried away and she is a young girl once again. When we come to the verse about the MacDonalds she begins to laugh.

"Dòmhnullaich 'us gu'm bu dual dhaibh
Seasamh direach ri achd cruadail,
A bhith diann a' ruith na ruaige,
Dheas, cruaidh gu dòruinn."

The MacDonalds were always wont
to stand boldly in the face of hardship,
eagerly putting opponents to rout,
faithful, intrepid in adversity.

Some of the older residents come to the door and join us. Instinctively they reach for one another's hands. And then some of the younger staff as well, their strong young voices blending easily into the rhythm. The brown dogs look up from the floor, as if once again everything is right with the world.

"Falbhaidh sinn o thìr nan uachdran;
Ruigidh sinn an dùthaich shuaimhneach,
Far am bidh crodh laoigh air bhuailtean,
Air na fuarain bhòidheàch."

We shall leave the land of the lairds
we'll go to the land of contentment,
where there will be cattle in the folds
and around the fine pools.

When we are finished she looks at me admiringly. "You even sing like our friend," she says, "only you're not quite as good. But then nobody was. It is too bad you never met him. I think you would have liked him."

I can no longer bear it. "He was my grandfather," I say. "Grandma, it's me, *gille beag ruadh*."

She looks at me with bemusement, as if I am beyond the preposterous.

"Oh, the *gille beag ruadh*," she says. "The *gille beag ruadh* is thousands of miles from here. Yet I would know him if I met him anywhere in this whole wide world. He will always have a piece of my heart."

All of us are better when we're loved.

42 And now it is dusk turning towards darkness as my car moves deeper southward. Not far away, across the river the United States – that country born of revolution – sends its towers thrusting to the sky.

On Monday in my office I will offer solace and change and perhaps hopeful improvement to those who seek me out. We will talk about retrusion and occlusion and the problems caused by overbite. "Don't bite off more than you can chew," Grandma used to say.

When I first started practising dentistry, I sometimes saw myself in my white coat with my dentist's drill as an extension of my earlier self, with the jackleg drill. Leaning towards the surface that I drilled while the cooling water splashed back towards my face. Drilling deep but not too deep. Trying to get it right.

In the landscape around me, those who harvest the bounty of the earth are stilled for the day. Yet they are there in the near-darkness with their own hopes and dreams and disappointments. On the East Coast, the native peoples who move across the land, harvesting, are stilled also. Tomorrow they will cross back and forth across the borders, following the potato harvest and the blueberries, passing from New Brunswick into Maine and then back again. They are older than the borders and the boundaries between countries and they pay them little mind.

In Kenya, at the base of Mount Kilimanjaro, the tall and arrogant Masai follow their herds. For strength they drink the blood of their cattle. They follow the cycle of the seasons and pay no heed to the boundaries of the parks and game preserves. They were there first, they reason. Unlike the Zulus, they have not yet been confined to certain "homelands" which are really not their homes at all. Perhaps the Masai do not know that others are planning "to do something" with them. "Soon," perhaps.

In Kingston Penitentiary, Calum said, a disproportionate number of the prisoners were from the native population. In many cases they did not fully understand the language of those to whom they were entrusted or condemned. They would hang their woven dreamcatchers on the walls of their cells, he said. There were not many dreams in Kingston Penitentiary. It was the only thing he ever said about his years of incarceration.

In the language of the law, a life sentence is really twenty-five years and one is eligible for parole after ten. That is why I am able to visit him on these days. I try to do so faithfully.

In the waters near Glencoe perhaps the mythical "king of the herring" still swims. If he exists, perhaps he is as complicated as many other leaders. He is regarded as a friend to some, but those who follow him may do so at their peril. In any case there are no MacDonalds who wait for him and his bounty, and perhaps without their beliefs he is just another fish, who should be careful where he swims.

Ahead of me, at home, my wife and children wait. In the hell of eastern Europe an official visited my wife's home when she was just a little girl. The official had a list which contained the names of her father and her two older brothers. They were commanded, said the official, to be at the station the next morning. When the door closed, her father said that he and his two sons should leave during the night. They could be far away by morning, and later they could work something out. Her mother argued that they should follow the rules and regulations that were laid out for them. She said it was not good to break the law, even if you did not trust it. They argued deep into the night. In the end her father reluctantly agreed to take her mother's advice. In the morning she said goodbye to her husband and her sons and they left for the station. She never saw any of them again.

My wife is supportive of my journeys. "We never know what lies ahead of us," she says. "There is never time enough."

I turn off the cruise control and the air-conditioner as I enter the "estates" where I live. My wife is already dressed for our dinner engagement.

"How was your trip?" she asks.

"Oh, fine," I say.

"Did anything happen? You look tired and pale."

"No, nothing happened."

Grandma used to say, "Everyone's tired."

I shower and change my clothes. I go to the phone book to check the address of our dinner engagement. In the margin of one of its pages I see the words "*Le pays des Laurentides*" and a phone number. Underneath the notation, in my son's handwriting, is the message, "Tell Dad."

"What's this?" I ask my son. "When did this come?"

"Oh," he says in embarrassment, "a long time ago. I was going to tell you but I forgot. The man sounded French. He had a name that sounded like 'gingerale.' He made me spell out that '*Le pays*' stuff. He said you would understand."

I dial the number and a pleasant woman answers the phone. I make my inquiries.

"Oh," she says. "This was their boarding house. They only stayed here for a little while. They said the money wasn't good enough so they went across the border to the States. I remember some of their names, Gingras, MacKenzie, Belanger. Do those names ring a bell?"

"Yes," I say. "Those names ring a bell. Thanks anyway."

43 *A*nd now it is six months later and the phone rings. It is evening. Outside my window the blustery snow swirls. "March may come in like a lamb, but it goes out like a lion," Grandma used to say.

"Hello," I say.

"It's time," he says.

"What do you mean?"

"It's time," he says. "Time to go." He coughs into the receiver.

"You mean now?" I ask. "It's snowing outside. It's dark. It's March."

"I know all about March," he says, "and so do you."

"Are you sure?"

"Of course I'm sure," he says. "I was never one to fool around. Have I ever called you before?"

"No, you haven't."

"Well then."

The operator comes on, asking for the deposit of more coins. Of course he is at a pay phone.

"Hang up," I say, "and call collect."

"No need for that," he laughs. "Always look after your blood," he begins to say, but the line goes dead.

There is no way to call him back.

"Be careful," says my wife. "The road report is bad."

"I will do the best I can," I say. "Perhaps I should take some liquor?"

"Take all you want," she says, "but be careful."

I take a bottle of brandy. We embrace and say goodbye.

Highway 401 is not as bad as it is reported to be. Often the weather reports are exaggerated to keep unnecessary travellers off the road. Sometimes my car fishtails, but I am able to keep it at a steady pace. The snowploughs with their flashing lights come and go. The salt trucks spray their pellets on the white roadbed. There are not many cars out tonight.

In Toronto, he is sitting on his bed. His white hair is combed and rises in waves upon his head. He has had a haircut. He has a small club bag at his feet.

"Thanks for coming," he says. "Are you ready for this? I'll help with the driving."

We leave his door open so that the desperate may take whatever they wish.

"Do you want this brandy?" I ask.

"No," he says. "Leave it on the windowsill. It won't last long."

We go forward into the night.

He is quiet beside me in the car. Sometimes I think he is sleeping or dozing, but when I look at him, his eyes are open. He coughs again and again.

The night goes by as does the highway as we head north and east. Sometimes there are snow squalls but then they clear. The leaden sky begins to lighten. Deep into Quebec we stop for breakfast. The breakfast special consists of eggs, toast, bacon or sausage, and beans.

The waitress brings us our order. She does not bring us the beans but instead an extra sausage. The French Canadians around us are having beans.

Calum laughs. "They think we make fun of them for having beans for breakfast," he says. "I suppose it's like us with our porridge."

We ask for the beans. The waitress looks at us. "You want beans?" she says. "Okay, I just looked at you and well, you know. . . ."

She brings the beans in two dessert bowls.

"No extra charge," she says.

"*Merci*," we reply.

Highway 20 is flat and fast. We move beside the ice-caked St. Lawrence.

At Rivière du Loup we turn south towards New Brunswick. The road becomes two lanes and our progress is not so rapid. Still, we go forward. We drink coffee from Styrofoam cups and when we are finished Calum throws them out the window, where they blend with the whiteness of the snow.

When we approach Grand Falls, I raise my eyebrows in a question. "We will go through Plaster Rock," he says. "It will be shorter and there'll be no traffic. I'll drive through that section of the trees."

"Do you have a driver's licence?" I ask.

"No," he says. "I let it lapse a long time ago. I had no need for it."

He drives steadily and surely. There is no traffic. The signs warn us to be aware of moose. "This is a good road," he says. "I wonder when they paved it. It used to be just gravelled. It was that way the time we came from Timmins. With the compressor and the kitten."

We pass Renous, home of the penitentiary. We pass through all the small communities with their disused schools and abandoned halls. We come to Rogersville.

"This place always struck me," he says. "The graveyard is so big and the community so small. More people in the graveyard than in the village. When we worked in the shafts there were never any graveyards. People never lived in those places long enough to die."

"Although some of them did," I say.

"Yes," he says. "Some of them died. Died in different ways. Here, you drive for a while."

We approach Moncton. After Sackville we cross the border into Nova Scotia. There is no piper on hand to welcome us, as is the case in summer. There are only wisps of blowing snow.

It is dark when we pass through Antigonish and the wind tries mightily to lift our car. The road signs warn us of blowing snow. The storm has increased. When we come to the base of the Havre Boucher hill, he says, "I'll drive now. I'm more experienced on hills and in snow than you are."

We begin the long ascent. It is a two-mile climb. There are no other vehicles on the road. The car slides and bucks, but he holds it to its course. The red light comes on to indicate that the engine is overheated. We make it to the top and begin the short descent. The mountain from which the Canso Causeway was built looms ahead of us and to our right.

"Do you know that song?" he says. "'Causeway Crossing' by Albert MacDonald?"

"Yes. I know it."

"Good song," he says.

The flashing lights of a police cruiser appear before us. The police officer waves us to the side.

"Where are you going?" he asks. "It's not often that we see an Ontario car around here at this time of year."

"To Cape Breton," we answer. "We're trying to get across."

"You can't get across," he says. "The waves are washing right over the road. The causeway's closed."

He speaks with an accent that is not local to the region.

"What are your names?" he asks.

"We're MacDonalds," we say.

"MacDonalds?" he says. "Are you the guys who make the hamburgers?"

"No," says Calum, "we're not the guys who make the hamburgers."

The snow increases and the wind blows so that the officer has to hold on to his hat. He runs for the safety of his cruiser.

Calum starts the car.

"What are you doing?" I ask.

"We're going across," he says. "That's what we came for."

As we approach the entrance to the causeway we can see the waves breaking. There is a shroud of mist in the air and dirty balls of brown foam fly before us. "This end is the worst," says Calum. He takes the car to where he can assess the situation. The waves are coming from the left, breaking and then receding. When they break, the roadway is invisible, buried under foaming depths of water.

Calum begins to count the waves.

"After the third big wave," he says, "there will be a lull and then we'll go. If the motor gets too wet the car will quit. The third time is the charm." Above the roar of the gale he says, "Here we go!"

The car springs forward. The red engine light is on, the engine is roaring, and the water comes in at the bottom of the doors. The windshield wipers are thick with ice and stop dead. He rolls down the window and sticks his head out into the gale to see where he is going on the invisible road. We are hit by one wave and then another. The car rocks with the force of the blows. The causeway is littered with pieces of pulpwood and dead fish. He weaves around the obstacles. The wheels touch the other side.

"Here," he says, "you can do the driving now. We're almost home."

We exchange places. Away from the pounding of the waves it is relatively serene. We can see the lights of some of the houses. I begin to drive along the coast. He settles into the passenger seat. The road we travel now is not directly in the path of the storm. Gradually the windshield thaws and the red engine light goes off.

Grandpa used to say that when he was a young man he would get an erection as soon as his feet hit Cape Breton. That was in the time, he said, when men had buttons on the front of their trousers. We, his middle-aged grandchildren, do not manifest any such signs of hopeful enthusiasm. But we are nonetheless here.

Tomorrow when the day breaks we will see what is now invisible around us. It will not all be pretty. Near the open water the bald eagles will pounce with mighty talons upon the white-coated baby seals. They will scream in different voices as they rise above the blood-stained ice. "You've got to take the bitter with the sweet," Grandma used to say. "No one said life was going to be a bed of roses."

I recognize all the familiar landmarks, although it is dark and there are mountains of snow. Here is the place where Grandpa threw the top of his whisky bottle out the window the day we were returning from my graduation. The day the red-haired Alexander MacDonald was killed, although we did not know it then. The day his mother bought him the shirt.

I turn to Calum and he is still, though his eyes are wide open, looking at the road ahead. Once we sang to the pilot whales on a summer's day. Perhaps we lured the huge whale in beyond his safe depth. And he died, disembowelled by the sharp rocks he could not see. Later his body moved inland, but his great heart remained behind.

By the glow of the dashboard lights I can see the thin scar on Calum's lower lip beginning to whiten. This is the man whose tooth was pulled by a horse. This is the man who, in his youth-ful despair, went looking for a rainbow, while others thought he was just wasting gas.

The car crests a high hill and in the distance, across the white expanse of the ice, I can see the regulated blinking of the now-automated light. It is still miles away. Yet it sends forth its message from the island's highest point. A light of warning or, perhaps, encouragement.

I turn to Calum once again. I reach for his cooling hand which lies on the seat beside him. I touch the Celtic ring. This is the man who carried me on his shoulders when I was three. Carried me across the ice from the island, but could never carry me back again.

Out on the island the neglected fresh-water well pours forth its gift of sweetness into the whitened darkness of the night.

Ferry the dead. *Fois do t'anam*. Peace to his soul.

'All of us are better when we're loved.'

Acknowledgements

I would like to acknowledge the spiritual assistance that came my way during the completion of this novel. I would like to express my appreciation to Hawthornden Castle International Retreat For Writers, Lasswade, Scotland, for providing me a place "to be at peace in decent ease."

My thanks to Doug Gibson for his caring persistence, and to Ed. Ducharme for his help and concern.

A.M.
Cape Breton,
August 1999

About the Author

Alistair MacLeod was born in North Battleford, Saskatchewan, in 1936 and raised among an extended family in Cape Breton, Nova Scotia. He still spends his summers in Inverness County, writing in a cliff-top cabin looking west towards Prince Edward Island. In his early years, to finance his education he worked as a logger, a miner, and a fisherman, and writes vividly and sympathetically about such work.

During the winter months Dr. MacLeod is a Professor of English at the University of Windsor, Ontario. His early studies were at the Nova Scotia Teachers College, St. Francis Xavier, the University of New Brunswick and Notre Dame, where he took his Ph.D. He has also taught creative writing at the University of Indiana. Working alongside W.O. Mitchell, he was an inspiring teacher to generations of writers at the Banff Centre.

He is such a careful and painstaking writer that his reputation in literary circles around the world is based on only fourteen short stories, collected in two books: *The Lost Salt Gift of Blood*, published in 1976, and *As Birds Bring Forth the Sun*, which appeared in 1986.

As a result of the admiration excited by these books, Alistair MacLeod has given lectures and readings from his work in many cities in Canada and around the world. He and his wife Anita have six children: they live in Windsor.